Tulips
FOR Tilly

Tulips for Tilly

In Bloom Series Book 4

KASEY KENNEDY

Tulips for Tilly
In Bloom Series, Book 4

Copyright © 2023 by Kasey Kennedy

ISBN-13: 978-1-958942-12-3 (paperback)
ISBN-13: 978-1-958942-11-6 (hardcover)
ISBN-13: 978-1-958942-10-9 (e-book)

Cover and interior design by Alt 19 Creative

Author Website:
www.kasey-kennedy.com

Published by:

For my sister, Sarah, and brother-in-law, Joe Erlenbusch,
Congratulations on your 25th Wedding Anniversary!
Looking forward to celebrating many more with you, I love you!

CHAPTER ONE

TILLY MILLER LET out a soft 'ope' as her ankle twisted in her teetering pink heels. She was walking up the aisle at the wedding of her friend, Paige Bell. Soon to be Mrs. Paige Morrison.

The teenager escorting her snickered at her jerking movement. Behind her she heard her disaster-of-a-date ask if she was all right.

She nodded her head quickly, trying not to draw any more attention to herself. She couldn't believe she'd had to resort to asking her brother's best friend to be her date. Her original plan was to ask the teacher's assistant in her Psychology 201 class, but once he let her down, not so gently, she had to fall back on the old standby.

And by old standby, she meant the guy she'd double-dated to prom with. And there was that date she'd needed for her cousin's wedding last fall. And that time he asked her to go to his college fall formal—just as friends!

It had become a crutch for both of them. If they didn't have a date to something important, they'd call the other one up. The conversations usually went like this:

"Hey, it's me."

"Hi. What's up?"

"I need a date."

"For what and when?"

"For XYZ on such and such day. Can you make it?"

Deep sigh. "I guess."

End scene.

Tilly's heart was still bruised from her breakup with Kyle, her boyfriend of two years, last October. She'd tried a few first dates since then, but they all felt forced and garnered no second dates. But it was time to get back in the game and find someone, so she wouldn't need to keep relying on Ronin. Now that he was moving to Bloomington to go into business with her brother, it would be too easy to fall back on the old standby.

They reached an available aisle and the usher gestured for her to sit. She had to walk sideways to get past a couple of ladies who were clutching purses the size of small animal carriers. Tilly wondered if they'd brought their cats with them. *Might be a better date than Ronin*, she thought.

Ronin McGuire was a good guy, but when you've known a person since you were four years old, the allure tarnished somewhere among the hair pulling, training bras, braces, and acne.

It seemed Ronin had been there for every important occasion that she could remember in her life. He was there when her brother Michael fell out of the tree and broke his arm. No one was sure, but they all suspected the two boys had gotten into a tussle when Michael fell.

Ronin's had been the shoulder she cried on when she found out her Grandma Debbie had died. The three kids had been watching *Friends* reruns in the Miller's living room, when Tilly's mom had walked in, visibly shaken, and said Ronin needed to go. The kids protested, until finally Irena said, "Grandma Debbie passed. I'm so sorry. Your dad is on his way home. Now, Ronin, it's probably best if you go on home."

But Ronin stayed. Tilly had burst into tears at her mother's announcement, and both Michael and Ronin tried to comfort her.

Michael started sharing his favorite funny memories of Grandma Debbie to get Tilly to laugh. Ronin scooted over on the couch and put his arm around her. She laughed at Michael's stories through her tears. Ronin squeezed her shoulders and patted her arm when she sobbed. She couldn't count the number of tears that landed on his T-shirt.

Tilly finally made it to an empty seat and turned to Ronin. "Will you step past me?" He was tall, and she didn't want him blocking her view when Paige came down the aisle.

"Certainly, Emmy."

Tilly smiled at the old nickname. He was the only one who had ever called her that. Having a name like Matilda Marie Miller did set one up for the nickname; she wished her parents had thought of that before giving her three matching initials. At least he used the nickname "Eminem" for her brother Michael and not her.

Ronin unbuttoned his suit jacket as he sat next to her. Twisting in his seat to look back up the aisle, his knee brushed hers.

Sighing, she asked, "Would you scoot over? You're crowding me."

"Sorry, trying to see what's happening."

"Nothing will happen until the music swells, then they'll all march in."

Tilly wasn't sure why she was so annoyed with him—he was doing her a favor by coming to this wedding as her date. She hated the thought of going to a wedding alone. It seemed to say *Hey, look at me, someone I love and care about is tying the knot, and I'm here without a date. Poor pitiful me.* After two years of dating Kyle, she thought they were getting to the point where he would ask her to marry him. Instead, he dumped her, saying she wasn't ambitious enough. Sure, the spark had fizzled, but it was a steady relationship. One she thought would build a good, strong marriage.

3

She'd felt that spark once before, with a high school boyfriend, Jesse, but that had turned ugly when her best friend, Claire, became infatuated with him, too. Not only did Tilly lose Jesse in the breakup, she lost her best friend, as well.

Tilly told herself to chill out with Ronin. It wasn't his fault that she didn't have a real date for this wedding. She should be thankful that she wasn't alone.

Ronin's arm draped across the back of her seat. The warmth felt good against her skin. It was cool for a June afternoon, and she wished she had brought a sweater or jacket.

"Is my arm bothering you?" Ronin asked.

"No. It's nice and warm."

"Are you cold? Do you want my jacket?"

"No, I'll be fine."

Ronin whispered. "When you're ready for it, just ask."

The music swelled and they both turned to watch the wedding procession. Trevor, the groom, walked down the aisle with his mom on his arm. His mother wore a sage-green dress with tiny crystals that caught the light. She had a beautiful, bronzed tan and Tilly remembered Paige saying that Trevor's mom lived in Florida. *I'm so jelly,* Tilly thought. *I could use a tan.*

Next, Paige's mom was escorted down the aisle by Paige's oldest brother, Jack. Tilly read all the names in the program. It was a beautiful book-like pamphlet with a deep green cover featuring a light pink peony flower. The elegant writing on the thick, cream-colored pages inside was handwritten calligraphy. There was a table of contents pointing to the correct pages for wedding party, ceremony, music choices and the meaning behind them, "the story of us", and even some recipes: for the Bell family famous Fourth of July sugar cookies, Paige's London Fog Tea Latte recipe, and a recipe for Trevor's homemade lollipops. It was the wordiest wedding program Tilly had ever seen. Not surprising, since the bride was a bookworm.

The rest of the wedding party made their way down the aisle and into their places in front of the altar. Everyone stood when Paige appeared on the arm of her dad. Tilly grinned when she saw her friend. After hours of talking about this day with Paige, it was a blessing to be here to celebrate the marriage. Paige was so sweet and kind, and she'd snagged a handsome guy that was just crazy about her. Tilly's heart swelled with emotions, and she was thankful her tiny purse had room for tissues.

Tilly teetered on her tiptoes to see Paige's dress and nearly toppled forward. Ronin wrapped his forearm around her and held her waist. "Easy there, Em."

Tilly gripped his arm and righted herself. "Thanks," she murmured, twisting to look him in the eye and smiling. "You're always watching out for me."

"Someone's got to," he whispered back.

Tilly turned her attention back to Paige and sighed as she saw the sweet, ethereal dress. It had a tulle overlay sprinkled with pale pink floral appliqués. Tilly squinted and could see that they were peonies. *Her favorite flowers,* she thought.

As Paige reached their row, Tilly beamed when she saw the bouquet. She had helped Anna Lee, the owner of In Bloom, the flower shop where she worked, create the masterpiece of deep pink peonies, white roses, pale-pink roses, and deep green foliage. Within the bouquet were thin wires with multi-faceted crystal beads that sparkled as they caught the light.

The minister led them in prayer and asked that the guests be seated. Ronin let Tilly sit before he settled next to her.

The minister shared several funny stories about Trevor and Paige. It was cute to see Trevor bow his head in embarrassment more than once.

Before the rings were exchanged, the minister called for a blessing of the rings. He walked the ring box over to Trevor's side of the aisle. Each of the grandparents and parents in turn touched the box to their heart or gave it a kiss before passing it on. After the box had made it over to Paige's family, the minister walked over to take it from Paige's grandmother. Tilly thought about her own family and felt a rush of emotions. Her mother had been adopted, and Tilly felt there was a small hole in her own heart, missing the knowledge of her maternal grandparents by blood. Yes, she loved her adoptive grandparents, but there was still a gap there that she hoped would be filled someday.

She pulled a tissue from her handbag and dabbed at her eyes. Ronin put his arm around her and gave her a comforting squeeze.

ON THE WAY to the reception, Tilly recapped the wedding like a play-by-play announcer, and Ronin added a couple of pieces she'd missed. She appreciated that he went along with her review and didn't try to force her to talk about something else. It wasn't every day one of your friends got married. Besides, a girl had to take notes and think about what she would do the same and differently for her own wedding.

At the venue, Ronin parked and told Tilly to wait before getting out. He said he was worried her heels wouldn't fare well on the gravel parking lot.

He came around to the passenger door and opened it for her. When he reached out his hand to her, Tilly didn't hesitate to grasp it. She was dreading the walk across the lot in the tricky shoes herself. She wished she'd brought a second pair of shoes for the reception.

"Watch your step," Ronin said as she stood.

"I'm watching. This may be a minefield for my heels."

She took two steps before her right heel twisted and she nearly toppled over. "That's not gonna work," Ronin said.

Next thing Tilly knew, she was scooped up and carried in

Ronin's arms across the parking lot. She let out a gasp and put her free hand beneath her backside to keep her skirt from flying in the breeze, exposing her unmentionables. Her dress was too short to be cradled like this!

"Ronin! Put me down!"

"Just hold on," he barked. "I'd like to make it across the parking lot without you breaking an ankle or taking me down when you fall."

Tilly's eyes scanned the lot. No one else was walking in. *Thank goodness for small favors!* She stopped worrying about the dress and put both hands around his neck, tightening her grip on him.

Once he reached the sidewalk, Ronin put her down, leaving his hand on her lower back as she steadied herself. As he slowly raised himself up, her gaze lingered on his face. *When did he get so handsome? Gah, stop! This is Ronin, silly!*

She smoothed her dress. Looking up at him, she silently bemoaned their height difference; he had a good seven inches over her petite, five-foot four-inch frame.

She huffed. "Was that really necessary? I would have made it."

"Eventually," he agreed. "I just sped things along."

"You're so helpful."

"It's a pleasure to serve." He bent forward in an exaggerated bow.

Tilly shook her head and walked through the door of the venue. They were greeted by a server who told them the reception room wasn't open yet, but they could grab a drink in the bar while they waited. They found seats at the deeply polished oak bar with a brass footrest.

"What would you like?" Ronin asked, reaching for his wallet. He leaned against the bar, and Tilly had the distinctly odd thought that if this weren't Ronin, she'd probably tell a girlfriend he was H.O.T. hot. He'd started keeping his hair long on top, very short in the back, and he sometimes put some product in his hair to slick it back. He'd shaved today and his jaw line would make a male model envious. She really should try to set Ronin up with one of her single girlfriends.

"Hey, I invited you; I'll get the drinks." Tilly pulled her debit card out of her purse.

"No, you won't." Ronin set a twenty on the counter. "What do you want?"

"Fine. A diet soda, please." She wasn't twenty-one yet and didn't want the bartender to card her.

When the pretty bartender approached, Ronin ordered her soda and a craft beer for himself. Tilly's eyes narrowed when the woman patted Ronin's arm and said, "Coming right up."

If she'd been on a real date and the bartender did that, Tilly would have probably given the woman a piece of her mind.

Once their drinks were delivered, Ronin held his up and toasted, "To weddings. To lifelong friends. And to open bars," he added with a wink.

"Cheers," Tilly responded, clinking his glass. "Thanks again for coming with me."

He leaned toward her. "I'm glad to be here." His voice was low and husky.

Whoa. That was hot. Yuck. Time to change the subject. "When do you move into your apartment?"

"July first. You ready to help us move?"

"I told Michael I'd help. But I'm not carrying heavy stuff up two flights of stairs."

"You're so dainty," he teased. "I can't believe we'll be right down the block from you."

"Don't remind me. You and my brother will be too close for comfort."

"I disagree. When you need a last-minute date, you can be at my door in minutes. Or if you need a cup of sugar or laundry detergent."

"More like when you need help doing laundry or cooking, you'll be happy I'm down the street."

"Just like growing up."

Tilly shook her head. "Growing up we were right next door. I'm glad you won't be that close now."

"Ah, come on. Wouldn't you like to open a window and just holler at me like we used to?"

"No. Having you guys a half a block away will take some getting used to. But I am happy that Michael is moving here. I've missed being close to him. It'll prevent any further homesickness."

"You've been here three years. You still get homesick?"

"Not often. But it's hard being away from family and not seeing them for weeks or months at a time. I miss my parents. You're lucky."

Ronin's parents had moved from their shared hometown of Roselle, Illinois to Bloomington the previous year when his dad took a promotion to join the local hospital. His mom was a freelance writer and could work anywhere. His family was thrilled when Ronin said he planned to move to Bloomington as well. Tilly was thankful that his move was bringing her brother Michael closer, too.

"Yes, it'll be great being only a few minutes from them versus a few hours. Speaking of my parents, Mom told me to invite you to their place on the Fourth of July. Their backyard faces the park where the city launches their fireworks. It will be a lot of fun. Michael's coming. There's a chance the roads will be closed to traffic, so get there by three p.m. if you can. And bring a swimsuit because the girls will want to swim."

"Really? I don't have plans yet. Let me talk to Mom; they might be disappointed if neither of us comes home for the holiday."

"Sure. I get it. What are the plans for your birthday?"

"Nothing yet. You know how it goes. Everyone parties hard for the Fourth of July, and my birthday is always an afterthought."

Ronin's eyebrow lifted. "I'm thinking about it before. And I know your parents do, too."

"Sure, but I'm talking about my friends. Seems like everyone wants to relax the weekend after the Fourth. But I'm not complaining. It's fine. Mack and I will have a little get-together—"

Ronin stood up straighter and his forehead furrowed. "Who's Mack?"

"Mackenzie. My roommate. I told you about her."

"Oh, right. You said 'Mack' and I thought you were talking about a guy. I forgot that was your roommate's name. What's she like?"

Tilly beamed. "She's great. She's funny, charming, super-cute."

"A college student, I assume."

"Yes, we were dorm mates our first couple of years and then decided to get the apartment together."

"What is she studying?"

"She's a theater major."

"Uh oh. Sounds like trouble. All that drama."

Tilly laughed. "She's a hoot. You'll like her." Changing the subject, she said, "I bet your parents will be happy when you move off their couch."

"Ouch. I have my own bedroom."

"You didn't have to kick one of your sisters out of her room?"

"Nope. I got the guest bedroom. Luckily, no guests were planned for this month. I'll be glad when I'm in my own apartment again, though. Living with my sisters is driving me crazy. I love them and everything, but they're a handful."

Tilly nodded. "Your sisters are sweet. They keep me updated on what's going on."

"They're your spies, huh?"

"Well, I didn't hire them, but they do share with me."

"Even more reason for me to be out of the house."

"Are you worried they'll give me the inside scoop on your love life?"

"What love life?"

"Oh, come on. You're always dating a new beautiful, smart lady who's trying to get her claws into you. Your mom tells me that all the time." Tilly laughed, but it sounded fake even to her ears. She'd rather not know about Ronin's love life, but his family sure liked to keep her informed.

"Going on dates doesn't make a love life. Trust me." Ronin's shoulder twitched and he looked away from her. Tilly got the feeling that he was trying to hide something with the flash of pain that crossed his face.

"Well, I have to agree with you there."

"What about your love life? What happened to the loser you were with for two years?"

"How did you remember that?" she asked slowly. "Are you keeping track?"

"Not trying to. Just remembered. What happened to him? Good riddance if you ask me."

"I don't really know. We went to dinner, and he broke up with me. I thought things were going fine. It caught me off guard."

"Fine? Just fine?"

"Yes."

"Then I know he was a loser. Emmy, don't settle for fine. Don't settle at all until you find a guy that makes your life wonderful. Who shows you and tells you that he'll do anything for you. Someone who makes you laugh and who treats you like a queen. That's the guy you want. Not some guy that makes life 'fine'".

Tilly stilled and her mouth went dry. She didn't know what to say. Ronin was right. She hated it when he was right. Why couldn't she find a guy like that? Someone who looked at her the way Trevor had looked at Paige during the ceremony. Like she was his whole world, not just a piece of it.

She wanted the stars and moon to align and bring her that kind of guy. The fact that Ronin recognized and named it was unexpected.

"Ready for another drink?" he asked.

"Not right now."

He ordered another beer and asked for two glasses of water. She thought about what Ronin had said. Could she be so lucky as to find a guy like that? Someone who treated her like his queen? A girl could wish.

DURING THE RECEPTION, Tilly and Ronin were seated with her friends and coworkers from In Bloom. As the DJ announced the bride and groom's first dance, Tilly clasped her hands and leaned towards Ronin. "Ready to dance?" she asked.

He nodded and she turned to Nica. "We're going to go closer to the dance floor during their dance."

"We'll be there soon." Nica shifted her eyes towards her boyfriend, Grady, who was in a deep conversation with John Peerson, Anna Lee's beau.

Anna Lee saw Tilly push her chair back and held up a finger, telling her to wait. Anna Lee whispered something to John and came around the table to Tilly.

"I suppose you young people are ready to bust a move," she said.

Tilly laughed. "In these shoes and this dress? I don't think so. I am ready to dance, though. What about you, Anna Lee?"

"Well, sure. If the music is tight and I'mma feelin' right."

"Can I get either of you ladies a drink?" Ronin asked.

"I've reached my limit, young man," Anna Lee responded.

"Emmy?"

"I'll have another wine, please." Now that they were in the reception, she wasn't worried about being carded.

He rested a hand on her waist as he passed behind her, a gesture that caught Anna Lee's eye. Once he walked away, she turned to Tilly. "Mighty fine young man you got there."

"Oh, I don't 'got' him," Tilly protested. "He's just a friend. We grew up next door to each other."

"Well—" Anna Lee patted her arm, and Tilly found comfort in the gesture. "You've got a very handsome, very polite, very personable *friend*. I hope you find a boyfriend who is that charming and sweet. And he's not hard on the eyes, either, is he?"

Tilly fiddled with her bracelet, not wanting to meet Anna Lee's perceptive eyes. "I suppose so. Never thought about him that way before."

"And now?"

Tilly was saved from answering when Lauren Largent approached. She was one of Paige's bridesmaids and a former employee at In Bloom.

"Oh, Lauren!" Tilly squealed. "You look so amazing! You're radiant. Paige is radiant. Everything is perfect."

She glanced over to the dance floor where Trevor and Paige beamed at each other.

Lauren hugged them both before responding. "Thank you so much. And I agree, no hiccups today. Paige is ecstatic, so I'm happy. But we need to catch up. I want to tell you about my job and Hawk and things."

Tilly raised both eyebrows. "This sounds interesting! Breakfast tomorrow?"

"Sorry, can't. Have plans. How about Monday?"

"You're on."

Ronin returned with their drinks and Tilly introduced him.

The couple's first dance ended, and the room cheered.

"I've got to go. The wedding party dance is next," Lauren said. "Nice to meet you, Ronin." She winked at Tilly before walking away.

Shoot. She's got the wrong impression. I'll have to clear that up when we meet.

Ronin snickered beside her. He put his hand on her lower back and leaned down to whisper in her ear. "She thinks we're a couple."

"Yeah, well. Looks can be deceiving."

But touches can't, and his touch was sending a tingle up and down her spine. She willed herself not to jump away. *Weddings make everything seem romantic, and people can get tricked into thinking they're in love. Watch yourself.*

Nica and Grady joined them as they watched the wedding party sway across the dance floor.

"Ready to dance, *chica?*" Nica asked, bouncing on her toes.

"I am!"

"Your date is ready to go."

Tilly glanced over to Ronin who was talking to Grady and tapping his foot to the beat of the music. She laughed.

"I guess he is."

Having attended other weddings with Ronin, she knew he was a great dancer. It was one of the things she looked forward to. Seeing him interact with her friends today, seeing his charm and kindness on display with some of the people she cared most about in this world, was chipping away at the walls of the "friend" box that she'd put him in a long time ago, and it was disconcerting.

Her head swam with so many images of him from over the years. It was like watching a "This is Your Life, Ronin McGuire" montage. She had to admit, she really liked the more recent images of Ronin as a thoughtful and handsome man, not the gangly kid who used to tease her all the time.

CHAPTER TWO

THE GUEST BEDROOM was beginning to feel claustrophobic. Ronin had shoved all the decorative pillows under the bed and put the fake flower arrangement on the table in the hall, but the room still felt too much like grandma quarters. He was counting down the days until he could move into his new apartment with Michael.

He and Michael had big plans for their new business venture. They would start touring buildings with the appropriate space for their drop-in and co-working rentals just as soon as they were settled in their apartment.

When Michael suggested an apartment building that was literally feet away—all right, a couple hundred feet away—from Tilly, Ronin was uncertain at first. It had taken a few years, but he finally felt he'd gotten her out of his system once he went away to college and didn't have to see her every day.

He thought their wedding "date" had gone well. He'd worried when he picked her up. Seeing her in her too-short, too-tight black dress caused his breath to catch. She was so beautiful. On the outside and the inside. On the way to the wedding, he made sure their conversation focused on her brother. It reminded him that he couldn't let his crush on Tilly reignite. He couldn't imagine dating his best friend's little sister. He worried that doing so could cause a fight with Michael.

The thought of causing either Michael or Tilly pain was unimaginable. As much as it hurt him, he had to stuff his feelings for Tilly back into the deepest recesses of his heart and mind, never to be accessed, no matter the cost to his own happiness. He unconsciously squeezed his computer mouse, but stopped when he heard a cracking noise. "Dang it," he muttered.

When they'd slow-danced, he'd made sure to keep a couple of inches between their bodies. Being too close to Tilly, catching a whiff of her musky, sweet perfume or the freshness of her shampoo, could unravel the progress he'd made while being apart from her. Luckily, the DJ's playlist was mostly upbeat, and there were only a few slow dances. As the night wore on and she became tipsy, he knew he had to beg off any more of the slow dances. He was able to encourage her to take breaks and get water and fresh air during the last couple of slow songs.

He'd enjoyed meeting her friends and her boss at In Bloom. Anna Lee was a no-nonsense lady, and he loved how fondly she talked about Tilly. When Tilly beat herself up about how she couldn't decide which career path to take, Anna Lee said, "Nothing wrong with figuring it out later. Why do all you young people think you have to have a plan, or a hustle, by the time you're twenty? No one's got it figured out by then, even if they say they do. Heck, I'm almost seventy-one, and I still haven't figured anything out. I do what I love and don't worry about the rest of it. No grind. No hustle. No bustle. No thank you."

Everyone nodded along with Anna Lee's words. She was right, and Ronin knew it. He wasn't confident that what he was doing next—going into business with his childhood best friend—was the right thing to do, but it was right for now. He was excited about the chance to build something from the ground up. With so many people working remotely after the pandemic, creating a shared office space that was vibrant, hip, and professional seemed like a smart endeavor.

Meeting the other young ladies that Tilly worked with had been fun. Remembering the challenges she had experienced with her best friend Claire in high school, it was great to see her warm and genuine friendships with Paige, Nica, and Lauren.

A knock at the door pulled him out of his musings. His sister, Shevaun, walked in and plopped on the foot of his bed.

"So, how was the big date last night?" she asked, as she began to pick at the finger polish on her nails.

"It wasn't a big date. I went to a wedding with Emmy."

"Yes, I know. And it's Tilly, you big dummy. You're not fooling me. You may say it wasn't a date, but…it's Tilly, and I know you. Plus, you wore your special suit. It was a date."

"We went as friends. She needed a plus one."

"Ronin plus Tilly equals three. Couple goals."

"If you think our relationship is couple goals, then it's obvious you have no idea what you're talking about. We've never been involved romantically. I hardly know her anymore. I've only seen her a handful of times since I left for college."

"You're lame. It's been more than a few."

"Are you keeping tabs or something, Vaun?"

He stood, hoping Shevaun would follow his lead and exit. He didn't want fingernail polish chips on, or in, his bed.

"Not tabs, but I think about these things. I can't help thinking that if you didn't have the feels for her, you would be in a serious relationship with someone else, and you're not. So…"

"That logic doesn't work. I couldn't be in a serious relationship and move here."

"Whatever happened to Kristy? I thought you might have had a chance to get serious with her."

"We wanted different things."

"Like?"

"She was talking marriage, and I wasn't ready."

"You only dated for a few months, right? That seems fast."

"It was. Too fast."

"I guess some girls would think you're a catch. Though you don't have a job, and you are living in the guest room of your parents' house. And all your clothes are in plastic storage boxes."

"Hey, I'm not going to be here long enough to unpack. It's efficient. What about your love life?"

He needed to change the trajectory of this conversation and fast. He'd do anything for his sisters but didn't like being on the receiving end of their endless questions. He had Shevaun pegged for a lawyer; her cross-examination was intense.

"I'm too young for a love life."

"You're nineteen."

"Too young. I go on dates, but I don't want to get serious. Enough about that. When are you and Michael going to start your business so I can get a job?" Shevaun started thumbing through the books in the bookcase—books his parents had bought, read, and kept around for guests.

"What makes you think we'd hire you? Go get a job at McDonald's."

"No. Gross. You'd hire me. I can make life difficult for you if you don't. Especially the next time Tilly comes over."

He reached under the bed, grabbed one of the decorative pillows, and tossed it at her. "Get out, Vaun."

She left, laughing over her shoulder.

He groaned. The conversation had done exactly what he didn't need right now—created small fissures in his heart and his mind where those carefully guarded feelings for Tilly were liable to slip out. This was not good; he needed to do something to get his mind off of her. He changed into swim trunks, telling himself that several laps in the pool should get his mind off her—physical exertion should help.

ELIZABETH MCGUIRE LOVED to make a huge Sunday dinner. It was her way of regrouping and preparing the family for the week ahead. No devices were allowed at the table, and everyone was expected to contribute to the conversation in a loving and supportive manner.

Ronin's youngest sister, Trinity, came to his room where he was working at the desk creating a list of areas around town to scope out with Michael. She let him know that it was time to wash up and come to dinner.

In the formal dining room, Ronin took a moment to close his eyes and take in the smells of baked chicken, homemade baked beans, and yeast rolls. His mom loved to cook, and he realized how much he'd missed her cooking while away at school, getting first his undergrad degree and then his MBA at Loyola. As much as he was looking forward to being in his own apartment, he was just as glad he'd be close enough to come home for Sunday dinners.

Shevaun walked into the room, carrying a homemade apple pie to the sideboard, and Ronin's mouth watered as the scents of cinnamon and other spices wafted by.

"Wanna go for a bike ride after dinner?" Shevaun asked.

"Yes, that'd be great. Think you could go for ten miles without whining?" he teased.

"Absolutely, loser. You'll be eating my dust."

"Yeah, right."

Trinity was putting plates on the table. "Can I go?"

"Will you slow us down, Tiny?" Ronin asked, using the nickname he'd given her when she first came home from the hospital.

"You're funny if you think I'd slow you down. Just try to keep up."

Elizabeth walked in, carrying another dish. Ronin smiled at his mom and the patch of flour on her apron. Though her cooking was great, she was not the neatest of chefs. "I think all of us should go, so no one is left behind."

"Sounds great," Ronin replied. It had been years since they'd all gone on a family bike ride. "What can I do to help?"

"Get the basket of rolls and we will be ready. Bruce! Dinner!" Elizabeth untied the apron and called down to the basement for her husband.

Once they had all filled their plates and started eating, Elizabeth asked what everyone's plans were for the week. Trinity was a lifeguard at the community pool and worked every day that week; she was a frugal kid and was saving for college.

Shevaun was applying for jobs, but this late in June, she wasn't sure that she would find anything. According to Elizabeth, she had plenty of housework to keep Vaun busy and earn her keep. Ronin noticed the look of disdain that flashed over Vaun's face before she gave him a pleading look. Yeah, she was definitely going to be after him for a job.

Ronin would be drafting the business plan he and Michael needed to get a bank loan for their business. He'd already secured his parents' support in a sizable financial investment, and they loved to hear about the progress he was making.

"Did you get a chance to talk to the insurance agent I recommended?" his father asked.

"Not yet, but I have an appointment with her on Tuesday. I'll let you know how that goes."

"Good. Why don't you have Shevaun tag along with you? It would be a good experience for her, and she has nothing better to do." Bruce grabbed another roll.

"I was going to have her reorganize my craft room," Elizabeth said, "but you're right, it would be a great experience for her."

"I'd rather NOT have to organize the craft room." Shevaun rolled her eyes but smiled at her mother. "Maybe Tilly would like to come over and help with the craft room. I bet she and Ronin would have it organized and cleaned, in no time."

"She has a job, smart Alice." Ronin said.

"It's part-time. I know she loves to organize—"

"Why would I pay someone to do that when I have you, dear?" Elizabeth said, reaching over and patting Shevaun on the back.

Ronin suppressed a laugh. It was always good to see his parents put Shevaun in her place. When he did it, he usually got scolded.

The truth was, he wouldn't mind doing a project like that with Tilly. She liked to make games out of chores and always kept the conversation going. He'd missed that.

"Has Tilly been visiting you guys since you moved here?"

"Yes, not like when we lived next door to her family, but she stops by— I think when she gets lonely or needs advice," Elizabeth said.

"Definitely not as much, but it's great when she does," Trinity added. "She helped me get ready for prom last month. She came over and did my hair."

"That was nice of her," Ronin replied.

"I can't believe you'll be right down the street from her, Ronin," Shevaun said, a little gleam in her eye. Ronin tensed in anticipation. "Can't keep you two apart for long."

"It's been five years. Michael wanted to be close to his sister."

"Right...Michael did..."

Elizabeth looked at Ronin across the table. There was a question in her eyes that Ronin didn't want to answer. He needed to change the subject.

"What are you working on, Mom?" Ronin asked, shooting Vaun a look that clearly said, "drop it".

"I'm researching my next book. It will be a thriller with a romantic element. A case of mistaken identity—children switched at birth. I'm exploring the themes of nature versus nurture and the meaning of home."

"Sounds fascinating." Ronin turned to his dad, not wanting Shevaun to pick at the Tilly wound. "Dad, what about you? What's new at the hospital?"

Bruce put down his fork and swiped his napkin across his mouth. Ronin noticed that his dad's salt-and-pepper hair needed a trim. The man was a bit absent-minded when it came to personal care; his focus was on his family and his patients. "Lots of good things. Like your mother, I'm researching—the use of machine learning and AI in the treatment of hypertension. The administration has applied for a grant, and if approved, my team will take the lead on a new study."

"Wow. I hope you get the grant."

"Thanks. I do, too."

The talk moved on to dinner-planning for the rest of the week. Ronin was thankful that he'd successfully steered the conversation away from Tilly. He'd have to play offense the next few days to make sure Vaun's suspicions about his interest in Tilly died down before she came over to celebrate the Fourth with his family. She hadn't committed yet, but he was fairly confident she'd come. He'd been surprised when Vaun suggested he had a thing for Tilly. He'd briefly regretted inviting her—he feared it would be like opening Pandora's box. Not only could it fuel Vaun's suspicions, but it could reignite the feelings that he thought he'd successfully extinguished. After spending so much time with her yesterday as her platonic plus one, he wasn't so sure.

Ever since he'd left for college, there might be months between the occasions he saw Tilly. But it never took long to fall back into the familiarity that came from knowing someone for eighteen years. She had acted slightly irritated with him earlier in the day, but by the time he took her home, it had felt like they were good friends again, sharing inside jokes and speaking to each other with just a glance.

She had dozed off in his car on the drive home, and when he pulled up to the curb in front of her building, she didn't stir. He put the car in park and turned to watch her sleep. Her face was turned towards him, and a strand of her soft, brown hair had fallen over her cheek. He carefully pushed it back from her face and watched her breathe in and out. He wanted to lean forward and kiss her lips softly but was afraid she'd wake up and slap him across the face. Instead, he put his index finger in the center of her forehead and smiled as she jerked awake, and he managed to catch her wrist before she slapped him.

"You're home, Emmy." He smiled at her confusion.

"I fell asleep?"

"Yes. It was a long day, and you danced your butt off tonight."

"Right. Don't do that finger on the forehead thing. It's the worst."

"I know. That's why it's so fun to do. Now, good night. I'll watch you walk to your door."

She picked her purse up from the floorboard and turned back to him. "Thanks for going with me. And for driving." She paused, and her sleepy eyes searched his for several moments.

Ronin's heart skipped as she leaned closer. Was she going to kiss him? She raised her hand and he braced himself. She was a little unsteady, but she managed to put her index finger in the middle of his forehead. He held her gaze.

"What are you doing, Emmy?"

"See? Annoying." She smiled and turned toward the passenger door. "Night, Ro."

"Night, Em."

He watched as she walked up to her door, searching in her purse for the keys. Letting out a sigh, he wondered if he should have walked with her. A moment later, she opened the door and turned to wave him off. The porch light framed her in a soft glow. He knocked his head against the headrest. He thought he'd gotten her out of his system. He'd been lying to himself.

CHAPTER THREE

TILLY SHARPENED HER snips and sat back down. It was Saturday morning, and she was working at In Bloom. The back door was propped open to let the breeze in, and the wind caused the baby's breath in front of her to sway.

"Anna Lee," she asked, "did you say we needed eight or ten of these centerpieces?"

"Only eight. Thank goodness! We're going to be cuttin' it close."

Nica walked in with the coffee pot.

"Oh, good. Fill 'er up. I need more caffeine!" Anna Lee said, raising her cup.

Nica filled the indicated cup and offered to fill Tilly's. "No, I'm okay for now. Any more coffee, and I'll be shaking, and that won't work very well."

"I guess I need to hire some more help. But I'd need to hire five people to replace Paige and Lauren." Anna Lee smiled, the love and pride she had for the girls on her face.

"I had breakfast with Lauren on Monday. It was great to catch up with her about her trip to Greece, her new job offer in Chicago, and Hawk. Sounds like things are going really well for them."

Nica and Anna Lee were happy to hear the update. Tilly put the final rose in the arrangement she was working on. "Oh, Anna Lee, my roommate, Mackenzie, is looking for another job.

She's waiting tables, but she wants something different. She's a theater major, so she's pretty artsy. I think she'd be a good fit."

"Really?" Anna Lee tilted her head, her shoulder-length, gray hair bunched on her shoulder. "Well, send her in as soon as you can, so she can fill out an application."

"Will do." Tilly turned back to the task at hand. They were short-handed, and with two weddings today, they needed to work faster and talk less.

Two hours later, they'd done it. All centerpieces, bouquets, and boutonnières were ready to go. Tilly and Nica loaded the van as Anna Lee helped customers in the retail space. Tilly had volunteered to drive the van, and Nica was going to ride shotgun to help her unload.

After the first stop, Tilly checked the time on the dashboard. Considering Anna Lee's habit of keeping the clock exactly ten minutes ahead, she decided they had time to stop for a to-go coffee, and she pulled into the nearest coffee chain drive-through.

Nica changed the radio to the university station, which was playing the latest release from The National. "Oh, turn it up," Tilly said.

The band always reminded her of Ronin. He'd been the one to introduce her and Michael to their music back in high school. She couldn't remember how he'd discovered them, but once he had, the three of them were always watching the band's videos on YouTube.

The song ended, and Tilly wanted to text Ronin to ask if he'd heard it yet. It'd been a week since Paige's wedding, and she hadn't heard from him. Other than a quick thank-you text the day after, she hadn't contacted him either. It was just as well. Soon, he and her brother would be living down the street, and she was sure he'd be around more often. The boys would probably visit every night looking for food. She was not going to play that game. No way.

"Right, Tils?" Nica asked.

"I'm sorry. What was that?" Tilly had been daydreaming. Again.
"It's the next left-hand turn ahead."

Tilly glanced at the GPS on the phone perched in a homemade phone holder that Anna Lee had made for the flower shop van. Anna Lee hated to drive the thing herself; she preferred zipping around town on her scooter. The girls had suggested a phone holder, and Anna Lee crafted one in a day, made from heavy-gauge wire and repurposed glass beads for "flare". "Got it. Thanks. I might have missed that turn."

Driving back to In Bloom after the second delivery, Nica talked about helping Paige pack and move out of their apartment after the wedding. Nica and her cousin Izzy had opened an ad for a new roommate but didn't expect to get anyone, since it was summer break. Nica said that wasn't a problem; Paige's old bedroom was going to be used as a workroom to refinish some furniture Nica had picked up at an auction. The furniture would be used as staging pieces for properties that she and her boyfriend, Grady, were flipping.

"Grady will have to find a storage unit once I'm done with the furniture, and then we'll be ready for a new roommate," Nica said.

"That works out." Tilly was envious of Nica's drive and passion. She knew what she wanted and wouldn't let anything get in her way. Tilly certainly wouldn't want to get in her way. Nica might be even shorter than her, but she was a feisty woman.

"I can't believe Paige is married," Nica said. "From engaged to married in less than seven months! Kind of *loco* if you ask me."

"When you know, you know. So, you and Grady haven't set a date yet?"

"No. And we won't for a long time. There's no rush."

Tilly sighed. There were so many things she didn't know about life. She knew she didn't *need* a man to take care of her. She could manage on her own. But she loved the idea of being in a long-term relationship, and she hoped marriage and kids were in her future. She didn't know what she wanted to do professionally; there were so many options, and she didn't want to be stuck on one path. She wanted to explore many different things. But she knew she wanted a family!

"So, who was that hunky guy you were with at Paige's wedding?" Nica asked.

Tilly was shaking her head before Nica finished. "An old family friend. He's super-close to my brother. They're starting a business together. He's just my stand-by plus one, and I'm sometimes his. He moved to Bloomington a month ago. We're not a thing. It wasn't a date."

"Looked like a date to me. He only had eyes for you, *chica*."

Tilly laughed as she pulled into the In Bloom parking lot. "No way. You must have been wearing your love-colored glasses. Maybe he had dust in his eye."

Nica clicked her tongue. "Maybe you don't see it, but I do. He's got a thing for you, Tilly.'

Tilly turned off the van and pulled out the keys. She turned her head, studying Nica. She didn't appear to be teasing, and she was usually a good judge of character. But she couldn't be right about this. Not about Ronin.

Nica's lips pursed, then spread into a slow, lazy smile. "Deny, deny, deny, all you want. I saw what I saw."

Nica opened the door and hopped out. Tilly was still staring at the passenger door when it closed.

She must have imagined it. A wedding is a romantic event; everyone has hearts in their eyes. Nica just got caught up in the romance of it. She doesn't know our history. She can't see that there is NO WAY Ronin would be interested in me.

Convinced that Nica must be wrong, Tilly gathered her things and locked the van. She wanted to get home and tell Mack about the open position at In Bloom. She wouldn't think any more about Ronin McGuire and his potential feelings for her.

TILLY PACED UP and down the long hallway in her apartment. It was late Wednesday afternoon, and Mackenzie should be home from her interview with Anna Lee at any moment. Tilly had told Mack to not text or call her after the interview—just to come home so they could discuss it face to face.

She'd prepared a large salad for their dinner and baked fresh bread in a Dutch oven. Since the weather service predicted rain all evening, they had planned to stay in and watch movies. Mackenzie had a list of the top one hundred movies of all time that she was trying to watch over the summer. They had checked off twenty-two so far. Tilly was supportive of Mack's goal, but hoped they could watch her favorite movie of all time tonight: *The Wizard of Oz.*

She heard a car door slam and peeked out of the curtain on the back door where she had a view of their parking spaces. Mack wasn't home yet. She regretted telling Mack to stop for a celebratory treat if the interview went well. But she hoped her roommate's lateness meant she was doing just that.

Her cell phone rang with her brother's ringtone, the March of the Winkies from *The Wizard of Oz.* She hurried to the kitchen counter to answer it.

"Hey. What's up?" she said, glancing at the clock again.

"Making plans for Saturday and wanted to check in," he said.

"Oh, sure. What do you need?"

"I should arrive with the moving van at noon. Ronin will start moving in earlier. He said he hoped to be there by nine. Can you check in with him to see what he needs help with? And can you plan to bring us lunch around one thirty? That should give me time to unload the moving van before stopping to eat."

"Won't you be famished by one thirty?"

"I'll have a few snacks for the drive. I'll be fine."

"Okay. Yes, I can do both of those things. Did you and Ronin decide which bedrooms you'll get already, or will he get first dibs?"

"We decided when we viewed the apartment. He gets the front bedroom, and I'll get the back."

"All right. Any requests for lunch?"

"Check with Ronin on that. You know what I like."

She did. All meat, all the time. And no raw tomatoes—ever. "Got it. Are you excited for the move?"

"I'll just be glad when it's over. I hope I don't have to move again for a couple years."

"We'll have to find you a girlfriend, and maybe you can settle down in a couple years."

"I don't know about that. I'm about as unlucky in love as you are, Sis."

Tilly sighed. She didn't know how anyone could be as unlucky as she was. She wanted to give encouraging advice, like she would to any of her girlfriends. She could be the spunky cheerleader for all her friends, but her brother knew her better than anyone. He'd know if she said anything she didn't mean. "Well, there's that. The unlucky-in-love siblings. UIL Sibs. Maybe that's our super-duo name."

Michael laughed softly. "Like the Wonder Kids. Superpowers, activate. We're not hopeless. Let's not give up on ourselves. I'll see you Saturday. Hey, maybe being in the same city, we can help each other find someone special."

"Be your wingman? Ew. No. You've got Ronin for that. I've got Mackenzie. I'll call Ronin and be prepared to help with the move and lunch. Love you, big bro."

"Love ya, little sis."

They hung up and Tilly glanced at the clock again. *Ugh, this waiting is hard.*

She picked up a few odds and ends in the living room and added a few things to the grocery list posted on the fridge. She put a reminder alarm on her phone to call Ronin. She'd wait until Mack got home; she didn't want to be on the phone when Mack walked in with her news.

She didn't hear her roommate's car pull in, but she heard the back door open. She jogged down the hallway and searched Mack's face for an indication that she had the job (or not). Mack, being an actress, wasn't easy to read. There were times when she'd have the deepest scowl on her face, and when pressed, would say she was perfectly happy, just doing facial expression exercises.

"Well?" Tilly asked, stopping Mack's progress into the apartment.

Mack smiled, and her pale blue eyes crinkled at the corners—a genuine smile. "She said I could start on Saturday. Since you took the day off and all."

Tilly squealed. "Yay! I knew you'd get the job. It'll be fun working together. I'm so excited. What did you think of Anna Lee?"

Mack handed Tilly a plastic grocery bag as she shifted her backpack. "Take this," she started. "Anna Lee was so sweet. She's an old soul. I dig her so much. Reminded me of my grandma."

"I know," Tilly said, leading the way down the hall. "She is the sweetest. I'm glad you liked her. She can be a little…eccentric. Is that the right word? I don't know. But she's full of advice and laughs. Did you see her cat, Salty?"

"Yes; the cat was sprawled out over the table during the interview. Anna Lee had a list of questions, but she didn't take a single note during the interview. When we were finished and she offered me the job, she walked to the register and pulled out a small notebook from the cabinet underneath. She flipped it open and then asked me a few tactical questions about the schedule. She scribbled a few notes then, but that was it."

"She's like that. Her memory is sharp; she doesn't need a lot of notes. I'm sure if it was a work order, she'd take notes, but when it comes to people, she remembers their stories. If you mention something that happened to you in the past, she won't ever forget what you said. She's brought up some things I've said over the years, things I've completely forgotten I mentioned to her. If the right situation comes up, and it makes sense to mention it again, she will."

In the kitchen, Tilly set the grocery bag on the counter. "I have a salad and fresh-baked bread ready for dinner. It's a little early. Want to eat now?"

"No, not yet. I bought a small tiramisu cheesecake at the bakery to celebrate."

"Oh, yum! Well, change and get comfy, and we'll start a movie. What do you want to drink?"

Mack tossed her head side to side as she decided. "A seltzer. On ice, please. I'll be right back."

Tilly poured a lemon-lime seltzer for Mack and a berry one for herself. She prepared a snack plate of sliced cheese, crackers, grapes, and olives that would tide them over until they took a break for dinner. She pulled down the blinds in the living room and turned on her collection of decorative lights: the frog with the glowing eyes, the three small houses with light shining from their windows, and the large stained-glass egg that shone from inside. The little lights set the mood for a night curled up on the couch or in the recliner watching movies.

Hours later, having watched *Vertigo* and *Rear Window*, Tilly clicked off the TV and turned to Mack, who was lying prone on the couch, a thrift-store afghan covering her legs. "You awake?" When Mack didn't respond, Tilly whispered, "I'm turning in." She got up, turned off the decorative lights, and went to bed.

CHAPTER FOUR

*E*VEN THOUGH IT was summer break, Tilly liked to set an alarm and wake up consistently at seven thirty. It was easier than when she let her sleep schedule get out of whack.

She crept out to the kitchen/living room area to see if Mack was still on the couch. It was empty, and Tilly was glad that Mack had made it to her comfortable bed at some point.

Humming to herself, she filled the coffee carafe and poured it into the maker. Pulling the plastic basket that housed the coffee supplies down from the cabinet, she selected a medium-roast *crème brûlée* and a French vanilla coffee. Putting four scoops of each into the coffee maker, she replaced the plastic basket in the cabinet and turned on the machine.

Pulling her phone from her back pocket, she considered the time. She had to call Ronin to coordinate Saturday's move-in activities, but she worried it might be a little too early to call. She didn't know what kind of schedule he was keeping.

"I can always leave a message," she told herself as she selected his number and pushed send.

Ronin answered on the second ring. "Good morning, Emmy!"

"Good morning, yourself. I hope I didn't call too early." *Though he sounds way too chipper to have been asleep.*

"Not at all," he said. "I've been up for a while."

"Ah, you're an early bird." She'd always told herself that she knew Ronin about as well as you could know a childhood friend, but now it occurred to her that after the five years he'd been away at school, she needed to reevaluate just how well she really knew him. College and graduate school were behind him. Who knew how much his world view had changed in that time?

She could hear the smile in his voice as he said, "You must be, too."

"It's easier if I keep consistent sleep hours."

"Same." He paused, and the image of him in bed, shirtless, popped into her mind. *Whoa, not going there.* "What's up?" he asked.

"Oh, I wanted to call about Saturday. I talked to Michael yesterday and he asked me to make lunch and thought lunch at one thirty would work. I wanted to see if that was okay with you, and if you have any food restrictions that I don't know about."

When they were kids, Ronin had said he had a peanut butter allergy, but Tilly always suspected he just didn't like peanut butter. Of course, that wasn't something she'd mess with; she wouldn't try to sneak peanut butter into anything she was giving him.

"No food restrictions. Thanks for offering to make lunch."

"Sure thing. Now, Michael said he'd be here around noon. Do you want any help before then?"

"As far as moving, I think I'm covered. I hired some of Shevaun's friends to help with the heavy lifting. Since you offered, I would love some help unpacking. Maybe you could unpack books or kitchen items and put them away."

"You trust me with putting your stuff away?" Tilly asked.

"Of course. I mean, we're talking about books and dishes. I'll handle my underwear myself."

Tilly's cheeks flared; she was thankful he couldn't see her. "I should hope so. I wouldn't touch your underwear with a ten-foot pole."

Great. Now she sounded like an eight-year-old.

Ronin's deep laugh caused Tilly to smile. She realized how much she'd missed it. When she had seen him during the last few years, it had usually been at holiday gatherings with both their families around. Their interactions felt moderated and watched. She felt like she was on the set of a TV sitcom—there were laughs, but it felt canned, forced. The jokes that could be made in front of their parents were chaste, never off-color.

"Is that a no to the books and kitchen stuff?" he asked.

"No. I'll help." She thought about several devious ways she could help—she could switch the jackets on some of the books or put them on the shelves backwards. She could put plates in drawers and silverware in upper cabinets. "What time do you want me there?"

"Eleven-ish. That gives us the chance to unload the truck and get boxes into the appropriate rooms."

"Sounds good."

"Em?" He paused. She waited. "Thanks for helping out. It's going to be fun to live down the street from you."

"We'll see about that."

She hung up and grabbed a coffee cup. Smiling, she thought about the exchange with Ronin. Yes, it was going to take a little getting used to, having him and Michael close by again, but it could be fun. She could picture impromptu barbecues in the backyard, talking and listening to music late into the night. Or movie nights. Or doing things together around town.

There was the bonus that if she had car trouble and needed a lift, they would be close by. It would be like having two big brothers half a block away.

Well, one big brother and his friend. She considered Ronin her friend, too. Though he got on her nerves like a brother at times, there were other times, like when he picked her up for Paige's wedding and stood at her front door in a dark suit and tie with still-damp hair, when the sight of him made her toes curl and her ankles go weak. And when he'd carried her across the parking lot at the wedding, she couldn't help the exhilaration that had coursed through her body. But she'd reminded herself that he wasn't an actual date, just a friend doing her a favor. She forced herself to think about wet chickens—anything to stop her body's reaction to him. Just friends. They couldn't be anything more. She'd repeated the mantra in her head as she followed him out the door that day, and as she lowered the coffee cup, she found herself practicing it again.

UNABLE TO WAIT any longer, Tilly left for Ronin and Michael's apartment at ten on Saturday. She'd dressed comfortably in denim shorts and a bright pink T-shirt with matching pink tennis shoes. Her hair was pulled up into a high ponytail, and she wore small diamond stud earrings that her parents had given her for her eighteenth birthday.

Grabbing the casserole dish of baked mostaccioli and the loaf of fresh bread she'd bought at the bakery, Tilly started towards their apartment building.

She saw Shevaun walking out the front door. The girl's bleached white hair was spiked with gel, and she wore a Metallica T-shirt, probably a hand-me-down from her dad. Mr. McGuire might be a kindly doctor by day, but that man loved his heavy metal.

"Tilly!" Shevaun shouted, spotting her. She ran across the tiny front yard and threw her arms around Tilly. Tilly laughed as she gripped the casserole dish tighter.

"Hi, Shevaun. It's so good to see you."

"You haven't come by in forever," the young woman chided.

"Hey, you were away at school. I've been to your parents' several times this year."

"It's not enough. I miss you." Shevaun rested her head on Tilly's shoulder. "You're the best."

"Oh, that's the sweetest. You're going to make me cry. Here, take this bag with the bread and lead the way."

They walked up to the boys' apartment. Shevaun gave Tilly the recap of the morning's events and introduced her to the friends that Ronin had hired to help with the move. Shevaun said she was just there to supervise because she wasn't getting paid.

They walked into the living room where two young men were sliding a TV stand into place. She could hear Ronin talking from what she assumed was his bedroom down the hall. Shevaun led Tilly into the kitchen, tossing the bread onto a stack of boxes by the fridge.

Tilly grimaced slightly, hoping the bread didn't get crushed. It was fresh and supple, and she hoped it would stay that way.

"Ronin has been a pain all morning." Shevaun hopped up onto the counter, almost knocking over a large bottle of water. "I don't think he slept last night. He's a grouch."

"I'm sure he's had a lot on his mind, preparing for the move and the new business."

"Don't you stick up for him, too," Shevaun whined. "You should always take my side when it comes to Ronin."

Tilly laughed softly. "No sides, Shevaun."

She placed the casserole in the fridge. If Michael wanted to eat at one thirty, she had time before it needed to go in the oven. She turned to check out the stove. Footsteps alerted her to someone's approach. She didn't realize she was nervous about seeing Ronin until her heart sped up in anticipation.

A guy around Shevaun's age appeared around the corner. She didn't want to admit it, but she was disappointed it wasn't Ronin. He sported a flopped-over mohawk and had a large safety pin sticking through his ear. *Yikes,* Tilly thought. *Looks like that would hurt if it got snagged.*

"Hi," she said. "I'm Tilly."

"Oh," Shevaun said. "Tilly. This is Mai Tai. Mai Tai, this is Tilly. Be nice."

"Nice to meet you, Mai Tai," Tilly said, holding back a giggle.

"'Sup?" the young man grunted in return. "Vaun, Ro says we can go after the last load."

"Cool. But I'm staying."

"Cool." Mai Tai left, and Ronin walked into the kitchen.

He was dressed for a hot moving day in comfortable-looking basketball shorts and a tank top that showed everyone he was not a stranger to the gym.

Tilly blinked rapidly, feeling a little self-conscious, and worrying that she had overstepped by making herself at home in his apartment—standing in his kitchen and opening his refrigerator at his sister's direction, not his. Then there were his biceps and his long legs and his sweaty hair. *What was that mantra from the other day?* "Hi," she said, as confidently as she could.

"Emmy, thanks for coming to help. We'll have everything unloaded soon. I have to keep an eye on Vaun's friends. I'll be back in a few."

At his words, Shevaun rolled her eyes and dropped down from the counter. "I'll go. Keep the peace. Make yourself..." she paused. "Useful," she finished, leaving the room with a wink.

Tilly laughed and glanced around the kitchen. There were a few boxes placed about haphazardly. She could probably start unboxing. She wondered if anyone had thought to wipe out the cabinets first. She hated the idea of throwing his stuff into dirty cabinets. She should have brought cleaners. A guy might not think about that. She glanced at the boxes, hoping Ronin had brought some kitchen cleaners with him. "Ah ha!" she shouted, spotting a box labeled "cleaners and misc.". She wasn't sure what miscellaneous he'd have, but she hoped for a rag and a good liquid cleaner.

She quickly found what she needed and filled the sink with hot water, adding two squirts of the cleaner. The water bubbled up, and she dipped a white cloth and got busy. She lost herself in the work, humming to herself and wishing she'd brought earbuds.

Thirty minutes later, she had the cabinets washed out and all the doors open to dry. She'd start putting stuff away soon. She investigated each of the kitchen boxes and organized them according to where she planned to put everything. She wanted to tell Ronin her plan of attack and get his agreement before she got too far.

Surveying the boxes, she hoped her brother was bringing dishes, because she could not find any in Ronin's stuff.

Setting the cleaner under the sink, she jumped when someone cleared their throat behind her.

"How's it going?" Ronin asked.

She stood and spun quickly. "Good. I washed everything down before putting anything away. Glad you're here; I want to show you where I'm planning to put everything and get your approval."

His eyes looked tired. She could see what Shevaun meant; he must not have gotten a lot of sleep. She wanted to tease him about it but she couldn't do it. She had a sudden urge to make him feel better instead. *I wish I'd baked cookies.*

His shoulders rose and fell in a deep sigh. "Whatever you want to do, Em. I trust you. Have you heard from Michael?"

She glowed at his comment and grabbed her phone. She had a text from Michael. "Yes, hold on." She read the text and conveyed Michael's ETA. (She didn't convey the fact that he'd stopped to use a restroom when he sent the text).

Ronin nodded. "Good. Right on time. I'm going to return the moving van, and I'll be back to help. Shevaun is staying. Don't let her get in your way."

At the mention of her name, Shevaun ran and hopped up on the counter. Tilly was glad she hadn't scrubbed that piece of counter yet. Oh well, she'd put boxes there as she worked and scrub it later.

"What time's lunch?" Shevaun asked. "Tilly brought a casserole."

"Oh, yeah?" Ronin asked.

"Baked mostaccioli," Tilly confirmed to Ronin. Turning to Shevaun, she answered, "Whenever everyone is ready. I partially baked it at home, so it will only need about twenty minutes to finish."

Ronin grabbed his stomach and Tilly's eyes followed his hand's movement. His tank was slim-fit and hugged him in all the right places. As his hand pressed the shirt close to his body, she thought she could see the ridges of his abs. The idea that she could count them to find out if it was a six pack, (or an eight pack?) crossed her mind. She felt her cheeks heat at that thought. Ugh. She had to get over this little obsession with his physique. It wasn't healthy.

"Yum," he said. "It may be dangerous living so close to you, Em."

Her mind was still on his abs. Dangerous, yes. "I only cook for special occasions. Like move-in days. As Anna Lee always says, 'Don't be too good of a cook, or you'll never go out to dinner.'"

Shevaun laughed. "Yes! Who's Anna Lee?"

"My boss at In Bloom. She's amazing."

"Maybe you could get a job there, Vaun. You said you were looking," Ronin said.

"Why haven't you left yet, bro Ro? Don't you have a truck to return?"

Ronin shook his head as he walked away. "Back in a bit," he called over his shoulder.

"Are you looking for a job?" Tilly asked. She knew Anna Lee could use some more help.

"Sort of. I mean, I want a cushy job working for Ronin. I don't want to work too hard." Shevaun leaned back on her hands—her feet swinging back and forth, causing the pockets in her too-short cut-offs to wiggle—the epitome of a bored teenager.

"Hard work is good for you. Helps you build resilience and makes it easier to deal with the really hard stuff that life sends your way." Tilly grabbed a box of pots and pans and set it on the counter.

Shevaun yawned loudly. Tilly was used to dramatics from Mackenzie, but not from Ronin's sister. Tilly wondered what-all Shevaun had learned during her freshman year of college. "Life's hard. You grow old and you die."

"Ouch," Tilly responded. "You sound cynical. What's that all about?"

"Do you know how hard it is to live up to the expectations of my parents? My dad is a doctor, and my mom is a best-selling author. It's ridiculous. Now, Ronin is starting his own company—"

"With Michael," Tilly added.

"Yes, with Michael, and I just know they're going to be successful. Where does that leave me? I don't know what I want to do. I don't know what kind of degree to get. Most of the time, I just want to create chaos. Poke the bear, you know?" A look of sadness or hurt flashed across Shevaun's face.

Tilly was shocked. Shevaun always seemed to have everything figured out. She was a great communicator, confident, and creative. She had been a straight-A student through high school; her family loved to brag about it. Could one year of college have shaken Shevaun's belief in herself? Was Ronin aware of his sister's feelings? The friend with the floppy mohawk suddenly made more sense.

Tilly crossed the kitchen and threw her arms around Shevaun's waist, the highest she could reach with Shevaun sitting on the counter. "Oh, sweetie. It's okay. You don't have to figure it out yet. Heck, I'm going into my senior year, and I don't know what I want to do. I'm worried my psychology major is going to go to waste. Like you, I have successful, driven parents, and it feels impossible to live up to their expectations. But keep this in mind: our parents love us and want us to be happy. Yes, they have expectations. They aren't going to sit by and watch us make terrible decisions that ruin our lives. They want to see us successful, sure. But they're okay letting us figure out what success means to us."

She squeezed the younger woman's shoulders and stood back. Shevaun had tears running down her face. "Oh, no! I'm sorry I made you cry."

"It's fine. I needed that. I needed those words. Thank you. Now I know why Ronin has the hots for you."

"What?" Tilly's voice rose, almost a shriek. She jumped backwards from Shevaun like her words were white hot darts being thrown at her.

Shevaun smiled and wiped her cheeks. "It's okay, Ronin doesn't realize it, either. Well, I was going to stay for your baked pasta, but I'm going to run. I need to go think about things. Life. Big things. Tell Ronin I'll call later."

Hopping off the counter, Shevaun wrapped Tilly in a warm embrace. Tilly felt the girl's bony shoulder blades and thought she needed some pasta.

"Are you sure you can't stay for lunch?" Tilly asked. Not only did she want to feed Shevaun, she also wanted the buffer when Ronin returned.

"No. Thanks. More for Ronin. You know what they say, the way to a man's heart and all. But don't worry, you've already got his heart."

Tilly shook her head. "You're wrong. We're just friends, nothing more. I couldn't imagine dating him."

"Well, maybe I'm wrong." She shrugged. "But I don't think so. I'll see you later."

Shevaun walked through the front door and Tilly leaned against the counter, processing her words. First, the turmoil Shevaun was in, and second, the comment she made about Ronin having feelings for her. How could that be? They hadn't been around each other much in the last few years. Plus, Tilly knew Ronin had been in a pretty serious relationship; she got the updates from Michael. Ronin and his girlfriend had just split up in January, right after the holidays. She hadn't asked him about it, but maybe she needed to.

CHAPTER FIVE

RONIN EXPECTED TO hear Shevaun's voice as soon as he opened the apartment door. His sister was rarely quiet, and when she was, you had to worry about what she was up to.

"Hello?" he called, walking into what sounded like an empty apartment.

"Oh, hey." Tilly popped up from behind the kitchen counter. "I was just putting away your pans. I thought this was a good place, just steps away from the stove. What do you think?"

He glanced at the stove and back at her. A small strand of her light brown hair had come loose from her ponytail and swayed in front of her eye. As she stood there, she swiped at it several times.

A few beads of perspiration dotted her forehead. "That's fine," he said. "Is it too warm in here? You're sweating."

Tilly rolled her eyes. "Horses sweat, men perspire, and women glow. That's what Anna Lee says." She raised her arm and wiped her face on the sleeve of her loose T-shirt. "And no, it's not too warm. I was just…" She paused. "Dancing before you got here."

"Dancing? There's no music."

"There is in my head." She laughed, and Ronin wanted to record the sound so he could play it whenever he was feeling down. "How did the truck return go?"

"Easy. Mai Tai gave me a ride back."

"What kind of name is Mai Tai?"

"You get your nickname from memorable moments, I guess."

"What sort of nicknames do you have?" she asked.

"None that I know of."

She raised an eyebrow. "Yeah, right. I'll ask Michael when he gets here. He should be here soon."

Her voice sounded hopeful, and Ronin felt hurt that she wasn't happy to be alone with him for a while. "He's the one person you *can't* ask."

"If I ask, he'll tell me *everything*." She stressed the last word and he wanted to groan.

"No. Bro code."

"Ha, ha. Joke's on you. I get first dibs on the bro code. He has to tell me. We share DNA."

Ronin walked over and tossed his keys on the counter. They slid against the wall and he hoped they wouldn't get lost in the mess left by the unpacking. "We'll see. How much more unpacking do you have left in the kitchen?"

"Just two more boxes. Once Michael gets here and I get his stuff put away, I'll show you both where everything is. I just hope you don't have to rearrange everything when I'm gone." She laughed, but Ronin heard nervousness behind it. The sound was strange. Tilly was usually all light and laughter. She hadn't seemed nervous around him since her eighth-grade graduation when she was upset about having a mouthful of braces for so many important photos.

He had to stop fixating on her every mood. "Sounds good. I'm going to go to my bedroom and start putting stuff away."

"Do you still want help with your books?" Tilly asked as she tucked the loose hair back into her ponytail. "Will you and Michael share bookshelves?"

"Not sure. My bookcases went into my bedroom. And yes, I could still use help with that, when you're ready."

Meet me in my bedroom was the phrase Ronin could not add. He started to, but it got stuck in his throat. It would have sounded like he was coming on to her, and he could NOT think like that around Tilly.

"Okay," she answered. That nervousness was there again. When she came to work on the books, he was going to have to leave the bedroom. He'd better put his underwear away first.

Twenty minutes later, he heard a commotion at the door. Not a crisp knock, but a dull bang. He hurried out, but Tilly beat him to the door. She flung it open and squealed when she saw her brother. Ronin could tell she wanted to launch herself into her brother's arms, but Michael was holding a large indoor houseplant. Tilly bounced on her toes and clapped her hands, waiting for him to set the plant down.

As soon as he did, she threw her arms around him. Michael squeezed her back as he nodded at Ronin. Ronin felt a twinge of jealousy watching the siblings embrace. Tilly turned her head to rest it on Michael's chest, and he could see her face. Her eyes were closed, and her face wore a huge grin. She squeezed Michael tighter before letting go. *Man, what I would do to trade places with him right now!*

Michael smiled over Tilly's head. "How's it going, roommate?"

Tilly stepped back and Ronin held out his hand to shake Michael's. "Worse now that you're here, Eminem."

"Hardy har, man." Michael looked around the living room and kitchen combo, nodding his head. "You guys have been busy. Are you ready to help me unload the van?"

"You two have the muscles, so you can unload. I'm still unpacking a few boxes of Ronin's stuff in the kitchen," Tilly answered, making her way back to the kitchen.

"I'm ready," Ronin replied.

"Let's do it," Michael said, walking through the door.

Once Michael's things were unloaded, Ronin asked Tilly to heat up the pasta while he and Michael returned the rental van.

Back at the apartment building, Ronin teased Michael about his late arrival as they walked upstairs. Entering the apartment, he took a whiff of the spicy, creamy pasta that Tilly was pulling from the oven.

"Perfect timing!" she called, setting the dish on top of the stove.

"Smells delish," Michael said.

"Agreed!" Ronin chimed in. He gave Michael a light jab. "If that pasta is half as good as it smells, you'd better be extra nice to your sister, so she feeds us more often."

"I'm a broke-as-a-joke college senior; if you want me to cook for you, you're going to have to cough up some cash for the groceries."

"Yes, ma'am!" Ronin teased. "We may be eating ramen noodles until Michael and I get our business off the ground. I'm glad we're finally both in the same place so we can make some real progress."

There was so much planning, organizing, and executing to do. And he needed to throw himself into work to get Tilly off of his mind. There was no way he could date his roommate's little sister. Michael would never allow it. Sure, there were bro rules, and he didn't think Michael would tell Tilly about some of his more outrageous mistakes, but she was Michael's sister, and his loyalty would go to her first, as it should.

TILLY'S PLANS FELL through as soon as she got home. She was supposed to go to a new restaurant with Mackenzie, but Mack got a last-minute invitation to dinner with a guy from her drama program that she'd been crushing on all year.

As Mack rushed out the door, Tilly reminded her to call if she needed a ride.

The door closed behind her friend and Tilly sighed. *Hmm, now what to do about dinner?* she mused.

She decided to go for a walk to get some fresh air. Unpacking boxes of books and miscellaneous kitchen items had irritated her sinuses. She laced up her tennis shoes and grabbed her ear buds. She planned to listen to the new Taylor Swift album during her walk.

Her phone rang with her mom's ringtone. Since she was home alone, she answered it on the speaker.

"Hi, Mom. How are you?"

"Fine. Fine. Did your brother get moved in? I didn't want to bother him."

"Yep. I left there a little while ago. They were still unpacking."

"That's good. How's their apartment?"

"Good. So weird that I can see it from my bedroom. I like having a close relationship with him, but I hope this isn't too close. You know?"

"It'll be good for both of you. Just don't let those boys con you into doing their housework or cooking. They've got to learn."

"No chance of that!" Tilly laughed.

"That's good. What are your plans for this evening?"

"Mack and I were going to go out, but she got an invite from a guy and that took precedence, so I'm still deciding what to do."

"You could come home and visit us. Do you work Monday?"

Tilly considered. It had been a while since she'd been home. And if she got out of town, her brother wouldn't be able to rope her into helping with any more unpacking.

"No, but Tuesday is the Fourth, and Ronin invited us over for dinner and fireworks at his parents' place."

"That's fine, but why not come home? You could help me with my adoption research. I have a few new leads to work through, and two days—with your help—may lead to a breakthrough."

A thrill shot through Tilly. New leads? While her mom had talked for years about trying to find her birth parents, she'd only gotten serious about researching it this year when she had a spot that showed up on her annual mammogram. The doctor asked if she had a family history of breast cancer, and she had to say she didn't know because she was adopted. Since then, she had a new interest in finding her birth parents.

"New leads? That sounds promising! Umm…" If she packed a bag and left now, she could grab fast food on the road and be home in a couple of hours. She was thankful it was summer, with no homework in sight. "Sure, it'll take me a bit to pack and get ready. I should be home by eight."

"Fantastic! I'll make pancakes for breakfast tomorrow, and then we'll get busy. Maybe we'll take a break and go shopping at Woodfield."

Tilly smiled. Shopping with mom was always a good time. She had a great eye for clothing that was flattering, and she was happy to bring out the debit card and purchase clothes for her daughter.

"Sounds good, Mom. I'll see you soon."

"Call if you have any problems, sugar."

Tilly texted her brother to tell him that she was going home. Then she wrote a note for Mackenzie. Notifications complete, she packed a bag and headed out the door.

HOME. SITTING WITH her parents on the overstuffed couch in the TV room, Tilly sipped hot tea and waited for the movie to begin. Tonight, they were watching *Casablanca*, one of her dad's favorite movies.

As Chris Miller scanned the DVD cases for the movie, Irena told Tilly about the latest updates in her search for her birth parents.

"I finally received a copy of my birth certificate that does *not* have the location of my birth redacted. And, you're not going to believe this, I was born in Bloomington!"

"Wow!" Tilly leaned forward. This was a major update. "What else does it tell you? Parents' names? Hospital?"

"No parent names, but the hospital is listed."

"Which hospital?"

"Brokaw."

"Hmm, I haven't heard of it. Did you look it up?"

Irena looked down at the blanket in her lap, pulling on a loose string. Tilly wondered how far the blanket might unravel. "Not yet. Each step in this process brings me both joy and absolute terror. What if I don't like what I find? There are so many reasons why a mother chooses to give up her baby. So many bad situations, not many good ones."

"But what if you do? Like Anna Lee always says, don't borrow trouble. Don't worry about something you can't control or don't know the facts about. If it is bad news, deal with it then, not now."

"You sound wise beyond your years. I think your boss has had something to do with that."

"She is pretty amazing." Tilly sipped her tea and set it on the marble coaster on the end table. "What's the next step?"

"I need to figure out where the Brokaw hospital records went and see if I can get a copy of my original birth certificate. Maybe then I can find the names of my birth parents."

A shiver went down Tilly's back. For years, she had talked to her mom about this search. She knew Pops and Gigi had adopted Irena. Everyone was very open about it. It had been Gigi who'd suggested searching for Irena's birth parents when the laws changed. Irena had talked about it, but it wasn't until the mammogram that she started to get serious about looking.

"Wow," Tilly replied. "Every step is one step closer to the goal. It's so exciting."

"Exciting is mild. I'm still petrified, though." Irena smiled, and Tilly knew her mom was exaggerating.

Her dad put the DVD in the player and picked up the remote. "Ladies, do you need anything else before we start?"

"No, we're good," Tilly and her mom replied in unison.

Tilly thought about what her mom had said. Yes, she credited Anna Lee for putting a lot of life into perspective. Anna Lee was quick with advice and had a different way of looking at things. Tilly appreciated it and felt that she was better able to deal with avoiding "borrowed trouble" now. She still fretted about a career decision. She was interested in psychology because she liked talking to people and understanding what had made them who they were and how to help them improve their lives. But she wasn't sure about pursuing it far enough to become a licensed practitioner or doctor.

That felt like too much responsibility, and she worried she would be too stressed by taking on that kind of challenge. Her parents had high expectations for her and her brother. They were both bank executives, and while they didn't expect their kids to follow in their footsteps, they expected Tilly and Michael to succeed in whatever they chose.

The problem was that Tilly couldn't choose. Nothing seemed to fit her just right. Like Goldilocks but without blonde hair.

It was times like these that she struggled with envy. It seemed all her friends had their lives figured out. They knew what they wanted and were going after their dreams. Mack would become an actress, Paige a book editor, Nica a contractor, and Lauren had just secured a job at a Greek importing company in Chicago. Even Michael and Ronin were laser-focused on getting their co-working space business off the ground. It seemed risky to her, but she knew whatever the two of them set out to do, they would make it work.

Once her dad sat back on the couch, her mother snuggled into his side, and he stretched out with his feet on the ottoman. The bucket of popcorn—extra butter—was resting between her and her mom.

She studied the pair out of the corner of her eye for a moment. After all these years, they still seemed to be completely in love. Sure, they argued occasionally, but they were always respectful to each other.

Tilly hoped she would find someone like that someday. Someone who could read her mood as soon as she walked in the door. Who knew when to push and when to back off. Someone who was her best friend, her confidant, and her love.

HOURS LATER, THE boys' apartment was starting to look like home. Boxes were emptied, broken down, and placed in the recycling bin behind the building. They'd agreed on furniture placement for the shared living spaces. Tilly had shown them where everything was in the kitchen, and she'd even run to the store to buy groceries to stock the fridge and cabinets.

She'd left earlier, saying she had plans. When Michael asked if she had a date, she just laughed and acted mysteriously. Ronin felt his shoulders tense, and he had to resist the urge to follow her into the hallway and drill her for answers.

Once she'd closed the apartment door, Michael turned to him. "She's still a brat. Why did we move this close to her?"

"Don't look at me, dude. You're the one that wanted to be this close."

"Oh, right." Michael nodded. "That was on me. Well, she made herself useful for once. Not sure that will happen again."

"Come on, man." Ronin shook his head. "That's harsh."

"Sorry. Getting hangry, I guess."

"Want to heat up Emmy's pasta for dinner?"

"As delicious as it was," Michael countered, "can we order a pizza?"

"Sure. Maybe we should have asked Em for recommendations. Her neighborhood and all."

"Right. I'll call her. How does a meat lovers sound?"

"No veggies?"

Michael grunted. "I suppose. Which ones?"

"Onions, green peppers, and olives."

"Absolutely not on the olives. And sausage and pepperoni?"

"Sounds great."

Michael shook his head and walked towards his bedroom. "I wouldn't say great, but it'll be all right."

Ronin sorted through component and stereo cables in the living room. Another hour or so of unpacking, and he'd be ready to sit in front of the TV and relax. Once the food arrived, he'd be willing to call it quits for the day. They still had Sunday to settle into their new digs, though there was nothing stopping him from getting to his parents' house for Sunday dinner, unpacked or not.

He would text his mom in the morning to see if it was okay to invite Michael to dinner. He hoped she wouldn't suggest Tilly, too. No way did he want Tilly and Shevaun in the same room more often than he could help it.

When the doorbell rang an hour later, Ronin strode across the room to answer. It was the pizza delivery, so he pushed the button to unlock the downstairs door.

"Pizza's here!" He shouted to Michael.

He heard a grunt of acknowledgment from Michael's room.

The young woman delivering the pizza looked to be around Shevaun's age. He cringed inwardly thinking about Vaun delivering pizza. It didn't seem safe, especially on a Saturday night. She could be walking into a college frat party full of drunken jerks. She was a petite kid whose mouth was lethal, but her muscles were not.

Michael walked into the living room and Ronin turned to him as he took the pizza from the delivery girl. "Did you tip online?"

Michael smiled at the delivery girl. "I did."

"Thanks," she said as she gave a quick wave.

She turned to leave when Michael called out. "Hey, what's your name?"

The blonde turned back. "Reese. Have a good night."

She hurried down the stairs and Michael closed the door. "She was hot," he said.

"Sure. I guess," Ronin replied. *She was cute, but not nearly as pretty as Emmy.*

Dang. Why did his thoughts have to go there? Living this close to her was definitely harder than he'd thought. Add living with her brother, and Ronin was in trouble.

Seeing her as frequently as he anticipated, it was going to be even harder to get over her. And how was he going to hide his feelings from his roommate? No one knew him better than Michael. Yes, he had other close friends, but none as close as Michael. Now that they were living together, it wouldn't take long for them to be reading each other's minds.

And he could not have Michael guessing what he was thinking about Tilly. Because he knew if Michael had half the thoughts about Shevaun or Trinity that Ronin had about Tilly, Ronin would have to grind Michael to a pulp.

CHAPTER SIX

THE FOURTH OF July was a glorious, sunny day. Tilly took her time getting ready. Swimming in the McGuire's pool was a possibility, so she asked Mackenzie to French braid her hair. She wore a bright pink swimsuit under her patriotic T-shirt and blue denim shorts. She put sunglasses with bright red frames in the tote bag, along with a beach towel and sunscreen.

Michael had picked her up, and during the drive, he updated her on his and Ronin's plans for getting their business going.

"Ronin is passionate about making the business work. He's talked to a lot of people who started working remotely during the pandemic, and many of them said that their mental health took a dive because they couldn't socialize with others. It bothered him to hear that. On the other hand, it provides more opportunities to work for companies that aren't local. You can apply for remote-work jobs with companies that are based anywhere now."

"Really?" she asked.

"Yes. And companies can benefit from not requiring that space for employees. They have fewer rent and utility costs. Coworking spaces like ours will serve a lot of needs."

"That is wonderful. Sounds like Ronin did a lot of research."

"Absolutely." Michael nodded emphatically. "He took the lead on interviewing people. He was very thorough. He's more of a people person than I am. I prefer to work on systems. Once we figure out titles, I'll probably be the Chief Operations Officer and he'll be CEO. He's got the looks, and I've got the brain."

Tilly smiled thinking about the scarecrow in her favorite movie. "Ronin's smart, too!"

"Well, yeah, I know that."

As the conversation waned, Tilly thought about Ronin's research. It was interesting to hear that he was upset about people struggling with their mental health during the pandemic, as that was an area of interest for her, too. She wanted to help others deal with depression and anxiety, to find hope and bright spots. Interesting that Ronin also wanted that; that he wasn't just about the bottom line.

As Michael turned into their hosts' driveway, Tilly sighed softly. This house gave her the same feeling as going home. Comfort, safety, laughter. Living next door to each other for so many years made their old neighbors feel like extended family. Tilly sometimes thought that the two sets of parents conferred with each other on parental topics like boundaries, discipline, chores, and expectations. She knew she couldn't get away with things at the McGuire house—Ronin's parents were quick to correct her, just as her parents were quick to correct Ronin and his sisters.

Since the McGuires had moved to Bloomington, Tilly had visited, but not as often as she'd have liked. School, work, and socializing kept her busy. But when Kyle broke up with her last year, she'd made a beeline to the comfort and safety of the McGuire home. Elizabeth had grabbed a box of tissues, a cozy blanket, and an extra-large glass of water. She'd made Tilly curl up on the couch, tucked in under Elizabeth's arm, where Tilly proceeded to cry on her shoulder for an hour.

Reaching into the backseat, she grabbed the large container of chocolate chip, snickerdoodle, and sugar cookies that she had made, along with the flowers bought from Anna Lee the day before. The red roses, white peonies and blue hydrangeas were festive, and they'd added a mylar balloon on a stick that said, "Happy 4th!"

"Can I carry something?" Michael asked.

"Don't want to walk in empty handed? Want some of the credit?" She handed him the cookies.

"Yes and no. I won't take credit for your efforts."

Michael let her walk ahead of him and she rang the doorbell. Shevaun answered the door before the chime's dulcet tones had ended.

"Hi!" she said. Looking past Tilly, she added in huff, "Oh, you brought *him*."

"Hello to you too, Shevaun," Michael said. "Missed me, huh?"

"No, jerk. Saturday was the worst day of the year, knowing you were moving to town."

Ronin walked into the foyer, hearing the exchange. "And you want us to hire you, Vaun? With that attitude?"

"I was teasing!" she shrieked. "I love you, Michael, and I'm so glad you're here! At least it got Ronin out of the house."

"Here, let me take those," Ronin said to Tilly, gesturing for the flowers.

"I got 'em. I want to give them to your mom."

"Sure. This way."

Tilly followed Ronin and she took a moment to take in the sight of him. Since the wedding, he'd begun to grow a beard and she thought it looked great on him. He wore a pair of deep blue cargo shorts with a red T-shirt, white socks, and tennis shoes. He'd obviously gelled his hair—the long hair from the front was slicked back. She preferred his loose hair, but this was a good look for him, too. More professional. She wondered if he was trying to impress someone important today.

They found Elizabeth in the kitchen. Trinity and Bruce McGuire were outside on the large deck overlooking the built-in swimming pool. Tilly glanced out the window and smiled as she saw a large unicorn blow-up ring floating in the pool.

"Mom, Emmy and Eminem are here," Ronin announced.

Elizabeth spun from the sink where she was washing dishes. Soap bubbles flew from her hands and landed across Ronin's chest.

He jumped back in surprise.

Tilly and Michael laughed as Elizabeth reached for the dish towel. "Sorry about that, honey," she said. She hastily dried her hands and wrapped her arms around Tilly, giving her a tight squeeze. "I'm so glad you could both join us today. I wish your parents could have made the drive, but your mom told me they were packing for a trip."

"Yes, they said to send their love. I went home on Saturday for an impromptu visit. Here." Tilly held out the flowers once Elizabeth released her. "These are for you."

"Oh, they're gorgeous. I suppose they came from In Bloom. You don't get this quality at the grocery store."

Tilly smiled. Anna Lee would agree with the sentiment. "Yes, they're from In Bloom."

Michael leaned over to hug Elizabeth. "Tilly made a bunch of cookies. I'm just carrying the box. I did nothing but show up."

Elizabeth smiled and pulled Michael's ear. "You know you can always just show up. Tilly, put those beautiful flowers on the table. Michael, you can put the cookies on the counter. I'll plate them later. Now, go say hello to everyone outside, and I'll join you in a few minutes."

Tilly appreciated Elizabeth's directness. It was almost like home.

Ronin followed her into the dining room.

"How was the drive over?" Ronin asked, and Tilly wondered about the small talk. It wasn't like him.

"Fine. Holiday and all. So, what's it like living with my brother? Are you at each other's throats yet?" Tilly shifted the vase side to side to find the perfect placement.

She heard Ronin chuckle behind her. "So far so good, but you can still count the time we've lived together in hours, so too soon to tell."

Satisfied with the flower placement, she turned to him. "Were you able to get started on any of your business tasks?"

Ronin leaned against the doorway, blocking it. "We spent a few hours yesterday viewing retail spaces online."

"Oh? Any luck?"

"One promising location, but the price was too high. We are thinking about looking for a realtor if we don't find something on our own by Friday."

When Ronin didn't move, Tilly looked to the door and raised an eyebrow in question. His eyes stayed fixed on hers, and she felt a tingle race along her shoulder blades. She shivered.

He finally shifted and turned sideways for her to pass. Passing him so closely, she could feel the heat from his body and smell his cologne. She wanted to lean closer still and have him wrap his arms around her. *Snap out of it, Tilly! What in the world are you thinking?*

AFTER A COUPLE hours spent swimming and goofing around in the pool and a delicious dinner of hamburgers, brats, potato chips, and yummy pasta salads, Shevaun and Trinity were responsible for dinner cleanup. Bruce and Elizabeth walked across the backyard, greeting their neighbors.

Tilly volunteered to set up an ice cream sundae bar on the kitchen counter. She filled small red, white, and blue bowls with all sorts of toppings—broken peanut butter cups, M&Ms, crushed peanuts, gummy worms, chocolate covered raisins (she shuddered thinking about them on ice cream, but Bruce loved it), cherries, and sprinkles. She arranged bottles of caramel, strawberry, butterscotch, and chocolate syrups.

Michael started building a Fourth of July playlist on his phone and asked everyone for suggestions.

"Miley's "Party in the USA" must be on the list," Shevaun said, drying her hands on a towel.

"'Born in the USA', the Boss," added Ronin.

Tilly thought Ronin had stepped outside when his parents had. The sound of his voice startled her. She turned and found him leaning against the counter, his arms crossed. *Whoa! His muscles are de-FINE-d. Oops, don't go there.* He must have been keeping an eye on his sisters.

"How about Tom Petty's "American Girls"?" Tilly asked.

Michael nodded. "You bet. That's a good start. I'll go do a search and finish the list. It'll be ready to go before the fireworks."

Shevaun stepped next to Tilly. "That looks like yummy goodness. Hey, we've started a family bike ride. You and Michael should join us."

"Really? That's great, but I don't have a bike."

"Not even at your parents'?" Ronin asked.

"No. Dad is into the minimalist movement and cleaned out the garage. He asked if I wanted my bike, but I told him to sell it. It was over ten years old, and I hadn't ridden it in forever."

"We have an extra one you could borrow." Shevaun pressed. "It would be great if you'd join us. Give Ronin something to focus on besides me."

"Knock it off, Vaun," Ronin said. "Yeah, we do have an extra," he said to Tilly. "You guys should join us. I saw Eminem's bike. It's pretty beat up but looks like it'd do a few miles."

Trinity shut the door of the dishwasher. "Should I run this now, you think?"

Tilly glanced at Ronin, assuming he'd give the direction, but it was Shevaun that answered, "Go for it. I'm grabbing a beer while the parents are gone."

"No, you're not," Ronin's voice was quiet, menacing, and firm.

"Am."

"No. Don't start something I have to finish."

Tilly busied herself by taking spoons out of the drawer and arranging them with the sundae cups.

"Don't be a d-"

"Hey!" Michael exclaimed. "Vaun, help me start a fire in the pit. I'm making s'mores."

"We're having sundaes."

"I'll have a s'more sundae."

Michael succeeded in getting Shevaun outside, out of Ronin's line of sight. Trinity pushed a button on the dishwasher, and it swooshed to life. "I'm heading outside, too," she said.

Tilly wanted to add a few more bowls of toppings. She reached into the grocery sack of candies and chocolates that Elizabeth had left for her to use and grabbed a bag of Snicker bars. She looked around for the knife block.

"What do you need, Em?" Ronin asked, advancing toward her.

She felt him still radiating irritation from Vaun pushing her boundaries. "I'll find it. Ah, there are the knives."

She pulled out a medium-sized knife that would easily slice the chocolate bars. "Oh, where's a cutting board?"

"Here." Ronin pulled out a cutting board from a cabinet and brought it to her.

He leaned against the counter as he placed the board on it.

"You can go on out, I'll just be a few more minutes."

"I don't mind. I'd like to avoid Vaun for a few more minutes. She's getting better at ticking me off. She's nineteen and acts like she's thirty."

"She's maturing."

"Too fast. She's a *TEEN-ager*."

"You're a good big brother." Tilly started unwrapping the mini candy bars and laid them on the cutting board.

Ronin grunted.

Tilly smiled at him. It was fun to see him like this, protective of his sisters. When they had last lived next door to each other, he'd been indifferent to the younger girls, just as he'd been indifferent to her.

"Hey." Tilly began slicing the chocolates. "Reminder, we're having a party Saturday night for my birthday. Come any time after eight."

"After eight? What are you doing for dinner?"

"Mack is taking me to dinner."

"Oh."

"Anyway, come to the party. I can introduce you to my roommate. Who knows? Maybe you'll hit it off." Tilly meant to say that in a teasing tone, but it came out a little stilted, and her stomach churned. She had thought it was a good idea, but her body didn't seem to agree.

"Don't meddle in my dating life, Emmy. I can manage just fine on my own."

"Can you?" She raised an eyebrow. She really wanted to know more about his dating life. Could he have met someone since moving to Bloomington?

"I can. No setups."

"Yes, sir." She cut up the last of the chocolates and scooped them into a bowl. Ronin grabbed a couple of pieces and popped them in his mouth.

"Mmm," he hummed. "Can't wait for the sundaes."

The noise of absolute pleasure that came from somewhere between his chest and his throat caused a flood of heat to wash over her. "Do you want one now?" she squeaked out.

"You'd make one just for me?" His right eyebrow, the one with a tiny white scar above it, lifted, and he pinned her with a look that stoked the fire covering her skin.

If she didn't know better, she would have thought he was

flirting with her. Before she could process that thought further, the words "in a heartbeat," flew out of her mouth.

Ronin opened his mouth to say something but shut it quickly when his mother stepped through the patio door. "We'd better wait for the others," he said.

ELIZABETH HAD COME in to see if the sundae bar was ready. Seeing that it was, she called everyone in to build their own treat. Everyone stood around eating ice cream and chatting. They dismantled the sundae bar before the fireworks began. The evening was turning chilly, and Tilly borrowed Shevaun's Southern Illinois University sweatshirt before they moved outdoors.

A row of Adirondack chairs was lined up at the edge of the stone-paved patio. Tilly laughed as she saw everyone start to line up by age, starting with Bruce at one end and Trinity on the other. With Tilly's observation, everyone shifted, and she found herself on one end, with Ronin to her left. Michael was in the middle, with Shevaun and Trinity on either side of him. The sisters had been arguing over chairs, and Elizabeth asked Michael to separate them.

The sky was completely dark with storm clouds rolling by. The weather forecast said storms would occur after midnight, and everyone was holding their breath, hoping the fireworks would go on as scheduled.

When the first firework went up, Tilly felt anticipation surge through her body. She smiled as she tilted her head back to watch the bursts overhead. She was glad they were on the far side of the park from where the fireworks were being launched. She loved the sights and sounds—from a distance. She didn't like worrying about wayward fireworks landing on her head or super-loud explosions.

She could hear Trinity and Shevaun bickering; Michael was doing a poor job of mediating. Ronin leaned toward her and made the same observation. His breath tickled her cheek and Tilly wondered why she'd put the sweatshirt on. Ronin's nearness was causing her blood pressure to spike and her temperature to jump.

An extra-large boom made her jump in her seat. Ronin reached over and squeezed her hand. "Startle much?" he asked. His question was comforting, not teasing. She appreciated the gesture and smiled at him. After a few seconds, she tried to pull her hand back, but Ronin held on tighter and turned his gaze back to the sky.

Accepting his touch, she turned her hand over and squeezed back. He didn't look at her, but she saw the corner of his mouth twitch up. She leaned back in her chair and sighed. The day had been perfect. Spending time with Ronin's family and Michael felt like stepping back in time. She'd been to the McGuires' house many times since they'd moved to town, but this was the first time she'd been there with her brother and Ronin. It felt like old times, except there was no hair-pulling and teasing from Ronin, just the comfort and warmth of holding his hand.

She hadn't thought much about Ronin moving here. He was just her brother's best friend, someone she had played with and hung out with through the years. In the last few years, he'd become a handy plus one, but she hadn't thought of him as a possible love interest before. He'd always just been there, a friend that she could count on.

But the last couple of weeks, ever since Paige's wedding, she'd felt something new. She was more aware of him; she noticed things about him that she never had before. And her body's reactions to him were telling her something.

Why did he clasp her hand? To calm her nerves, or was there something else? Was *he* trying to tell her something? Could Shevaun and Nica be right? Did he have feelings for her?

Could that explain Shevaun's side glances and giggles and Ronin's attempts to hush his sister when she was teasing him?

It was too much to think about. For now, Tilly was going to sit back and relax and enjoy the warmth and strength she felt from Ronin's hand holding hers.

CHAPTER SEVEN

TILLY COULD HEAR Mackenzie hang the last party
decoration, a life-size cutout of a Munchkin from *The
Wizard of Oz,* on the hallway wall across from her room.
There were twenty-one cutouts of various Oz characters hanging
around their apartment and the building's back patio.

Tilly was in her room, putting on a coat of soft pink lipstick.
She took a final glance at the mirror and shrugged. She wished
she hadn't allowed Mack to talk her into having a big party.
Everyone would expect her to get wasted and act like a fool. She
didn't want that kind of attention.

She was looking forward to introducing Mack to Ronin. She
was still confused about her growing feelings for him and thought
Mack could help her figure things out. Ever since the Fourth of
July celebration, Tilly kept analyzing the meaning behind Ronin
holding her hand.

She'd finally decided that it had just been a kind gesture meant
to comfort her, nothing more. Though that was her final verdict,
she wasn't sure how she felt about it. She was partially relieved;
it was easiest to keep Ronin in the box he'd always been in as
her brother's best friend.

But there was something comforting about holding his hand.

It wasn't a protective touch. It was a touch that said, "You got this, but I'm here just in case you need me."

She liked that. He wasn't trying to minimize or find fault in her fear; he just wanted to comfort her.

Mack knocked on her open door. "Ready for your first shot? I brought some tequila!" She held out a small shot glass of clear liquid. Tilly swallowed a lump. She dreaded this. Why was taking shots of liquor such a "to-do" on one's twenty-first birthday? *A rite of initiation? More like a rite of humiliation.* Her friends were coming, and she did not want anyone holding her hair back as she leaned over a toilet seat.

"Just one shot. Okay?"

"Yeah, right." Mackenzie leaned her head back and laughed, causing the long dangling chain earring with three silver stars that she wore on her left ear to fall behind her shoulder. Her right ear had two stud earrings, one slightly larger than the other one. "On the count of three. One, two, three!"

Mack lifted her shot glass to her mouth and let the liquid flow down her throat. She finished and smacked her lips.

"You like the taste of it?" Tilly asked.

"Hey, you didn't shoot it on my count. And no, I don't like the taste, but mind over matter. Bottom's up, buttercup!"

Tilly decided to get it over with and swallowed the shot in one go. Shot glass empty, she shivered. "Yuck! That's disgusting!"

Mack laughed. "I know. But you gotta roll with it. Hey, you told everyone to just come to the backyard, right? I was thinking we should lock up and head down."

"Yes, that's what I told everyone. What do we need to take down?"

"The coolers are there and loaded. I have two boxes with snack foods that we'll set out. And we need to grab the speaker. Everything else is down there. Let's go!"

Tilly followed Mack to the kitchen to get the necessary items.

As she stepped into the backyard, Tilly smiled. Mack's theater friends had come over earlier in the day, and they'd decorated the patio area with bales of hay, a faux yellow brick road, several pairs of ruby-colored shoes, rainbows, and poppy flowers.

She was thankful she had such a great roommate. Mack was outgoing, creative, and fearless, traits that Tilly wanted to work on for herself. Life was never dull with Mack around.

"This is gorgeous! You did an amazing job! Thank you so, so much!" Tilly grabbed Mack and pulled her into a hug. The smell of Mack's baby oil and musk wafted to Tilly's nose, and she smiled. She would always associate those scents with this time in her life and her amazing roommate.

"I had help, don't forget. Oh, hey!" Mack pulled away from the hug. "We have guests! Hi! Welcome! I'm Mackenzie, everyone calls me Mack."

Tilly turned to see Paige, Trevor, Nica, and Grady arriving. She hugged each of them and introduced them to Mack. "So glad you could come! Welcome!"

"We wouldn't miss it!" Paige exclaimed, holding up a bottle of orange-flavored vodka. "We are stocking your bar."

Nica nodded. "I brought my favorite tequila, *chica*. Hope you like it."

"I bet it's better than the swill I was just forced to drink," Tilly said. "Thank you both. There are drinks in the coolers. Beer in the red one and seltzers in the blue."

Trevor jumped into action. "What does everyone want? I'll get the drinks."

As her friends settled in, Tomas, who lived in the apartment on the ground floor, came outside. Mack handled the introductions. Tilly glanced at her watch. She hoped Michael and Ronin would arrive soon.

Some of Mack's friends arrived, and a couple of people from Tilly's classes. She was sitting in a folding chair talking to Nica when she heard a tinny bell sound. She glanced up to see Ronin pushing a bike towards her. Michael was following closely behind him.

Ronin smiled broadly when she met his eyes. "Happy birthday, Emmy!" he said.

Tilly heard Mack murmur "Emmy?" behind her. She hoped Mack wouldn't get any ideas about using the nickname that only Ronin used.

Tilly tilted her head. "Are you giving me a bicycle, Ronin?"

"Yes, this is your new bike. Check out the basket."

He turned the bike slightly and Tilly shrieked when she saw the large picnic basket sitting above the back wheel. "It's like Miss Gulch's bike! I love it!"

He put the kickstand down and pointed to the picnic basket. "Take a look."

She opened the lid and peered inside. It took a moment for her eyes to catch up to what she was seeing. "Ronin! It's Toto!" She reached in and pulled out a small gray and black stuffed terrier. She tucked the plush dog under her chin and rocked side to side.

"I have a feeling that the little Toto dog you carried around when you were five has moved on. But who knows, maybe that little guy is still sitting on your bed."

"Wouldn't you like to know?" The words were out of her mouth before she realized what she was saying.

"I was hoping for a tour of your apartment. I haven't seen it yet," Ronin responded. Her saucy statement hadn't fazed him at all. In a teasing voice, he added, "You didn't invite me in when I picked you up for the wedding."

"I didn't? Oh, right. Well, we're trying to limit the number of people traipsing in and out tonight, but I'll show you around in a little bit."

Tilly felt her cheeks flaming again. Why was that always happening around Ronin?

She turned to Michael and gave him a hug. "Hey, Michael. Let me introduce you guys to everyone."

She managed to get through the introductions without additional slip-ups. Maybe it was the tequila. When she introduced Ronin and Michael to Mackenzie, it seemed to her that Michael and Mack started flirting. *No, this won't do,* she thought. *If Michael and Mack start to date, my brother will be over all the time. No, thank you!*

After her brother and Ronin got drinks, everyone settled into a chair. Tilly kept stealing glances at her new bicycle. Now she could ride with Ronin and his family on Sundays without needing to borrow a bike. She was already looking forward to it, but she didn't think tomorrow would work—she assumed she was going to have her first official hangover.

An hour went by before she found herself sitting next to Ronin again. "Thanks again for the bike. I'm over the moon! It was so thoughtful. I can't believe you remembered my obsession with the Wiz."

"Em, how could I forget? I think I've watched that movie fifty times with you."

"Want to watch it again? Got plans for tomorrow night?"

Ronin chuckled, that low, throaty sound that warmed Tilly's heart.

"Maybe not tomorrow, but soon. I haven't seen it in years."

"You're missing out! Oh, you know what else you've missed out on? Oz Fest!"

"Oz Fest? The heavy metal rock tour?"

"No, *The Wizard of Oz* fest. It's a thing. In Mapleton, about ten miles south of Peoria. In August. Promise me you'll go with us. I need to recruit Michael, and it will be easier to get him to agree if you agree."

"And by agree, you mean…"

"Well, you have to dress up. Mack is going as Glenda, I'm Dorothy, and one of her friends from theater will be the lion. You can be the tin man or the scarecrow. We'll help with the costumes."

"Em," he said, raising an eyebrow. Tilly's finger itched to reach out and trace it. Her arm rose slightly, and she clenched her fist, forcing her hand back to her side.

"Are you serious?" he continued. "You want me to put on a costume in August and walk around all day? It'll be hotter than Hades. I think I'd rather perform a root canal on myself."

"Mack is a theater major. She knows all the tricks to creating lightweight, cool costumes. It'll be fun. Please?" She didn't want to beg, but she would, if necessary.

"All right. But you owe me. Big time."

"Yes! I owe you."

"And I will cash in that favor."

"Okay."

Mack approached with a bottle of clear liquid again. "Uh oh," Tilly whispered.

Ronin leaned over. "You can always say no."

"Tilly!" Mack stopped in front of Tilly and waved the bottle back and forth. "Time for another shot!"

Tilly thought about Ronin's words. Yes, she could say no, but Mack would tease her mercilessly. She gave Mack a thumbs up.

"Thumbs up, bottoms up!" Mack called, pouring the liquid into a plastic shot glass, and handing it to Tilly.

Mack turned to the crowd in the yard. "Hey everyone, let's all sing Happy Birthday to Tilly, and then she will take another shot. On three!"

Leading the crowd in song, Mack rocked back and forth on her feet. Tilly was thankful for her outgoing and kind friend. Except for the shots—kind except for that.

Once the loud and obnoxious singing was over, Tilly downed the shot. "Yuck," she said. "I think I hate tequila."

Ronin laughed softly. "Try saying no next time."

"I will." Another shiver rippled across her shoulders. "I'm going inside to get something else to drink. Ready for that tour?"

Ronin nodded and stood. She led him through the back door that was painted purple. Tilly was sure the door was purple because of someone's love of the TV show *Friends*.

They trekked up the stairs to her apartment, and Tilly pulled the key out of her back pocket to let them in.

"We're coming in from the back, of course. This hallway runs between the bedrooms. Mack's bedroom is on the right." She indicated the door with the theater comedy and drama masks. "Then my room is here on the left." She was thankful she'd pulled her door shut before she left. She hurried past.

"You're not going to even open the door?" Ronin asked. "I want to see if that worn out Toto is still on your pillow."

Before she could stop him, Ronin opened the door and flipped on the overhead light. She glanced around, relieved that nothing was out of place. Since she'd had the day off from work, she'd cleaned the apartment thoroughly, just in case someone needed to use the bathroom or wanted to see their place. But she'd never thought Ronin would be looking in her bedroom. *Yikes!*

He nodded. "No Toto. Glad I bought you a new one. You'll go to sleep each night thinking of me."

"No, I won't!" *Well, now I will.* Her cheeks flared. "I'm too old to sleep with stuffed animals."

He smiled and she felt lightheaded. She hated it when Michael and Ronin teased her. But was this lightheaded sensation from his smirky smile or the tequila shots?

Ronin crossed over to her bed, and she worried he was going to sit on it. Instead, he looked out the window above it. "You can see our apartment from here." He pointed down the street.

"Yeah, I know. I thought it was cool when Michael said he wanted to move close by."

"And now?"

"Maybe you're too close."

"Show me the rest of the apartment."

"Right. This way."

She led him into the kitchen and living room combo. He looked around carefully, like he was studying for a quiz.

"It's eclectic. I'm trying to discern how much of it is you, and how much is your roommate."

Only Ronin would use the word discern in casual conversation. "I think we're both eclectic, but Mack is the creative one." Tilly leaned over the kitchen counter and straightened the bouquet of vibrant raspberry-colored tulips that Anna Lee had sent her for her birthday. She cherished the card that came with the flowers. It wasn't the standard two-inch by three-inch card. It was a full-sized greeting card, a print of Claude Monet's Waterlilies. Inside, Anna Lee had written a beautiful note that had brought tears to Tilly's eyes.

Just thinking about the note caused a tear to fall. Ronin moved closer to her, and she brushed the tear away.

"Hey, Emmy, what's wrong?" he asked, leaning closer to look her in the eyes.

"Nothing. Just thinking about a sweet note that I received from my boss today."

He took her chin between his thumb and index finger, tilting her head up so their eyes met. "Hey. No tears on your birthday. I can't handle it."

Tilly looked into his light blue eyes with the dark edges and felt lost. The overhead lights were off, and a string of Christmas lights above the kitchen cabinets cast soft colors about the place. Lamps glimmered in the living room, washing Ronin's face in a warm peach glow.

He can't handle it? I can't handle this. She thought about the stuffed dog and the bike that Ronin had brought her. They were perfect gifts showing careful consideration. To be honest, Tilly thought they were better, more thoughtful gifts than anything Michael had ever given her.

Ronin continued to gaze into her eyes, his own eyes darting back and forth like he was willing her eyes to dry up and spill no more tears.

Before she knew what she was doing, Tilly threw her arms around his neck and kissed him full on the mouth. She groaned when her lips touched his and his hand quickly moved from her chin to the back of her neck, holding her in place. He tilted his head to deepen the kiss she'd started.

A moment later, Tilly pulled her head back. "What did I do?" she whispered.

Ronin leaned his forehead on hers. "You kissed me. I didn't see that coming."

She dropped her arms and took an exaggerated step backward. What if Michael had walked in? What if Mack had? She'd never hear the end of their teases and taunts.

"Ugh. I'm so sorry. I don't know what came over me. I can't drink anymore."

"Weren't you coming in for something else to drink?" he asked, not addressing the kiss or her comment.

"Right. I was. Thanks. Um…" she strolled to the refrigerator and yanked the door open. She grabbed a can of tomato juice and held the can to her flaming cheeks. *I'm probably as red as the tomatoes on this can.* "Here we go! Let's get back outside before we're missed."

Ronin's forehead wrinkled. "Are you sure about tomato juice?"

"I like tomato juice."

"It's a fine juice, but I'm just thinking if you get sick later on, you may regret the tomato juice."

"Oh." Tilly considered. "You might be right about that. What should I drink instead?"

"Do you have a clear soda? Lemon-lime?"

"No, but we have ginger ale. I'll drink that."

"Good plan."

CHAPTER EIGHT

RONIN FOLLOWED TILLY back through the apartment, stealing one more glance into her bedroom as they passed. The room was frilly and neat, just like Tilly. *Her kiss wasn't frilly and neat, though,* he thought. *More like wild and messy.* He fisted his hand, remembering that it had just been used to bring her lips closer to his—a gentle pull on the back of her neck, bringing her closer to him.

Two dressers, a closet door, a large desk with a stack of books. There were movie posters in simple black frames lining the walls: *The Wizard of Oz, Breakfast at Tiffany's, Singing in the Rain,* and *Casablanca.*

Ronin knew Tilly's mother was a movie buff; she had frequently hosted movie nights when they were kids. The parents would mostly hang out in the kitchen while the five kids were sprawled around the family room with a classic musical or comedy playing. There were even Disney nights, but those were more casual nights, without all the parents and the gourmet food spread.

Mrs. Miller would provide a little introduction to each movie and would create fun games for them to play while they were watching. It might be a multiple-choice quiz, a true or false questionnaire, or an "opportunity" to draw a character. Ronin liked those the least; he struggled with drawing or anything artistic, much to his writer-mother's disappointment.

He wanted to explore Tilly's room further—he suspected there was more than one stuffed animal in there somewhere; she was a sentimental, tender-hearted person. Even if she had no stuffies here, he was sure she must keep some in her bedroom at her parents' house.

Stepping onto the patio, he felt everyone's eyes turn towards them. He was thankful it was dark, with only soft lighting from Edison bulbs and lanterns hanging about the space. A nice touch. He hoped no one would have a good view of Tilly's face; he imagined she was still as red as a firecracker. He followed the yellow brick road design across the patio and saw an open seat next to Michael.

Stopping at a cooler, he grabbed a beer, thankful he could walk home from here. That thought stopped him for a moment. *Emmy is just a short walk away and will be for at least another year.*

He sat next to Michael, who was talking to Trevor. He realized he could see Tilly if he stayed engaged in Michael and Trevor's conversation, so he twisted slightly and chimed in when appropriate.

But his eyes and mind were on Tilly. Someone had made her—*or did she do it herself!* he wondered—a T-shirt that read, "Cheers to 21 years!" He hoped she wouldn't be saying too many more "cheers", or she'd regret it in the morning. He didn't want her to miss Sunday dinner at his folks' or her first bike ride with his family afterward. He hoped she'd enjoy the new bike, then maybe they could do little rides in the evening, just the two of them. Oh, Michael, too. He supposed Mackenzie could go as well. *What's with all the M names?* he thought. He might have to come up with a nickname for Mackenzie too. *Emmy, Eminem… Emzee…. that might work.*

He took a swig of the beer and his eyes caught Tilly's. He was certain she blushed even deeper. That kiss. He'd tried to push it from his mind. Not the kiss itself, but his reaction to it, which had not been to push her away or to pull back, but to pull her closer and deepen the kiss. What had he been thinking? After just one beer, he certainly wasn't drunk. She might have been. All the more reason to have shown restraint and gently push her away.

As it was, his reaction was a clear indication that he was attracted to her. After all these years keeping his feelings hidden, thinking he'd gotten over those feelings, even that kiss had brought them flooding back. *So much for getting over her.*

The guilt he felt over those feelings was crushing. She was his best friend's little sister. Their families were close and shared so many holidays and special occasions together. Though his parents had moved away from Michael and Tilly's parents, they still made plans to get both families together. What would happen to the dynamics between their families if Ronin pursued his interest in Tilly, and things went sour?

But why did she kiss me? That question was going to play on repeat in his mind. *Was it an expression of gratitude that got out of hand or something more? Will we talk about it, or pretend it didn't happen? Will Emmy even remember it in the morning?*

As hard as he tried to forget the feel of her soft lips against his and the way her arms had wrapped around his neck like she'd done it a hundred times, those sensations and memories kept demanding the attention of his brain.

He closed his eyes and leaned his head back. The image of Tilly's dark green eyes flecked with gold as she tried to hold back the tears was front and center. She shouldn't be crying on her birthday. He didn't want her to be sad on her birthday. He wanted to absorb any and all hurt disturbing her day. *Not just today, though,* he thought. *I want to do that every day.*

"Right, Ronin?" Michael asked.

"I'm sorry. What?" Ronin had completely tuned out the conversation as he reminisced about Tilly's kiss.

"I was telling Trevor about our plans for a co-working space and said that if we need any plumbing work, he's first on our list to call."

"Sounds good to me. We need to build our list of trusted contractors. Good to start with friends of Emmy's."

Trevor leaned forward to see Ronin better. "Who's Emmy?"

Michael laughed. "My sister, Tilly. Ronin named her Emmy because of the triple M initials."

Trevor nodded. "Got it. Like it. To get her goat, I call her Tils. She's fun to tease. Keep in mind, too, that Nica is a highly creative and competent contractor, if you need something remodeled or refinished."

Ronin considered those words. He hoped Tilly's friends didn't tease her too much. He didn't want her to feel hurt. *The real question is what do I want when it comes to Emmy?*

Michael responded, "That's good to know. Now, if we could just find the right property, we could get started. Is there a realtor in your circle of friends?"

"Sorry, man. No." Trevor shook his head. "Grady invests in property, mostly residential, but he could probably help with some connections."

Ronin's interest piqued. "Who's Grady again?"

"The stiff-looking guy with the cute, short Latina, Nica. She works with Tils."

Ronin looked at Michael. "I think we should go talk to Grady."

"Let's do it."

While Michael took the lead, Ronin thought about the tin can "telephone" he and Michael had strung between their bedrooms as kids. It was impossible to truly understand what the other was saying through the string, but he knew when Michael was tugging on the line.

He thought about the view from Tilly's bedroom to their apartment. He smiled to himself, thinking about stringing some kind of wire from their building to hers. He wouldn't tie a tin can on each end, but a small bell, just to say, "thinking about you".

He could probably recruit Michael to help him out. He'd just have to mask his emotions when telling Michael about the idea. *No sense in making Michael suspicious about my feelings for Emmy.* Ronin realized he needed to find a way to squash Shevaun's suspicions before she let something slip to the wrong person.

Ronin groaned internally. As much as it pained him to recognize it, his feelings for Tilly had just been repressed. They hadn't gone away. Maybe in a year or two, maybe when she was out of college, he would feel more comfortable pursuing something with her. Maybe once he and Michael weren't living together, and the possibility of them falling out over a relationship between Ronin and Tilly was reduced. More waiting. Ronin had done it for six or so years so far, what was another one or two?

The real risk was that she would fall in love with another man because Ronin was too afraid to speak up and put everything on the line now. Ronin fisted his hand. He had the urge to throw a punch into the fencing behind Michael. *Settle down, you idiot. Now's not the time or place for caveman-like displays of emotion.*

HOURS LATER, RONIN lay in bed thinking about the party. From a business perspective, it had been a success. Talking to Trevor and Grady had given a boost to their business plans. Grady had mentioned an excellent commercial realtor, and he would make the introduction on Monday over lunch.

Everyone he'd met was open and engaging. Good midwestern stock. It strengthened his belief that this was the right move for him and Michael. They had spent weeks analyzing various mid-sized towns in terms of population, demographics, median incomes, industries, housing, and availability of shared workspaces. He'd argued for Minneapolis, but Michael preferred Bloomington. Proximity to his sister was just a tiny factor. He didn't want to move any further north than the Chicago area because he hated winter and snow. Not that he'd be entirely free of it in Bloomington, but it snowed much less here than in Minneapolis.

Ronin checked his phone. No text messages. He'd sent Tilly a text when he got home thanking her for a fun party and reminding her about Sunday dinner.

The party was winding down when he'd left, but there had been a few revelers still talking and laughing in the girls' apartment. He'd helped Michael carry Tilly's bike, the coolers, and the small table that had housed booze and snacks up to the apartment before they'd left.

Tilly was looking a little sleepy when he left, and he'd hoped there would be no more shots for her before she went to bed. It could make for a rough day and bike ride otherwise.

Thinking about Sunday dinner reminded him that his parents' twenty-fifth wedding anniversary was coming up in six weeks. Shevaun had asked him for ideas last week. As the oldest, he needed to step up and create a plan—find a venue, hire catering, decorations, a gift. All the things. With his sisters' help, of course.

His phone beeped. He picked it up and looked at the time. Two a.m. He quickly navigated to the messaging app.

He groaned. Shevaun. He hoped she didn't need a ride home from a friend's house because she was drunk. Or even worse, a couch to crash on.

He read the text and smiled. She was just asking how Tilly liked the bike. He responded, *Ask her yourself later today.*

Tossing the phone back on the nightstand, he rolled over and closed his eyes. He hoped Tilly was sleeping soundly and wouldn't be hurting and hungover later.

CHAPTER NINE

TILLY WAS THANKFUL she'd taken the bike for a spin around the block by herself. She wasn't completely comfortable yet, but she wasn't as shaky as she'd been that morning.

When Michael and Ronin picked her up, she was embarrassed to remember that she hadn't replied to Ronin when she'd gone to bed the night before. She'd seen his sweet text, and intended to reply to say good night, but her pillow had drawn her like the Pied Piper leading children to candy, and she fell asleep with the phone still in her hand.

This morning, she had texted Ronin to tell him she was fine, no hangover. Just thankful for the fun evening, being surrounded by friends, and for the super-snazzy bike. *I'm also grateful that he didn't mention that ridiculous kiss! I practically jumped the poor guy's bones just for telling me not to be sad. What's wrong with me?* Yes, she'd been a little emotional thinking about the card from Anna Lee, but why had she thrown herself at him like a puppy excited her owner had come home?

She worried that she wouldn't be able to meet Ronin's eye when she saw him, but she'd managed just fine throughout dinner. It felt like it always did, fun and casual. Everyone was laughing and sharing stories about their week. Bruce and Elizabeth said they loved having Michael and Tilly join them, saying it was almost like they lived next door again.

After dinner, the plan was for the group to bike three miles to an ice-cream store for dessert. Tilly winced when she saw the group speed off. She was too unsteady for that pace, and resigned herself to being last, maybe even missing dessert.

She'd biked a few blocks when she looked ahead and saw Ronin waiting for her. He was straddling his bike with an amused look. She let the distance and the sunglasses hide her eyes as she took in all the details of his impeccable attire; a plain white T-shirt that looked like it had been pressed, khaki shorts, white tennis shoes that looked polished. He wore a baseball cap with the Loyola University Chicago logo and dark aviator glasses. He still hadn't shaved, and his beard was tantalizing.

Darn, he is scrumptious! Maybe that's why she'd kissed him so passionately last night.

She wished she could see his eyes as she pulled up next to him, but it warmed her to see the half-smile twisting his mouth.

Ronin lifted his hat up and adjusted it before setting it back on his head. "I was beginning to worry about you, Em."

"I'm all right. Just out of practice and trying to not wipe out. You didn't have to wait for me." She took advantage of the stop and hopped off her bike to stand with her feet flat on the ground for a moment.

"Happy to wait for you. How is the bike working out? Is it the right height? Having any issues?"

"It's fine. I took it for a test drive this morning."

"You did?"

"Yes, after coffee with Mackenzie. I wanted to practice so I wouldn't fall and look like a mess in front of you and your family. Or Michael. He'd never let me hear the end of it."

"You're right. He's a jerk."

Tilly laughed. "Glad we can agree on something."

Ronin dramatically threw a hand over his heart. "Emmy, your words wound me."

"Oh please, I get enough of the dramatics from Mackenzie. Not you, too!"

Ronin chuckled. "Ready to go? The others may eat all the ice cream if we don't get there soon."

She looked down at the pedals. It was now or never. She had to say something.

"Um, Ronin?"

"Yeah?"

"I'm sorry about the kiss last night. I don't know what came over me." She winced. This was awful. "Maybe it was the alcohol." *Yes, yes! Blame the booze!*

Ronin shook his head slightly. "I didn't think you'd had that much to drink."

"Well, I guess I'm a lightweight." She laughed nervously. This wasn't going the way she wanted it to. She wanted to scream at him, *Why did you kiss me in return?*

"Maybe I owe you an apology." When she didn't say anything, he added, "For kissing you back."

"Oh, you kissed me back?" She smirked. This was better, teasing was better.

"I'll get you for that, Tilly!" He straightened to his full height in a mock-threatening manner.

"Wow, you used my actual name. Didn't think you knew what it was." All right, they'd each apologized, they could move on. Back to normal. Back to pretending it hadn't happened. She could do that, right?

Hopefully.

Maybe.

Shoot, I'll probably never forget that scrumptious kiss!

She sighed. He'd never see her as anything but Michael's little sister. Probably for the best.

"Of course, I know your name. Emmy. Ready?" he asked.

"Sure. Let's go."

They continued in a comfortable silence; Ronin mostly matched her pace but would ride ahead and circle back occasionally.

When they reached the ice-cream store, their group was sitting at a picnic table eating cones, shakes, and sundaes and chatting about the ride.

Tilly and Ronin parked their bikes and walked up to the order window. Tilly ordered a swirly cone, Ronin a vanilla cone. Ronin paid while Tilly reached for the money she had in her back pocket.

"I got this."

"Ronin, you're spoiling me. I can get my ice cream."

"You deserve to be spoiled. It's your birthday weekend."

"Well, thank you. I appreciate it."

A girl who looked about fourteen slid open the delivery window and held out Tilly's ice cream cone.

Taking the cone, she turned to Ronin and asked, "Do you think she's old enough to work?"

"A part-time job working in an ice-cream store? Every teenager should be so lucky."

"True. I would love to work in an ice-cream store. Though I'd have to do a lot more bike riding to keep the pounds off."

"Exercise does a body good."

Tilly thought Ronin must do a lot of exercising to keep his body in such great shape. He wasn't afraid of carbs or sweets, so he must do something to counteract the effects. She remembered the weight bench he'd moved into his apartment. That must help. She considered getting herself some free weights. *Maybe Ronin could give me some workout pointers.*

They joined the others at the picnic table, and Tilly slid in next to Trinity. Ronin took a spot across from her. Trinity was eating an orange slushy sundae. It reminded Tilly of a melty orange push-up.

"Trinity," Tilly began, "are you ready for your senior year? I am!"

"Tilly, it's July! No talking about school until August, okay?"

"Hmm, well, that kills my next question. I was going to ask about college choices."

"Nope." Trinity shook her head hard, causing her teardrop shaped leather earrings to bounce back and forth. Trinity loved making her own jewelry. "Not ready for that conversation, either. How was your birthday party?"

Tilly smiled. "It was great. Good turnout. Lots of laughs. I didn't get wasted. All good."

Ronin cleared his throat, and Tilly's cheeks warmed as she thought about the kiss and their earlier awkward conversation. She asked Trinity about her summer job as she slid her eyes slowly to Ronin, who was talking to Michael about their meeting with a realtor on Monday. Had he intentionally cleared his throat because of what she'd said, or was it unrelated? She couldn't tell if he was paying attention to her conversation, but she glanced over again and was certain he was smiling at her. She kicked him lightly under the table. When her brother hollered, she realized her kick had been misplaced.

"Who kicked me?" Michael put his hand on the table like he was ready to rise and go to battle.

"Oops. I was just adjusting. Didn't mean to kick." Tilly said.

Ronin laughed softly. She turned to him. He knew that kick was for him.

Bruce stood to throw away his sundae bowl and spoon. "Everyone ready?"

The others stood, and Tilly looked at her cone. It was only halfway gone. "I'll be a few more minutes. Go on without me."

Ronin was still eating his ice cream, too. "I'll ride back with Emmy. Don't want her to get lost."

Shevaun gave Ronin a wicked look. "Lost? Yeah, right."

Tilly's face flushed. Now that she'd kissed him, and he'd kissed her back, Shevaun's telling her that he liked her held more weight.

CHAPTER TEN

RONIN PUSHED HIS empty plate away. He'd eaten every bite of his patty melt and French fries. Michael was describing the ideal space for their co-working business to the realtor, Noah Bondel. Grady was there and listened intently; he'd remarked that he would consider investing in the business but wanted to have a deeper review of the business plan, which Ronin promised to set up later that week.

The restaurant, La Playa Vida, seemed misplaced here in Central Illinois, but Ronin appreciated the downtown location and the laid-back vibe. If they found a space to lease nearby, he could foresee many future lunches in this casual, eclectic place.

"So, Noah. What do you think? Do you know of any such spaces that are available now?" Michael asked, leaning forward, and stirring his nearly empty iced tea.

"I have a couple places in mind, but I would like to refresh my search. Let's plan to meet on Wednesday and I'll take you around. That will give me time to reach out to a few potential owners and other realtors. Can we plan to meet at ten?"

Michael looked at Ronin and raised an eyebrow. "Good with you?"

"Absolutely," Ronin answered. Turning to Noah, he said, "We

appreciate your willingness to jump right into the search. Should we meet at your office?"

"That works for me. Hopefully, we'll find the perfect location for your purpose quickly. If you'll excuse me, I'm going to go and start searching."

Noah stood to shake hands and left.

Grady looked at his watch. "I need to run, too. What did you think of Noah?"

"He seemed to be on top of his game," Ronin responded. "Very personable. Thanks for the introduction."

"Glad you liked him. I've worked with him for a few years. I trust him to be straight with me, and he hasn't let me down yet. I wish you luck in your search, and I look forward to talking again soon." He stood to leave. "Oh, Nica's always asking me about potential dates for Tilly. I hadn't thought of Noah before; he's a bit older, but like I said, he's trust-worthy…"

"No!" Ronin interrupted.

Michael laughed. "Hey, I don't know, Ro. Seemed like a good guy to me."

Grady held hands up. "Well, I'll let you two debate the issue. If you find him acceptable, you can do the introduction. I'll stay out of it. But if Nica asks, you have to vouch for me—I did come up with a decent suggestion. Take care."

Grady left, and Michael gave Ronin a light punch. "What was that all about? I thought you liked Noah?"

"Sure, as a realtor. We didn't get enough information to consider setting him up with one of our sisters. I certainly wouldn't set him up with one of mine."

"Your sisters are too young, I agree. But Tilly's twenty-one. Noah is thirty at most. That's not too much of a gap."

Ronin looked at Michael with a scowl. "That's nine years. Too many for a twenty-one-year-old."

"Fine. Fine." Michael finished his drink and leaned back in his chair. "Keep your jets cooled. Speaking of Tilly, she asked if she could tag along when we look at properties. Would you object if she did? Even if Noah is there?"

Ronin wasn't worried about Tilly being around Noah; he really didn't think she'd be interested in him. But if she tagged along, would he be able to concentrate on the properties, and not her? And what if she *did* find Noah interesting? There was a chance Michael could plant that seed even over Ronin's objection. Then what? He'd want to throttle Noah if there was any flirting between him and Tilly. It was a risk. But objecting to Tilly coming along after vehemently objecting to setting her up with Noah could cause other suspicions to rise in Michael that Ronin didn't have time to deal with.

"No, not at all. Ask her if she's available on Wednesday."

LATER THAT EVENING at their apartment, Ronin and Michael worked on a presentation to share with Grady to hopefully garner his support and financial investment in the business.

"How about this?" Michael said, pointing to the last slide of financial projections that they had used for their business loan.

"I think it's good; let's hope Grady sees the potential and comes on board." Ronin stood up to stretch. Sitting for an hour on the couch had caused his back to stiffen. "The slides are good; we can decide which of us will present each piece and practice presenting during the next few days. I'm ready for a beer. Want one?"

"Sure. I'm going to look for stock images to include before I shut down," Michael said, typing on his laptop. "I'm looking forward to seeing properties this week. I hope we find the right place."

Ronin strolled to the kitchen to grab two bottles of beer. "Agreed. Everything will start to accelerate once we acquire the right space. We'll have to think about potential expansion options, too. If this takes off like we hope, we may need more square footage or a second location."

"Truth." Michael grabbed the proffered beverage.

Ronin started pacing back and forth from the windows to the dining table. He needed to move. On his third pass to the window, he looked down the street towards Tilly's building. He remembered the idea of stringing a line from their apartment to hers, a way to get each other's attention without calling or texting.

"Hey, Eminem," he began.

Michael grunted, preoccupied with his image search.

"I have a crazy idea."

"What's new?" Michael laughed. "This business was your idea."

"Yes, and you were stupid enough to join me. Anyway, remember when we were kids, and we had the tin-can "telephone" between our bedrooms?"

"What?" Michael paused, thinking. "Oh, yeah, I remember. That never worked right."

"True, but we knew when the other one was pulling on the string. Even with windows closed, you could get the can to shake."

"Yeah, I remember. What made you think of that?"

Ronin pointed out the window, towards Tilly's apartment. "I was thinking we could put up a similar contraption between us and your sister's place. Put a bell on each end of the string."

"No way." Michael stood and moved to the window beside Ronin. "It's too far away. There are tree limbs in the way. She's across the street and a few buildings down."

Ronin pointed. "If we tried to go directly, yes, the trees would be in the way. But look. If we go across the street to the house in front of us and tack a hook into the corner of their house, then go in front of the two buildings between that house and Tilly's, we're there. See?" He swept his finger, indicating the path.

"Well, maybe. I see what you're saying. No trees that way. But the bigger question is why. Why would we do that? We have phones."

"It would be different, creative. Something to talk about. A mini adventure."

"What do you mean by mini adventure?"

"Well, we can't just walk up to the house across the street and say, hey, we want to string a wire to your house, do you mind? We'll have to do it in the dead of night. Stealth-like."

"Great. We'll get busted for trespassing and vandalism, and we could get called peeping Toms. No, thanks. You're on your own."

"I can do the heavy lifting, but I'll need a helper."

"Do we tell Tilly?"

"No, not beforehand. Let's make sure we can get the string to her place first. Then one of us will have to go and put the bell on her side."

Michael stared out the window, and Ronin worried he would start to question Ronin's motive. "Her bedroom is on this side of the building. You can see her window from here. Probably best to go to her window versus a living-room window."

Ronin smiled; grateful Michael's back was turned. "Sure, that would work." *That's what I wanted, anyway.*

"You work out the details, and I'll help." Michael shrugged and turned around. "It's late. I'm going to finish looking for images, then I'm calling it a day. I'll go to my room."

Ronin continued to stare out the window as Michael gathered his stuff and went to his room. He calculated the length of wire they would need and debated what type would work. He finally decided to try fishing line.

In his bedroom, he set an alarm for two a.m. He wanted to get up to check out how many people were about at that time of night—a reconnaissance mission.

Ronin smiled, thinking about Tilly's reaction to the idea. He hoped she'd find it funny and sweet. That was his intention. Just a friendly way to say, "Hi, I'm thinking of you" in a more personal way.

Of course, he couldn't ring her bell every time he was thinking about her or it would ring so often she'd find it incredibly annoying. That was the last thing he wanted.

CHAPTER ELEVEN

TILLY POURED A bowl of trail mix from the bag that Anna Lee kept in her office. Salty jumped up onto the ancient desk chair and sniffed the air.

"You don't want any of this, kitty," Tilly said. "It's not good for you."

Salty turned his head away, seeming to scoff at Tilly's remark.

Tilly returned to the back room where Mackenzie and Anna Lee were working on arrangements that would be delivered to several nursing homes in town. Tilly was expecting Anna Lee to ask her to deliver them, and she intended to take Mack along to show her what Anna Lee expected when delivering arrangements.

Anna Lee was explaining to Mack the different arrangement types—statement pieces, centerpieces, vignettes, and posies. They would be making several posy and centerpiece arrangements for today's deliveries.

Tilly placed the bowl of trail mix on the table near Anna Lee and Mack.

They heard the front doorbell ring, and Anna Lee left to take care of the customer, her long purple dress swooshing with her quick movements.

"She is such a character," Mack said, tilting her head and studying the bunch of carnations in front of her. She'd been tasked with trimming all their stems down to a uniform eight inches.

"I know!" Tilly agreed. "She's sweet, wise, and sassy at times. I love working for her. So, how was your trip home? It was too quiet in the apartment without you."

Mack had left Sunday morning after breakfast to visit her parents and younger brother in Moline.

"It was fine." Mack blew her pink bangs out of her eyes. "Allen wants to move into my bedroom, so I had to go through the rest of my stuff. Some we donated, some we put in the attic. I brought two boxes back with me, but they're still in my car. I'll unpack them tomorrow. Mom gave me a unique lamp that I thought would be cool in our living room—it's a lighthouse. She found it at a garage sale but hadn't decided where to put it. I was able to talk her into letting me bring it home."

"That sounds interesting."

"It is. Do you work tomorrow? I want to hit the thrift shops and look for a new bookcase. The pile on the floor in my room is getting tilty."

"Tilty?"

"New word, who dis?" Mack laughed at her own joke.

"No," Tilly drawled, thinking, "I don't work, but I have plans. I'm going with Michael and Ronin to look for commercial property. If you go thrifting in the afternoon, I could go with you then. If I get back in time."

"All right. Yeah. So, we didn't really get a chance to talk about Michael and Ronin after the party. I thought Ronin was pretty hot. Why don't you go out with him?"

Tilly rolled her eyes. "Oh, please. He's like another brother. I've known him since I was four or five. There's no way."

She thought again about the kiss she'd planted on Ronin Saturday night. That hadn't been brotherly. She couldn't believe he'd kissed her back. And he'd *definitely* kissed her back! The memory of that kiss scorched her lips—in a good way.

"To quote my man, Shakespeare, "The lady doth protest too much, methinks!" Come on, my lady." She shook her head playfully. "There are benefits to falling in love with someone you've known your whole life."

"Oh, yeah? What?"

"He should remember your birthday." She lifted a finger, counting. "You have shared history. He knows what you like and what you don't like. You know his parents. He knows your family. He knows you love *The Wizard of Oz*. The Toto dog was too cute."

"Wait. Now you're going from hypotheticals to reality."

"I switch fast, Tilly. Keep up. He's driven." She continued with the fingers on her other hand. "He's charming. He seemed kind. Plus, he is a dreamboat. That thick hair, those twinkly blue eyes. He's tall. Fit. I thought he filled out his pants nicely."

"Mackenzie!" Tilly protested.

"What? I'm human. I notice things. I bet you've noticed."

"Um, no." She knew her voice sounded shrill. Of course, she'd noticed, but she wasn't going to admit that to Mack. She needed to at least pretend to be indifferent to Ronin. For the sake of appearances. "Besides, how can you have that spark of something new with someone you've known a long time? You know? Getting to discover new things about the person. Being surprised all the time."

"Being surprised doesn't always work out."

At that moment Anna Lee walked in, and Tilly sighed in relief. This conversation would not go on with Anna Lee in the room.

"How's it going in here, ladies?" Anna Lee sat down, and Salty, who'd followed her into the work room, jumped from the floor to the tabletop, sliding into a pile of clippings next to Tilly.

"Good. We're making progress." Tilly indicated the cheerful red and white centerpiece as she tied on a ribbon.

"Looks good. How's it going with you, Mackenzie?"

"Almost done with the carnations. What's next?"

"You can trim up this bucket of lady's mantle. Same as the carnies, about eight inches. Well, girls. If you have things under control here, I'm going to the office to work on next week's schedule and pay a few bills. Holler for me if you need anything."

She stood slowly and looked at the finished arrangements on the side table. "Hey, Tilly, this one's a little cattywampus. Can you fix it?"

"Of course!" Tilly eyed the crooked arrangement and saw the issue that Anna Lee had caught. Her boss was a perfectionist when it came to flowers.

Anna Lee left again, and Tilly tried to change the subject. "Did you get your fall schedule straightened out?"

"Yes, the counselor took care of it when I called. I'm glad I caught the error early, or I might not have gotten into Mr. Lockhart's drama class, and I would have been devastated. I had him last year and loved the way he taught. But I know what you're doing, girly, and it's not going to work on me. Nice try. This conversation is going back to Ronin right now. I still think you should consider dating him. It's been long enough since your breakup with Kyle. It's time to get yourself back out there. It's our senior year. Let's make it the best one, full of great memories."

"What about you? You're not dating anyone." The last date she'd had with the guy from drama had not worked out; Mack said there'd be no second date.

"Let's make a pact. If there are no prospects for either of us by the start of classes, we each set the other one up on a date."

"You're on." At least this stopped Mack from pressing her about Ronin. For the time being.

CHAPTER TWELVE

TILLY CLIMBED INTO the backseat of Ronin's sedan behind Michael. She glanced up at Ronin as she fastened her seat belt. He was wearing black slacks and a light gray dress shirt. The shirt color complimented his skin tone. He'd gotten a tan since he first moved in, maybe from lounging by his parents' pool or all those bike rides.

A suit jacket lay on the seat next to her, and she felt a bit underdressed in her sandals, dark pink skirt, and light pink T-shirt.

"Morning, gentlemen," she said, sitting back as Ronin put the vehicle in gear. "Ready to see some properties?"

"Absolutely," Michael said, twisting in his seat to look at her. "I have a good feeling. I think we're going to find the perfect location today."

"Did you look into your crystal ball this morning?" Ronin asked.

"Good sleep is good for the attitude."

"I hope you're right." Tilly tugged on her skirt, wishing she'd worn pants. "I know you're both ready to launch your new business. Shevaun told me she asked you for a job, Ronin. Do you have something for her to do?"

"Not right now." Ronin turned on his signal and slowed down. "I think she may be back in school before we have any work for her. Maybe over winter break. Right now, Eminem and I can handle it."

"Makes sense. Well, if there's anything I can do to help, let me know."

Michael started reviewing the list of must-haves that he and Ronin had come up with for their workspace, and Tilly tuned out the conversation, studying Ronin from behind the safety of her sunglasses.

His left hand was steadfast on the wheel, and he tapped his right thumb on the gear stick, resting his right arm on the console between the seats. Nervous energy. Tilly imagined he was amped up, ready for the search.

He'd trimmed his beard this morning. Tilly tried to parse out the scents in the car. There was the leather smell from the seats, a fresh, clean ocean smell which she recognized as Michael's favorite cologne and an evergreen scent. Could that one be Ronin's cologne? She closed her eyes and tried to remember what Ronin had smelled like when she'd kissed him. She had been so close, she should have come away with the memory of his cologne, but all she could remember was the feel of his firm lips as he kissed her back.

Her eyes popped open at the memory. "Is the air on?" she asked, suddenly flushed.

"Yes, but I can turn it down, Em, if you're getting hot back there." Ronin pushed a button on the dash a few times, lowering the temperature.

She looked up at him; did she see a smirk on his lips? She wanted to throttle him. Thankfully, Michael didn't skip a beat as he droned on about their property must-haves and nice-to-haves.

I am hot, but did Ronin really guess why?

They pulled up in front of an office building, and Ronin parked the car. Michael jumped out to open Tilly's door for her. *Wow, where is this chivalry coming from?*

99

Inside, Michael searched a directory on the wall and announced that Noah's office was down the hall on the left.

Michael charged ahead, and Ronin gestured for Tilly to follow her brother while he brought up the rear.

In the office, Michael introduced Tilly to Noah, who held her hand a little longer than necessary, a flirty smile on his lips. He was a good-looking man, very confident and outgoing. Tilly supposed a good realtor needed those qualities—being confident and outgoing, anyway. It was a customer service business.

"It's very nice to meet you, Tilly," he said, his voice smooth, like melted chocolate.

"Likewise," she said.

Ronin cleared his throat, and Noah let go of her hand.

The realtor indicated two chairs in front of his desk and pulled up a third from a round table in the corner. Michael plopped into one of the chairs closest to the desk, but Ronin waited for Tilly to settle in before taking the other chair. *What a gentleman, letting me sit first,* she thought. That wasn't surprising, but she wondered if there was more to it than that. *Is Ronin trying to stay between me and Noah, trying to block me from Noah's view? What does that mean?* She smiled to herself. Would she ever understand men?

Noah handed Michael and Ronin a stapled stack of listings. "Tilly, I'll make you a copy," he said.

"That's okay. She can share mine," Ronin said, as he reached down and dragged the leg of Tilly's chair closer to him, as if she were lighter than a jacket. *He must be lifting weights.* He turned towards her and smiled.

"All right, then," Noah proceeded. "I found five potential properties. I put the packets in the order that I thought we should see them based on their locations, but if you'd prefer changing it up, that's fine with me. Take a look and let me know if you have any questions. I need to send a quick email before we go, then I'll be ready."

Tilly glanced at the papers Ronin was flipping through. She leaned toward him slightly and got a whiff of his cologne. *Definitely evergreen, and a warm spice, cinnamon perhaps.* Her stomach growled.

Ronin turned his head slightly. "Hungry, Emmy?" he whispered.

"I was so excited I forgot to eat. Just had coffee," she whispered back. Michael was asking Noah whether any of the properties included utilities in the rent, so he didn't hear their conversation.

"We'll get you food soon."

"Thank you," she replied. She felt bad; she didn't want to be a distraction at their work meeting. She glanced around the office, hoping for a fruit bowl, or even better, a box of donuts but she didn't see anything.

"Need something, Tilly?" Noah asked.

"No. Nothing!"

"Do you have a granola bar, Noah?" Ronin asked.

Noah was nodding before Ronin finished his question. "We have a well-stocked break area. We'll stop on the way out."

Ronin turned and looked Tilly in the eye.

"Thank you, again," she whispered.

"Anytime."

She took comfort in that. Yes, Michael was her big brother, and he would look out for her, but it was nice having Ronin's attention. *And after the kiss on my birthday, he's definitely NOT in the big brother category.*

THE THIRD PROPERTY was the charm. They decided not to even look at numbers four and five. They went to lunch, while Noah went back to the office to talk to the leasing management company on their behalf.

Tilly loved listening to Michael and Ronin's excitement over the property they'd found. It had been a debt-collection company and had a reception area with a secure door that led into a large open space surrounded by eight offices. It was the perfect layout and size for the business they envisioned.

"We need software," Michael said. "Something that allows us to schedule and reserve the offices. I would love to see electronic schedule pads on each office door, so people can see what's available and when the offices are booked."

Ronin nodded. "If that system could be tied into the billing system, it would be perfect. We could up-charge for office rental above their monthly time with the open space." He was jotting down notes from their conversation on a padfolio.

"I'll take the lead on researching software," Michael said, and Ronin scribbled task ownership on the list. Tilly could see what he was writing from where she sat in the back of the u-shaped diner booth where they were seated. Ronin and Michael sat directly across from each other, and Tilly thought they'd forgotten she was there. It was just as well; they were so excited about finding the right space, and Tilly was proud and thrilled for them. It was wonderful seeing those she loved make progress on life goals.

The waitress brought their entrées, and Ronin put his padfolio on the booth seat between them. He threw an apologetic glance. She smiled to let him know it was fine.

After the waitress left, Michael realized she'd forgotten his side of onion rings, so he went to track down the missing dish.

Ronin added pepper to his hamburger, looking at Tilly. "Thanks for tagging along today. I hope you didn't find it too boring."

"Not at all. I loved it. The space is great, and I can envision it thriving. It's exciting! Will there be a family and friends discount, so I can stop by and study when Mackenzie has drama buddies over using our living room as a stage?"

"Of course." He jokingly leered at her. "For a little manual labor, you may even get free access."

"Really? Tell me what kind of labor you have in mind. I don't mop floors."

"No?"

"It's my least favorite chore. I always beg Mack to do it when it's time to clean. Luckily, she doesn't mind it."

"What don't you like about it?"

"Wringing the mop out with my hands. Ick."

"You need one of those spinning buckets, then you don't have to touch it."

"Noted. But seriously. Anything I can do to help with the office space?"

"You saw the place and you've heard our long list of to-dos. What's missing?"

"Oh." Tilly considered. "I think you have a handle on it. But…"

"Yeah?"

"Everything I've heard is very traditional business-y. Masculine. You'll attract the dude-bros with your happy hours and sleek surfaces. But if you want the other half of the population to be interested, you need to add some softer touches."

"Like what?"

Michael returned, the booth bouncing slightly as he sat down.

"Artwork. Flowers. Soft seating areas. At least, that's what I would want to see."

Michael scoffed. "Are you talking about our co-workspace? Flowers? No way."

Ronin shook his head at Michael. "She's got a great point. It shouldn't be a cold, sterile environment. It's not a medical lab or a hospital."

Tilly nodded. "Even hospitals have warm, calming waiting rooms."

"That's true." Ronin took a bite of his hamburger and Tilly stabbed at a radish in her salad.

"All right," Michael conceded. "I hear you. But we have to watch the budget."

"Budget is a consideration," Ronin agreed, "but I would love to hear your specific ideas, Emmy. And for your consultation services, one-year free access to the co-workspace for studying. That will get you through graduation."

"What? A free year?" Michael protested. "Are you crazy? We can't give space away for free to all our acquaintances."

Ronin growled, "She's not an acquaintance. She's your sister."

Michael leaned back and held his hands up. "Right. Agreed. Sounds great."

Ronin reached under the table and squeezed Tilly's knee. A quick, soft motion, not obvious enough to catch Michael's eye, it was a comforting gesture saying, "We won this battle." Tilly looked into her salad bowl and smiled.

AFTER LUNCH, MICHAEL asked to be dropped off at an office-supply store. He said he'd take a rideshare home. When he got out of the car, Tilly moved to the front passenger seat, and Ronin backed out of the parking space.

They drove in comfortable silence for several minutes. Tilly started thinking about dinner; she needed to run to the store to get something to prepare. *Oh shoot, Mack wanted to go to the thrift stores. We can do that before dinner.*

Ronin cleared his throat, and Tilly turned to him and asked, "Did I miss something?"

"I have a favor to ask," he began.

"Yes?"

"My parents' twenty-fifth wedding anniversary is coming up and I could use some help planning a celebration."

"Really? You and your sisters are quite capable of pulling off that kind of party."

"Well, yes." He nodded. "But with getting our business off the ground, and how busy the girls are, I thought I would enlist some extra help. Besides, after hearing your ideas today, I know you would be a huge help in coming up with a memorable event."

"All right. You know I'm happy to help. I love your parents. When is their anniversary?"

"August nineteenth. We have about five and a half weeks to pull it off."

"Okay… that's not a lot of time. How many people are you planning to invite?"

"Don't know. Need to make a list."

"How formal or informal?"

"Something nice. More formal."

"Want to have it at your new workspace? Assuming you have access, and it's ready to go in five weeks."

"No. Don't want the workspace to overshadow their anniversary. It should be about them."

"Got it. So, you need a location to rent, then. I don't know much about rentals, but Anna Lee will have some ideas. We do centerpieces for a lot of weddings, parties, and stuff. We've delivered flowers to countless locations. I can ask her for a good list. Could you ballpark the headcount?"

"Let's say thirty to fifty, off the top of my head."

"All right. That will help. I work tomorrow, so I can ask her then."

"See? You're already adding value, Em."

He pulled up to the curb in front of her apartment building.

"Why didn't you just park at home? I could have walked."

"That would be the lazy way. I'm a door-to-door service kind of man."

"Well, I appreciate that," she said, grabbing the door handle. "I'll contact you tomorrow with the list."

"Why don't we get together over dinner and discuss it? My treat."

"I'm a broke college student; I never turn down a free dinner."

"See you tomorrow, Em."

"Later."

Tilly got out of the car, but instead of going in through the front door, she walked the narrow path between her building and the building next door to the back patio area. It was such a beautiful afternoon, she wanted to water the flowers and clean up any debris, just in case she and Mack decided to hang out there later.

Five minutes later her cell phone beeped.

> **RONIN:** You didn't go in the front door. You all right?

> **TILLY:** I'm fine. Needed to do some yard work.

> **RONIN:** Good

Tilly waited a moment to see if he had anything else to say. When he didn't text again, she slid her phone back into her pocket. *Odd. It's daylight. It's really sweet that Ronin is so concerned about me*, she thought. *Well, he's still new to the neighborhood; he doesn't realize how safe it is.*

CHAPTER THIRTEEN

THURSDAY AFTERNOON WAS unusually slow at In Bloom. They were caught up on premade arrangements, and all the shelves were stocked. Anna Lee had several consultations, and Tilly was managing the retail space on her own. To keep herself busy, she'd asked Anna Lee for some tasks and was given a large pile of supply catalogs and random mail fliers to sort through. Her directions were to save only catalogs that were less than six months old. Anna Lee had a habit of hanging onto more than she needed "just in case" and said it was easier to delegate the sorting and pitching task to someone else.

Once she'd purged the old items, the remainder fit into an antique coal bucket that Anna Lee had painted white and decoupaged with bright pink and purple flowers. Tilly put the bucket back in the office and searched the retail space for another project. When Anna Lee walked through, escorting a bride-to-be and her mother to the door, Tilly moved behind the counter to stay out of their way. Salty jumped up onto the counter, demanding petting and head scratches. He rewarded her effort with copious purrs.

Once the ladies had departed, Anna Lee straightened a display of fairy garden accessories and asked Tilly how her summer was going.

"Good. You know my brother Michael moved in down the street from me with his best friend, Ronin. They are starting a new business, a co-working office building where people working remotely can rent space, so they're not alone all day. We visited a few locations yesterday, and they found just what they were looking for. I'm excited for them to get going."

"That sounds mighty dandy. I bet you like having your brother nearby."

"I do. He's close, but I don't have to live with him, which is great."

Anna Lee laughed heartily, making Tilly smile; she loved it when she could make others laugh. "Oh, Ronin. The guy you took to Paige's wedding. I remember." Turning towards the counter, her boss said, "Ronin seemed like a good man. And handsome! He reminded me of Clark Gable. I thought the two of you looked mighty fine together."

"Oh, it's not like that. We're just friends."

"Friends is a great place to start. You build up that trust and compatibility as friends. Learn what the other likes and doesn't like." She began stroking Salty's back and was rewarded with his contented purring. "If you two decide to take things further, you've got a solid foundation to build upon."

Tilly thought about Anna Lee's words. She was right, of course. "I don't know. I think it would be hard to change the dynamic."

"Well, poo. What's so hard about that? I saw him looking at you at dinner. He hung on your every word. He smiled at the witty things you said. He never once poked fun at you to get a cheap laugh. I think there could easily be more there. Sometimes, chicklet, you got to go for it. Take a risk. You're too young to start racking up regrets."

"I hear what you're saying. I'll think about what you said." Tilly knew she didn't want to end up with a life full of regrets. But could everyone be right about Ronin? Was it so hard to imagine only because she'd thought of him as just a friend for so long?

"You do that." Turning back to the cat, Anna Lee said, "Salty, you are a lazy bum."

"Oh, Anna Lee, I have a question for you. Ronin asked me to help him plan an anniversary party for his parents. One of our first tasks is finding a location for thirty to fifty guests. Do you have a venue list, or can you think of a few locations that might work?"

Anna Lee nodded before Tilly had finished asking her question. "I do. I have a master list with a guest count. I'll sort it by size and give you a list. There are no more consults today, so I'll go do that now. Won't take me but a few minutes."

"Great. And I need something else to do. I finished the catalog pile."

Anna Lee paused. "Want to help me prep payroll?"

"Really? You'd trust me to help with payroll?"

"Of course, I do. I've been thinking about offloading some of the administrative work. Maybe I need an office manager to handle scheduling, payroll, ordering, billing, and other such tasks. The years are catching up with me, and I find I don't have enough energy to do the things I need to do around the house once I'm done with the business stuff. And with John in my life now, I want to do more socializing and supporting his family. Someday, I may need to think about retiring. Selling this place."

"What?" Tilly wanted to shout *"No!"* but restrained herself. "Really?"

"Oh, not right away. But someday. Give me a few minutes. I'll get that list for you and bring out my laptop. We can do the payroll prep here on the counter, if you can get that lazy cat down from there for me."

Anna Lee walked away, and Tilly gave Salty another long

backrub. "Salty, are you ready to retire? Would you miss riding back and forth in your backpack when Anna Lee rides her scooter?"

The cat refused to answer. Instead, he licked his paw and rubbed his ear.

Anna Lee soon returned and handed Tilly a list of venues, which Tilly folded up and stuck in the back pocket of her jeans.

An hour later, payroll prep was done, and Tilly felt confident that she could do it on her own, if asked.

"If you decide to create an office-manager position, I might be interested in applying," Tilly said, tamping down the flutter of nerves in her belly. What was she thinking? She had another year of college coming up, and though she didn't know what she wanted to do when she graduated, she wasn't sure her parents would approve of using her psychology degree to manage a flower shop. That concern aside, she loved the idea of running a business, being responsible for the people that worked there, and making sure the customer experience was superb. She thought about what Anna Lee did in terms of supporting people, some at their happiest, like the brides who practically skipped through the door to plan their wedding flowers, and some at their worst, like the grieving who needed to order flowers for a funeral.

If she talked to Anna Lee about that aspect, she'd probably find that Anna Lee used many of the skills that Tilly had been learning in her psych classes.

Anna Lee took off her extra-large red reading glasses and tucked them into the pocket of her dress. "Really? That's interestin'. I never had you pegged for office work. You are such a people person."

"I am. I love people. And I think about the way you work with your customers—I love that. And with my brother starting his own business, it's made me think about running a business myself someday. I thought it might be a therapy practice, but maybe retail is a better choice. I love being active, and sitting through hours of conversation might be a little draining. I don't know. It's a baby idea, not developed yet."

"Those gut ideas are usually the ones we need to act on. If you take too long to study anything, you can probably find some reason why it's not a good idea. You're searching for a reason to say no. But gut ideas— those things that sneak up on you and take hold—them's gold. Kind of like the idea of hiring an office manager; that snuck up on me. Haven't been planning it, just came to mind. Let me talk to John; he's a good sounding board for me. I'll get back to you, but I'm intrigued about this particular spark."

Tilly wanted that kind of sounding board. Mack was always great with advice, and they talked about everything. But having a significant other with a vested interest in your decisions was different. She loved the way Anna Lee talked about John, and if he was the reason she'd decided to slow down a bit, that was great.

Her mind wandered to Ronin. With his calm and steady nature, he would be a great sounding board. He wouldn't acquiesce and end a conversation in a huff like Kyle had when Tilly pushed back or challenged him. Ronin wouldn't run when things got difficult. She wasn't sure how she knew this, but she did. Maybe it was the way he and Michael had talked about their business dreams for years. They'd never backed off, even when others told them their friendship wouldn't survive working together.

A customer walked in, and Tilly helped her pick out a pretty bunch of flowers for a dinner party. Once the customer had left, Tilly texted Ronin, *I got the list of venues from my boss.*

Message sent, she began to sweep the runaway leaves and other debris on the floor. Anna Lee was in the office going through the day's mail. Tilly looked at the time on her phone—another hour to go on her shift. Ronin hadn't given her particulars about dinner; excitement filled her as she hoped he hadn't forgotten.

RONIN WAS CONCENTRATING so hard on the lease-agreement language that the sound of the text message indicator startled him.

Michael stood up from the other end of their couch and stretched. "Man, my eyes are crossing. I need to take a break."

Ronin put his laptop on the glass coffee table. "I could use a break, too. I think the lease looks good; I'll send it to the lawyer to have him look it over. If he's good with it, we can sign and lock in the date we get the keys."

"Sounds great. I have a task list for moving in ready to go. Let's go over that again. I think we are going to need to hire a few helpers. And we should consider getting a contractor in there to look things over, to make sure there are no challenges with the changes we want to make."

"Agreed. If you're going to the kitchen, will you get me a glass of water?"

"Yep."

Michael walked away, and Ronin looked at his phone. He smiled, seeing Tilly's name. Moving closer to her was *not* helping him get over the feelings he'd held onto for so many years. Working together wouldn't help, either. He'd be constantly reminded of their one and only kiss—that magical kiss. Even so, he wouldn't give up the opportunity to work with her. Maybe he needed exposure therapy. Hang out with her as much as possible and keep telling himself that she was just a friend...and reminding himself that since she was his best friend's little sister, nothing could ever come of the crush he had on her.

He didn't think Michael would allow it. He felt the same about his little sisters—no one would ever be good enough for them. No one would treat them like they deserved to be treated. *Someone generous, considerate, passionate—but not too passionate. Nauseating. Cannot think of the word passion in the context of my sisters.*

Ronin was happy to see Tilly had the vendor list. That was progress.

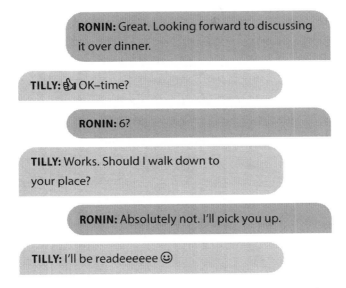

RONIN: Great. Looking forward to discussing it over dinner.

TILLY: 👍 OK–time?

RONIN: 6?

TILLY: Works. Should I walk down to your place?

RONIN: Absolutely not. I'll pick you up.

TILLY: I'll be readeeeeee ☺

Ronin laughed at her response. He could just imagine the sound of her sweet voice saying those words. He opened the picture app on his phone, scrolling backwards to find the pictures of Tilly and himself at Paige and Trevor's wedding. He'd asked Nica to take a picture of the two of them during the wedding reception, since they were all dressed up, and everything. He'd told Tilly that his mom would want to see it.

Looking at that picture, he felt both pleasure and pain. He was thrilled to have a picture of them together, looking like a couple, but he had to remind himself that they weren't a couple. She wasn't his and he wasn't hers.

Tilly was smiling brightly, but he assumed it was because she was at her friend's wedding, not because she was next to him. He had his arm around her and had pulled her close, causing her to lose her balance slightly, and she'd put her hand on his stomach to catch herself. The picture had been snapped just as she'd touched him. Anyone looking at the photo would assume they were a couple in love, not in a platonic plus-one date situation.

When Michael returned with the water and a bowl of tortilla chips, Ronin put his phone upside down on the coffee table, and they worked on the task list. Paint, lighting, technology, printers, office supplies, and break room inventory were top of mind for the space. They had already worked out a pricing model they were happy with that appeared to be on par with other co-working facilities in the Illinois and Indiana markets they had researched.

An hour later, Ronin declared he needed to shower before dinner. Michael didn't ask about dinner plans, and Ronin decided not to share. He wasn't hiding the fact that he was taking Tilly to dinner, but he wasn't going to offer the information either. Michael assumed Ronin was going to dinner at his parents' house, and Ronin didn't correct him. Another reason for picking Tilly up at her door and not letting her walk over.

This isn't a date, he told himself. *It's a business meeting.* He reminded himself of that again when he put on his cologne. *But I would want to smell good for a business meeting. Right?*

Since it was summer, and he didn't want to appear stuffy, he wore black shorts, a green polo shirt, and all-black tennis shoes. He planned to take Tilly to La Playa Vida but would confirm it was all right with her when he picked her up.

When he and Michael were reviewing the task list, they'd talked about asking their sisters for help. Ronin had brought it up first, remembering Shevaun pestering him for a job, but mostly for Michael to ask Tilly—and Michael took the bait. He said he'd talk to her about it that evening. Ronin hoped he wouldn't call her while they were at dinner, but if so, Ronin would use the opportunity to make sure she didn't say no.

CHAPTER FOURTEEN

TILLY PACED AROUND the living room. She was ready early and was trying to burn some of her nervous energy by moving around. She hoped Ronin wouldn't come up to the apartment to get her. Seeing him in this space would remind her too much of the night she'd kissed him in the kitchen, and she really needed to get the memory of that amazing kiss out of her mind.

She was trying, but the memory kept rearing up and knocking her down. She needed to come up with a good reason to lock that memory up in a vault—a very tight vault with no key. *Michael would be mad. Plus, I don't want to risk angering Ronin's family.* She even tried telling herself that it was a terrible kiss. *But that's a big, fat lie.*

Her heart raced just thinking about it. She'd wanted to run her fingers through his full hair when she'd reach around his neck, but the sensation of his lips on hers had thrilled and stunned her so much that her hands were immobile. His hands had moved to the back of her head, and she had felt each fingertip press against her skin.

"Gah!" she shouted; thankful the apartment was empty. She shook her head to rid it of the image of his blue eyes. Picking up the rose-scented candle from the TV stand, she inhaled deeply, wanting the scent to erase the memory of his woodsy cologne from her mind.

Breathing deeply to steady herself, she pulled on her sandals, adjusting them when the back strap snagged her long, ankle-length skirt. She'd paired the flowy skirt with a simple, silky pink sleeveless top. Her purse was vintage, an apple-shaped wooden box with a felt leaf on top; she loved its eclectic look. She'd found it at a yard sale. She and Mack loved to explore residential neighborhoods, and it was easy to get up close to the houses during yard sales.

A knock on the apartment door nearly caused her to scream. "Pull it together, Tilly," she whispered.

When she opened the door, her mouth twitched into a half-smile. Ronin had just showered; his hair was styling into a pompadour.

"New look?" she asked.

He smiled. "What do you think? The stylist showed me how to do it."

"I like it. It's a great look on you. Brings out your eyes—they were hidden behind the long mop top."

"I'm glad you approve. Ready to go?"

"Yes, let me get my purse."

"Got the list?"

"In the purse."

"Great."

He led her down the front steps and chatted about the work he and Michael had completed for the office space. Amazingly, the lawyer had approved the lease agreement shortly after they'd sent it to him, and they signed it. They would get the keys to the place on Monday, providing they had proof of insurance, which Ronin was expecting to get by Friday.

"Things are starting to move fast," Tilly said as they settled into Ronin's car.

"Yes, I'm thankful for that. There is only so much planning I can do before my head explodes. I'm ready to start finding clients and bringing the vision to life. Hey, I was thinking about La Playa Vida for dinner. Have you been there?"

"No, but I've heard good things. From Michael, actually. Sounds good."

They arrived at the restaurant and were seated in a corner booth. Ronin sat with his back to the wall, and Tilly was glad that she wouldn't be distracted by other people in the restaurant. She'd get to focus on Ronin and his new look throughout dinner.

After placing their orders, Tilly pulled Anna Lee's list out of her purse. "Here are the potential venues. I spent a little time researching online and made some notes in the margins. Here, I made you a copy."

She handed him the extra copy, and they started reviewing each location, "The David Davis mansion looks interesting. It seats up to forty for a sit-down dinner. The Vrooman Mansion is another old home turned venue. And it's a bed and breakfast."

"Who knew BloNo had so many mansions?" Ronin interjected.

Tilly laughed at his comment and the abbreviation for Bloomington/Normal. "Right. We've had some powerful families with lots of money here." Referring to the list, she said, "Then there's the Stanard Hotel. It's more of a conventional hotel with meeting rooms and onsite food service. Another benefit would be the rooms for out-of-town guests. Do you think you'll have a lot of guests traveling here?"

Ronin nodded. "Your parents, for one. And mom's sisters and their families. Probably more, but I need to get the list together."

"Right. Hurry up on that because we need a better head count."

"Yes, ma'am."

Charging forward, Tilly continued, "If you're thinking outdoors, there is a beautiful pavilion at Miller Park close to your parents' house. And then we have a couple of country clubs with golf or other activities for out-of-towners."

The waitress brought their salads, and they set the lists aside.

"Wow. This list is a great start. Maybe we should plan to visit a few locations and check them out."

"Oh, Ronin, do you really have time for that, while you're getting your business started? I could go with Shevaun and Trinity; we could do an initial review and then let you know our top two or three. That would save you some time."

"No," Ronin answered. "I want to see them with you. It'll be fun. We have a handle on the work for the business. Your brother and I talked about recruiting all our sisters to help with cleaning up, painting, stocking, and other stuff. Be surprised when Michael calls you. I, um." He looked down at his salad quickly. "I didn't tell him we were meeting tonight. He was under the impression I was going to my parents', and I didn't feel the need to correct him."

"Are you embarrassed you're meeting with me?" Tilly asked, her voice lilting in what she hoped was a teasing manner.

"No!" Ronin shook his head and reached across the table to take her hand. "No, Emmy. I'm not embarrassed at all. I just…" He shrugged his shoulder. "I just didn't want it to be awkward. Working with Michael and being friends with him, we are connected all the time. And I like being with you, Emmy, not Michael's sister. I'm not making sense. I don't know how to describe it."

Tilly looked at his hand resting on top of hers. It was so comforting and warm. She wanted to keep her hand in his, to feel that connection. She wanted more, so much more, from Ronin. But she couldn't go there. It would be too painful if he rejected her. As much as she wanted that kiss to mean something to him, she couldn't believe that it did. *If it had, he would have said something. He would have tried it again, right?* They'd been alone together during the bike ride on Sunday. They'd even talked about the kiss, but he'd just met her apology with his own. Then the moment was gone when she teased him. Teasing him was easier than professing her true feelings—less chance of getting hurt. And after Kyle, her heart was deeply bruised.

Putting the necessary distance between them physically, before her nervous system short-circuited, she flipped her hand over, squeezing his then releasing it. She replied, "I think I get it. It's easy to look at you and think, 'That's Michael's best friend, business partner, and roommate. But I want to look at you and just think, 'That's Ronin, *my* friend, my childhood friend who I never lost contact with. Who I...'"

She snapped her mouth shut before the wrong words could fly out.

"Who you..." Ronin's voice was soft but powerfully demanding, "...what, Emmy?"

"I don't know what I was going to say. I got ahead of myself," she managed to choke out.

Ronin grunted, disbelief and denial wrapped up in one small sound.

"ISN'T THREE O'CLOCK in the morning the witching hour?" Michael asked, pulling on his dark tennis shoes.

"Something like that. I've been scouting this out and we have about forty minutes before the early workers head out to start their day. For two nights in a row, I've not seen a single car on this street between three and four. This should be perfect."

Michael gave him a dubious look; he wasn't convinced Ronin's plan to string fishing line between their building and Tilly's was going to work.

Ronin had drawn the plan up earlier that day. He'd even installed the initial hook on the outside of their living room window and pulled their end of the fishing line through it, tying it to a small bell.

Ronin was confident that the fishing line would go unnoticed because it was so thin. It would only be discovered if someone was doing work outside one of the buildings that the line was attached to.

Dressed in all black, they crept quietly down the stairs of their building. They had met the tenant in the first-floor apartment, and the man had mentioned that he was a light sleeper. Ronin wasn't sure if that was true, or just something he'd said so they would stay quiet, but the night would go bad in a hurry if they woke him up now.

Ronin picked up the roll of fishing line outside their building. They dodged the streetlight in front of their apartment and dashed across the street.

"This is stupid," Michael muttered as he knelt behind a shrub.

"Hush," Ronin whispered. He had walked up and down this block fifty times this week, checking each of the buildings and houses, trying to decide the best placement for the wire. He'd decided on this house because of its high rail and low porch roof. He shimmied up onto the railing and paused, leaning against the wall, listening for sounds. The only sound he heard was Michael's breathing below him.

Taking a shallow breath, he put his foot on the windowsill closest to him, confident he could get onto the roof from there. He reached up, and with a soft grunt, pulled his body onto the roof, his legs stretched straight behind him with his chest on the roof.

"Need a push?" Michael stage whispered.

"No."

Ronin shimmied forward, slowly, trying not to make a sound. Seconds later, he was able to shift himself into a crouch. He pulled the hook out of his pocket and started screwing it into the wood siding, close to the corner. He turned the screw slowly, breathing a sigh of relief as he saw it making progress.

Once the screw was fixed, he gestured to Michael to toss up the spool. Luckily, Michael's aim was on point, and Ronin caught it on the first toss. He looped the wire over the hook and dropped the spool back to Michael.

Ronin slowly climbed back down and scurried to catch up with Michael, who was already at Tilly's building. Michael laid the spool on the ground, and grabbed the ladder that was always lying against the building—placing it beside Tilly's window.

Michael looked at Ronin and pointed to himself, then pointed at the ladder. *Yes, probably best for Michael to go. If someone is going to get caught peeping into Tilly's window, better her brother than me.*

Ronin handed Michael the hook and watched him climb up. It took him less than a minute to screw it in and wrap the wire over it. He dropped the spool, and Ronin quickly cut it with a pocketknife as Michael hurried down the ladder.

Silently, they replaced the ladder. As they walked beside Tilly's building toward the street, Ronin heard a car coming and paused in the shadows, plastering himself up against Tilly's building and signaling Michael to do the same.

A police car drove by, and Ronin was thankful for the timing and the shadows. Waiting a minute, he peered out from the side of the building. Nothing. They walked back to their apartment in silence.

Inside their apartment, Ronin turned to high-five Michael. "We did it!"

Michael let out a long breath. "That was too close. I thought I was going to have a heart attack standing on that ladder."

"Hey, you had the easy climb."

"True. I haven't had that much adventure in ages. Made me feel like I was ten again."

"Right. Let's see if your sister finds it as amusing as we do."

"So old school. Today we can text and talk and not move from where we're sitting or lying down. But being able jingle that bell to let Tilly know we're thinking about her, or just to irritate her, that's fun. Once school starts, we'll probably never catch her in her bedroom. But still, we can try."

CHAPTER FIFTEEN

*I*T WAS A glorious Friday afternoon, and Tilly and Ronin were strolling along the grounds of the David Davis mansion. When Tilly had researched the open hours online, she'd found that there was a Garden Walk this weekend, so they could tour the private gardens of several properties near the mansion in addition to the beautifully cultivated gardens of the mansion itself.

"This is just stunning!" she exclaimed, pointing to a water fountain surrounded by delicate blooms. "I feel like I'm in a European garden."

Ronin smiled as he pulled his phone out of his pocket. Tilly knelt to look more closely at the vibrant purple flowers, and he snapped a picture of her without her noticing. He glanced at the screen and was struck by her wide eyes, shining with enjoyment and happiness. He wished he could make her look like this all the time.

"European gardens seem like a cool thing to see." Thinking about a honeymoon trip, he shook his head. *Not going there.*

"I know, right?" Tilly stood and moved toward a four-foot-tall statue of an angel in the middle of a circle of hostas under the shade of a giant oak tree. "I was just talking to Anna Lee about gardens around the world. She said she's never been out of the

US, but she loves to look at pictures of all sorts of gardens, any-where in the world."

"Pictures aren't as good as the real thing." He thought about the picture he'd sneakily snapped of her. It was good, and he'd cherish having it, but looking at Tilly now, noticing her quickly shifting expressions, he knew he could study her face all day long and never tire of it.

An older couple holding hands walked past them slowly. The woman gave Ronin a sly smile; she must have read something in his face that he didn't intend for anyone to see. His features stilled as Tilly turned toward him again.

"Do you want to look around inside? See if it's big enough for the party?" she asked, swinging her tote bag back and forth.

Ronin loved her constant energy. She was always up for an ad-venture or for trying something new. Even when she was unsure of herself, like riding the bike on Sunday with his family. She willingly admitted that she might not be able to keep up, but she was going to hang in there and come along in her own sweet time.

"Sure. Let's take a quick look." He knew she was getting a kick out of looking at the flowers. She had taken a hundred pictures so far, and she would probably take a hundred more. She said she wanted to show them to Anna Lee.

Inside the historic home, they chatted with the events manager, who gave them a price sheet and checked availability for August 19th. The manager said it was currently open, but suggested they lock it in within a week to secure the date.

They exited the mansion and followed the signs to the next house on the Garden Walk tour.

"Well, what do you think?" Tilly asked.

"I think it would work, but I still want to see the other two locations that we liked."

He also appreciated the excuse to hang out with Tilly a couple more times. She'd agreed to visit the possible locations with him to give her opinion.

"Sure. Never go with the first one, that's my motto. So many choices; best to shop around."

"Do you apply that to the men you date, too?"

Tilly flushed. Ronin ached to take her hand and squeeze it, but he held back. *This isn't a date. This is just a scouting excursion.*

"Well, not intentionally. I don't like to date a new guy every week—I'm not that fickle. I was with Kyle for a long time. I thought we were happy. I loved the idea of settling down and getting married, and I thought he wanted that, too."

She paused. Ronin wanted to pull her close to him and soothe the hurt and frustration that showed in her face.

"So, what happened, exactly?" Ronin asked.

"He broke up with me. Said I wasn't ambitious enough. You know, I still haven't figured out what I want to do after college. Some people, like you and Michael, have known what they want for so long. I envy that, you know. I thought about being a therapist. I love talking to people, I love helping people. I want everyone to feel special and loved and in control of their lives. So many people need that. But I don't know. I don't see myself shuffling patients in and out the door. That's not how I see myself helping others. Fifty minutes at a time…" she trailed off as they approached the next garden.

There was an open iron gate leading to a backyard. A small bench sat just outside the gate.

"Let's sit for a minute," Ronin suggested. He knew she needed to get something off her chest, and she would be distracted by the flowers and features in this yard.

"Okay." She sat and placed her yellow-and-white-striped tote bag between them. It matched the yellow dress and white sandals that she wore.

The same couple they'd seen earlier walked out of the back yard, saying hello as they passed. Ronin nodded, and Tilly asked brightly how the garden was, not a care in the world in her voice. "Just lovely," the older woman answered, and the couple walked on.

Tilly turned to look at Ronin before continuing. "So, I don't know what's next for me. I haven't applied to grad school, and I don't want to. I look at all my friends who have a plan and are executing those plans as they are falling in love. They seem to be juggling so much so well, and I feel lost. I'm confused."

"What makes you happy?" Ronin asked. A part of him wanted her to include him on whatever happy list she shared.

"Being with my friends, my family. Work. I love working for Anna Lee at In Bloom. We interact with customers; we get to make the most beautiful arrangements. It's technical. It's artistic. It's…healing. That probably sounds weird. But if I'm in an odd mood when I get there, if I'm feeling down or worried about something, I can almost guarantee you, that feeling will go away before I leave work. That building is magical. It's old, you know. I think it's been filled with good people over the years. And it soothes my soul."

Ronin nodded. "That's fantastic. It sounds like a special place. Anna Lee sounds special."

"She is," Tilly agreed. "She's full of wisdom and experience and…magic. You probably think I'm nuts."

"Never. It sounds like you're happy there."

"I am. And you know what? She is giving me more responsibility and talking about creating an office manager position. I told her I'd like to apply if she does. Do you think my parents will be disappointed if I work as an office manager at a flower shop? Will they approve?"

"Emmy, they want you to be happy." Ronin leaned forward to emphasize his statement. "Have you talked to them about the idea?"

"No. I'm still getting my head wrapped around it. It's not something I've ever thought about before. But when Anna Lee talked about it, it felt right. Maybe I could take some design classes this year. Or business classes."

"Michael and I can help you with some of the business stuff. Maybe you could get involved with what we're doing and learn some of the business aspects. It's not the same, but there are similarities. Customer service, billing, scheduling, payroll, accounting. A lot of that will be similar."

"You're right! Are you serious? Do you think Michael would go for that?"

"Yes, I'm sure he will. We are going to be desperate for help during the first few months getting it launched. I may even have to hire Shevaun, heaven forbid. We're talking about a painting party the week after next. Would you be up for it?"

"Sure. I'd love to help. And I can make lunch!"

"Now you're talking. Ready to stroll through this garden?"

"Yes, let's!"

Ronin followed Tilly through the gate. Her step seemed a little lighter. Freer. He liked that she was comfortable enough to share a legitimate concern with him. He felt he'd helped her work something out. He was glad the conversation had focused on her career; if she'd brought up a love interest or lingering feelings for that jerk Kyle, he would have had a hard time thinking rationally. He might have told Tilly that he had been suppressing feelings for her for years.

He had so much on his plate starting a new business. He had hoped to put love off until later but he couldn't help his feelings for Tilly that were growing stronger and stronger. He prayed for the strength to get over the Michael hurdle. *I hope the stars will align and Emmy will have feelings for me, too.*

TILLY HOPED THAT their Friday-night-pizza-and-a-movie evening would become a regular thing with Michael and Ronin. It would be a great time to connect about the work week or school week and just relax before gearing up for fun weekends.

This was the first time since the boys had moved in that they were able to make it. Tilly had time after the garden walk and visiting the David Davis Mansion to come home, shower, and get into comfortable clothes. Of course, it was a matching running set. Not that she ever ran, but it was cute and pink with a white stripe running down the sides of the pants and jacket. Underneath, she wore a white tank top with a pink Barbie logo. News was out about the upcoming movie, and she was excited about seeing it.

With Barbie on her mind, she dried her hair and pulled it up into a high ponytail, curling the ends to give it a little flip. She finished the look with glitter pink eyeshadow and small pink hoop earrings.

She felt casual, comfortable, and cute—the three important Cs.

Mack called from her bedroom down the hall, "What time are they getting here?"

"Michael said seven." Tilly looked at her phone; it was ten minutes to seven. "Soon!"

She heard Mack curse and laughed. Mack was always running a few minutes late. "I'm getting in the shower now!"

At least the pizza was scheduled for seven-thirty. There was time.

Five minutes later, there was a knock at the door. Tilly slipped on a simple silver bangle and went to open it.

"Hey," Michael said, walking past her carrying a twelve-pack of beer. "I'll put this in the fridge."

"Hi, that's fine."

Ronin stepped forward, and Tilly gave him a shy smile. She felt bad about unloading on him that afternoon. He had enough on his plate; he didn't need to hear her whining about not knowing what to do with her life. Oh, well, it was time to chill out and not worry about those things until tomorrow. Or the next day. Next week was fine.

"Hi, there. Welcome."

"You look adorable, Emmy. Pink is your color."

"Thanks." She felt herself blushing. "I'm comfy."

Ronin's smile tightened. "You look it. I brought dessert."

He held out a bakery box.

"You did?" she asked, surprised. "What did you get?"

"Lemon-raspberry cheesecake."

"That's my absolute favorite!"

"I remember. You had it at your high school graduation party."

"Right! Because your mom had made one just before that, and I absolutely fell in love with it."

Ronin raised an eyebrow as he slid the box onto the kitchen counter.

Tilly glanced over at the empty flower vase that had held her birthday tulips from Anna Lee. She blushed, thinking about the kiss. That kiss! It flooded her memory and warmed her cheeks. She turned away from Ronin; she couldn't look at him right now.

Michael turned away from the fridge. "Where's your roommate?"

"She's in the shower," Tilly answered, busying herself getting plates out of the cabinet. "She'll be out soon. Pizza will be here in thirty minutes. Did you guys bring movie ideas?"

The plan was for each of them to write down two movie titles on a piece of paper. All eight choices would be thrown into a hat, and a random movie would be pulled out. The movies had to be accessible on someone's streaming service or on a physical DVD, to ensure whichever one they selected would be available.

"Of course, we're capable of following directions, Sis." Michael said, leaning against the counter and opening a bottle of beer. Tilly noticed his button-down shirt and pressed cargo shorts. She'd figured he'd show up in a T-shirt and gym shorts.

"You're right, they were very simple directions. I'm not surprised even you could follow them," she teased. Remembering she was hosting, she turned back to Ronin, more composed now. She refused to look at the vase. "Would you like something to drink?"

"I'm good for now."

Tilly leaned against the counter next to her brother. "Help yourself when you're ready. We stocked up for the weekend. Lots to drink in the fridge."

Ronin looked at Michael. "Did you forget something?"

Michael practically jumped to attention, facing Tilly. "Right. We have something for you."

"You do?"

"Yeah, come on. It goes in your bedroom." He started towards her door.

Yikes! There were clothes strewn about; it'd taken her a few outfit changes to decide what to wear tonight. "Just a minute. Let me straighten up. Hold on—what did you bring me that needs to go in my bedroom?"

"You'll see," Michael replied. "Hurry up and tell us when you're ready."

At her door, she turned back to look at them both carefully. "I'm not sure I trust you two right now."

Ronin gave her a lazy grin. "Trust is all you got, lady."

Whatever that means. She entered her room and grabbed all the discarded clothes, throwing them into a basket in her closet. She straightened her comforter and put the little Toto dog on top of her pillow.

Satisfied that the room was passable, she opened the door.

Michael walked in carrying a small silver bell. He shook it, and Tilly heard a soft tinkle. "Do you remember the tin can telephone Ronin and I put between our bedrooms when we were kids?" He crossed to the window on the other side of her bed.

"Yeah…"

"Well, this is similar, but no tin can. A bell. We've strung a line from our living room to just outside your window here." He unlatched and lifted her window, reaching outside. He pulled a barely visible wire inside and began tying it to a hole at the top of the bell handle. "And now…" He pulled the wire up and over her curtain rod so that the bell hung loose. "When we tug on the line in our apartment, it will ring this bell. And vice versa." He gave the bell a tug. "Our bell should have jangled."

She rushed to the window and looked out. "What in the world? How did you hang it?"

Michael pointed, telling how they'd run the wire. She shook her head in disbelief.

"We'll have to test it out. Make sure it really works now that your bell is in place," Ronin added from the doorway.

Tilly turned towards him, narrowing her eyes. "Whose idea was this?"

"Mine," Ronin said confidently, like it was perfectly ordinary to run wire between two apartments with multiple buildings between them.

"You're crazy!"

"Maybe," he shrugged.

Michael moved behind her, grabbing the stuffed dog off her bed. "Maybe we should take Toto here out to the living room for the movie. Just in case Tilly's favorite movie is picked."

"No, we can't watch *The Wizard of Oz* tonight. We need to save that for the night before Oz Fest. There will be no pulling out of a hat that night."

Michael groaned. "When is that again?"

"August fifth. You have to go with."

"Did I commit to that?"

Ronin answered for her. "Yes, you did. If I'm going, you're going."

"Fine."

Mack popped her head in from behind Ronin. "What's happening in here?"

Tilly pointed to the bell. "This. I'll explain later. Let's pick a movie. I can't wait to see what we're watching tonight."

Michael walked past Tilly and Ronin. He and Mack started talking in the kitchen. As Tilly began to follow, Ronin stopped her by blocking the doorway. "I'll text you later, and we'll test out the bell."

His enchanting blue eyes sparkled brightly. She gazed, wanting to get lost in them. *But I can't.* "All right," was all she said, walking past.

HOURS LATER, MICHAEL said he was going out for a bit before calling it a night and ordered a rideshare on his phone. Mack had gone to bed as soon as the movie was over; she had to get up and work her waitressing job at 6 a.m.

Ronin followed Michael to the door but paused as Michael jogged down the stairs. Tilly had followed them so she could lock up once they'd left.

"Emmy," he said, turning towards her.

Most of the apartment was dark. Only the string of Christmas lights above the kitchen cabinets and lighthouse lamp in the living room provided any light. Since Ronin was lit from behind by the hallway light, it was hard to read his face.

Tilly was ready for bed and covered a runaway yawn. "Sorry," she muttered.

"Think you can stay awake long enough to test the bell system?"

"Oh, right. Yes. How will we do that?"

"I'll text you when I get home and let you know when I've rung the bell."

"Oh, okay."

"Thanks for a fun evening."

It had been fun. Mack made friends easily, and it had soon felt like she'd known everyone for years, even though she'd just met Ronin and Michael the week before.

"You're welcome. I'm surprised you managed to sit through Mack's movie pick."

"Not something I would have chosen on my own, but it was interesting." Seeing her yawn again, he continued, "I'll get out of your hair. You need to get to bed soon. Hopefully you'll be awake long enough to try out the bells."

"Right. Good night, Ronin."

"Night, Em."

He left, and she quickly washed her face and put on her pajamas. Just as she crawled into bed, her phone beeped.

> **RONIN:** Ready?

> **TILLY:** Ready

A second later, the bell hanging from her curtain rod jingled softly. It worked!

> **TILLY:** OMG. It worked! I heard it.

She reached over to pull on the bell, hoping she was pulling hard enough for it to ring on his end. She waited a few seconds for Ronin's response.

> **RONIN:** That worked! I love when a plan comes together.

> **TILLY:** plan/scheme/world takeover/whatever

She smiled to herself. Yes, Ronin was capable of whatever he put his mind to. He was brilliant and creative and fun. He wanted success, but with all the right outcomes; he wanted to bring others up with him. He wasn't the kind to push others aside to get what he wanted. She loved that about him; his caring, protective, and watchful side. Seemed like he was always watching and observing. Like today, when he asked about her breakup with Kyle—it was as if *she* were in therapy, and Ronin her therapist. He'd asked all the right questions, encouraging her, telling her she didn't need to be so uptight about her future. It was comforting. That had been the first time she'd ever bared her soul to Ronin, and it felt nice. Like he cared deeply about her.

She blinked. She must be overtired; her imagination was running amok.

RONIN: You know me so well. Sweet dreams, Em

TILLY: Night, Ronin

CHAPTER SIXTEEN

*I*T WAS LATE Friday afternoon and Tilly had not seen her brother or Ronin all week. They'd received the keys to their coworking space on Monday and were hustling to get things ready for the grand opening in four short weeks.

Tilly flung shoes out of her small closet into the bedroom. She was on all fours seeking out the shoes from every crevice. She thought she had a pair of lilac-colored ballerina flats that she wanted to wear with her lilac linen slacks and white blouse. Today she and Ronin were touring the Vrooman Mansion, and she wanted her outfit to have an "old world charm" look. She'd poured over the pictures and the story of the historic mansion online and wanted to style herself appropriately. She would ask Ronin to take a couple of pictures of her in the beautiful setting. *Maybe it's time to create an online-dating profile. Time to get back out on the dating scene. Maybe it will even help distract me from these unrealistic feelings about Ronin,* she thought. It had been nine months since Kyle had broken up with her, and Mack was becoming impatient with her reluctance to date.

The bell in the window tinkled. "Ugh," she muttered, still not finding the shoes she wanted. The bell meant Ronin was ready and about to get in his car. Giving up on the lilac shoes, she slipped on a pair of white boots. They'd have to do.

She grabbed her cell phone off the charger and slipped it into her purse, a white clutch that Mackenzie had loaned her.

She grabbed her keys from the kitchen and turned off the ambient lighting in the living room.

Hurrying down the stairs, she exited the front door just as Ronin pulled up, idling the car in the street rather than pulling over to the curb.

"Hi," he said as she climbed into the blue sedan. "You look fantastic. Hot date tonight?"

"Just you, pretty boy," she chirped.

He was looking rather fine, she thought, sliding a glance his way. He was wearing chino pants and a short-sleeved blue oxford with a light white check. *Hmm, we sort of coordinate.*

"Watch who you're calling pretty. I'm handsome, not pretty."

"Insecure in your masculinity much?"

"Not insecure. Just think I'm too rugged to be called pretty. So, tell me more about the venue we're going to see today. I've had no time to research."

"Well, I've delivered flowers there for several weddings and ladies' luncheons. It is just divine. The rooms are pristine; you feel like you're walking into the turn of the last century. Julia Vrooman was born in the house in 1876 and lived there until her death in 1981! She was almost one hundred and five years old. That just amazes me. She and her husband never had children, and when she died, everything was sold at auction, and most of the money went to churches and charities.

"Anyway, her parents built the house. They were wealthy and had ties to a lot of prominent people. As did Julia and her husband. He served in some fancy position under President Woodrow Wilson, and they hobnobbed with a lot of famous people."

"Hobnobbed?"

"Yes, you know, rubbed elbows with, hung out with."

"Where in the world did you pick up 'hobnob'?"

Tilly tilted her head, considering. "Probably Anna Lee. She says all sorts of funny things. Like, the other day, we were making centerpieces for a party, and Nica was telling her about a dresser she was trying to make over to resell. She was explaining the numerous steps she needed to take for this particular project, and Anna Lee said, 'I don't know if that juice is worth the squeeze'. We all started cracking up. She's just so expressive. I think we've lost some of that in our everyday speech. Guess I'm trying to emulate her."

"Keep emulating, Emmy."

"So, you and Michael made good progress this week, yes? I haven't seen or heard anything from either of you."

"We did. We got a contractor in right away to reconfigure the office and the floor plan. He needs a couple more days to finish up. Then we will paint. Then new carpeting, and then we will open for business. We scheduled advertising—radio, print, and TV—to start next week. I feel like we made great progress this week."

"That's fantastic. Need help?"

"How are you with a paint brush?"

"Fair to middlin'."

"What?"

Tilly laughed. "Another Anna Lee-ism. I think it means "pretty good". Don't quote me though. When are you painting?"

"Tuesday or Wednesday. Depends on when the contractor finishes. His crew is working this weekend, so we're hoping for Tuesday."

"Neat. Oh, here we are."

They pulled into the parking lot next to the Vrooman Mansion. Once they parked, Tilly grabbed her clutch and stepped out of the car. She stood surveying the grounds as Ronin walked around to her side.

"Ready to take a look?" he asked, placing his hand on her lower back to guide her forward.

Tilly's mind went haywire at his touch, as if she'd stuck a knife into an electrical socket and all systems short-circuited.

She started up the stairs to the majestic, historic, mansion, and Ronin's hand fell away, leaving her with a sudden chill despite the eighty-degree temperature.

At the entrance, they met an events manager, who led them on a tour of the grounds, the dining rooms, and the bedrooms.

In the carriage house, Tilly oohed at the details carved into the wooden panels that lined the staircase leading to the two bedrooms upstairs. The first bedroom had dark wood crown molding, and the second bedroom had beautiful oak crown molding and wainscoting. The bathroom had a deep green claw-foot tub that she longed to bathe in.

"Oh, this is just scrumptious," she said, sitting on the beautifully carved bed in the second bedroom. "I think it would be amazing to honeymoon in this carriage house. Especially if you could have the whole place to yourself."

Ronin cleared his throat as he looked at the woman giving them the tour.

Their tour guide beamed. "We have families and even couples that rent out the entire carriage house for privacy."

"That sounds like perfection, don't you think, Ronin?"

"Sounds great."

"Have you two set a date?" the woman asked.

Tilly paused as she started to stand, caught between the current reality, in which she and Ronin were just friends, and a fantasy world, where she was discussing her wedding and honeymoon with a man with Ronin's confidence, humor, and stability. And excellent physique, amazing thick hair that she wanted to wash (to get the sticky gel out of) and run her hands through, soft beard, and perfectly firm but soft lips.

Standing upright, she turned to seek Ronin's face. The woman was straightening a throw blanket on the bed and didn't seem concerned at their lack of response to her question.

Ronin's gaze was fixed on Tilly when her eyes met his. *Why hasn't he responded?* It would have been appropriate for him to clarify that they were there to plan an anniversary party for his parents. *Why didn't he say that? Was he thinking about honeymoons and romantic escapes, like I was?*

"No," Ronin finally replied, the gravel in his throat apparent even in the short answer. "Not yet. For now, we're planning an anniversary celebration for my parents."

"Oh, lovely," the woman replied. "Which anniversary?" Without waiting for a response, she said, "This way, we can look at the grounds before returning to the mansion."

She started down the stairs and Tilly forced her feet to move forward as Ronin held out his hand in an "after you" gesture.

As she passed him, Tilly hissed, "Why didn't you tell her we're not engaged?"

"It was cute to watch you blush. Besides, what's the harm in letting her think that? She is showing us bedrooms and not just a reception room."

Outside, Ronin matched her stride and took hold of her hand.

"What are you doing?" she asked. A flutter rippled through her chest at his touch.

"Keeping up appearances, *sweetie*," he replied as the tour guide turned around and smiled at them.

It was surprisingly easy to return the woman's smile.

ONCE THEY'D SEEN everything, Ronin and Tilly thanked their guide and started for the car.

"Oh, wait," Tilly said as they started down the stairs of the mansion. "Would you do me a huge favor and take a couple pictures of me? I sort of dressed up for this. I need a couple of good pictures. Mack has been hounding me to start dating again. She thinks its time to create a profile on a dating app. She said she'll do it too, if I do."

She was smoothing her blouse as Ronin paused mid-step. "Sure." He put his foot down. He didn't like this. *Why is she getting on a stupid dating app? On the positive side, it must mean she's over the breakup with that jerk Kyle. On the negative side, it means she could start dating another obnoxious jerk and get her heart broken again.*

Ronin looked around. There was a row of blooming shrubs alongside the building. "What about over here?" he asked.

"That looks nice. Here, let me get my phone."

"I'll take them on mine and send them to you." Ronin was proud of himself for thinking on his feet. This way, he'd have the photos for himself.

"Oh, okay," she said hesitantly. "You won't mess with them, will you?"

The hesitation in her voice made him wince. "Of course not, Em. But I'm familiar with the photo settings on my phone."

She stepped in front of the shrubs. She seemed to think about what kind of pose to take and settled on putting her hands behind her, with a jaunty tilt of her head. *Oh man, she's so beautiful.*

Ronin wished he had more artistic flair when it came to photography. *Should have taken a course at some point.* He wanted to do this for hours. To be able to hide behind a camera while he got to watch her make cute, sensual, and serious faces at him was heaven on earth.

After snapping at least thirty photos, he looked around for another setting. "Hey, let's move over to that side. There's more sunlight, and that brick backdrop would look good."

"Okay." She followed him. "Thanks for doing this. I would have asked Mack, but she's been busy lately with both jobs. And I got dressed up today, so..."

"It's not a problem at all. Glad to help. Do you have plans for dinner? We could grab a bite."

"No, do you mind asking Michael to join us? I haven't seen him all week and would love to catch up."

Yes, yes, I do mind. He wanted an evening alone with Emmy; he didn't want to share her with anyone. Even if it was her brother.

Well, maybe there would be a silver lining. He could bring up the photos, and Michael would probably press her for information about the dating app. Ronin didn't think Michael would like the idea any more than he did.

"Not a problem," Ronin finally replied.

He took a few more photos. The sun was lower in the sky, and the heat created a shimmer that made Emmy's eyes sparkle even more brightly than usual. The last shot almost took his breath away. She was looking straight at the camera, a half-smile on her face. That smirk beckoned to his soul. It seemed to say that Emmy had a lot to offer him, if he was only brave enough to go after her. To open himself up and tell her how much he yearned to be with her. To protect her. To encourage her. To hold her and cherish her.

Now he was thinking about weddings and honeymoons.

In the car, Tilly reminded him to send her the pictures.

"Of course. I'll do it as soon as I can. Why don't you text Michael and see if he wants to join us for dinner? We can pick him up in fifteen minutes if he's ready."

"All right." Tilly began tapping on her phone. "What do you think? Do we need to see more properties, or do you want to go with one of the ones we've seen so far?"

Ronin considered. Both venues were beautiful properties. He could manage the cost. He had his hands full, starting his own business and didn't really have the time, but then he wouldn't have the enjoyment of visiting more locations with Emmy.

"Not yet. I'd like to keep looking. What's next on your list?" He stole a side glance at Tilly; she was reapplying lipstick. Which made him glance at her lips, which made him remember their kiss, which made him want to reenact it.

"Let me look." More tapping on her phone. "There's Broadview Mansion in Normal, and Ewing Cultural Center. What's your schedule like next week? I'll call and make appointments at both."

"Busy. But that's going to be a given moving forward. If you can make the appointments for later in the week, that will be fine. Late afternoon again."

"You got it. Oh, Michael just texted. Let's see." She paused to read. "He says yes to dinner and to pick him up. This works out perfectly!"

CHAPTER SEVENTEEN

ILLY AND RONIN slid into a booth at Hot and Sweet
BBQ, her favorite barbecue restaurant. Michael sat across
from them and began to update Ronin on the contractor's
progress that afternoon.

Tilly took the opportunity while the men talked to check her
social media accounts and exchange text messages with Mack.
She wanted to post the pictures that Ronin had taken on her
social media, and as soon as there was a lull in the conversation,
she nudged Ronin to send them to her.

While Tilly posted, Michael told Ronin that they'd received
several applications for a receptionist position.

"Are you going to let Shevaun apply?" Tilly asked.

"What? Why?" Michael asked. "Isn't she going back to school
in a few weeks?"

"Yes," Ronin started, leaning over the table. "And she asked
for a job. I wouldn't put her in the receptionist position, but there
will be other things she can help with."

"Maybe put her in charge of your social media. You both stink
at it," Tilly chimed in.

Michael tilted his head. "That's not a bad idea. What do you
think, Ro?"

"We need to finalize our business name and open social accounts, but I agree, she'd love that. Once we complete the remodel, we should hire someone to take high-quality photos to use in our advertising and social media. Emmy, do you have a photographer friend?"

Tilly considered. "Mack runs with all sorts of creative people. I can ask her." She started typing on her phone again.

"Mack seemed really cool," Michael said. "What's her story? Got a boyfriend?"

"No, are you interested?" Tilly asked.

"No. She's not my type, but maybe Ronin would be interested."

Tilly considered. She didn't think Mack was Ronin's type either, but maybe that was wishful thinking. Ronin was starting to fill her imagination in ways that he shouldn't. While he was taking her photos today, she'd felt a pulse of desire. Having to look into the camera meant she'd had to look at Ronin—at his tall frame, broad shoulders, and that longish hair that she wanted to smooth. After the miscommunication with the lady at the mansion who'd thought they were getting married, Tilly couldn't stop thinking about being in a relationship with Ronin. *What would it be like? He's always kind to me; what would it look like if he was into me? If he was trying to make me happy?* She thought about the things she would do to show him how much she cared. *Cook for him. Run errands. Listen to him when he's excited about his plans or frustrated with vendors or tenants.* She wanted to be the person, the special sounding board he turned to when he needed to spill whatever was on his mind.

This wouldn't do. He lived and worked with her brother. *How awkward would it be if things went sideways? Too awkward.*

She had to get over this crush on Ronin ASAP.

Maybe... Tilly had an idea. *What if I set Ronin up with Mack? Problem solved.*

She turned to Ronin. "I think you and Mackenzie would be a great match."

"She has pink hair."

"She's creative and smart and sassy. She's super-sweet."

"No."

"But why?"

"She's your roommate. It could be awkward."

Precisely how Tilly felt about dating Ronin while he was Michael's roommate.

"Why? I won't live with her forever."

She'd be Michael's sister forever, though. And while she couldn't imagine anything coming between Michael and Ronin, she didn't want to risk something that might hurt their lifelong friendship.

Ronin put his bottle of beer down with a thud. "Fine, Emmy. If you insist, I'll ask her out."

Tilly sucked in her breath. That hurt her soul more than she was expecting. She wanted to shout no. But she couldn't back down now. She couldn't tell Ronin—in front of her brother, no less—that she wanted him to ask *her* out.

"Okay," she finally said. "I'll talk to her. Are you busy tomorrow night?"

Better get this over with as fast as possible; the longer I have to think about it, the more it will hurt.

"I'll make it work."

"Great."

"Great."

Ronin asked Michael about the software they'd need to book the individual offices and bill renters. Tilly completely tuned out when Michael started a long explanation about technology. Her head was still spinning, thinking about Ronin going out with Mack. *How can I back this truck up? Maybe Mack won't go for it. I can only hope.*

Her stomach was churning, and she looked up at Ronin, with a scowl on her face. His facial expression matched hers. *What's he mad about now?*

ON SATURDAY NIGHT, Tilly was sitting on the couch when Mack got home from her date with Ronin. She'd been mindlessly clicking the remote and jumping from one silly show to another. Nothing was keeping her attention for long; her mind kept shifting to Ronin and Mack's date.

"Hi! How was the date?" she asked, as soon as Mack walked in.

"Oh, geez. We survived it. That guy's got it bad for you. I need a drink."

Tilly smiled in relief. "Oh, I'm sorry…"

"No. You're not." Mack shook her head, her long, choppy bangs brushing across her eyebrows. "I know you. You've got it bad for him, girly. Just be thankful he and I didn't hit it off, and things can go back to normal."

Laughing, Tilly stood and hugged her roommate. "Okay. I'll admit it. I'm relieved. But did you get along, at least?"

"Yes, it was fun getting to know him and hearing about his family. He shared a few enlightening stories about you and Michael. I had a great time. But as I suspected, there was no chemistry whatsoever."

"Oh, no. I'm sure he had a few stories to share."

"A few?" Mack scoffed. "Girl, he had some stories. Hey, I need another drink before bed. What say you?"

"Sure. I'll have whatever you're having."

Mack went to the refrigerator, and Tilly smiled to herself. *This calls for a celebratory drink, for certain!*

CHAPTER EIGHTEEN

RONIN IGNORED THE text message indicator; he wanted to finish painting this section of the wall. It was Tuesday, and the painting party was in full gear. His mom, sisters, Tilly, Michael, and several of the girls' friends were present. After assigning tasks to everyone, the painting party was under way. Ronin's mom, Michael, and Shevaun were painting the walls in the large open drop-in space, while Trinity, Tilly, and Ronin were working on the individual office spaces. Trinity would tape off an office, then Tilly would paint the edges with a tapered hand-held brush, so Ronin could roll paint on the walls with the long-handled roller.

The system seemed to be working, but Ronin knew he was going to need a long shower afterwards. Only three hours in, and his muscles were already complaining.

"Hey, bruh—," Shevaun interrupted Ronin's internal monologue of things they still needed to do to get the shared working space open. "We're breaking for lunch. Sandwiches are here."

Even though Tilly had offered to make lunch, Ronin insisted they order in.

"Cool. Be there in just a few." He dipped the roller in paint and turned his attention back to the last wall.

Everyone had gathered in the break room at the back of the open space by the time Ronin joined them. He grabbed a paper plate and two sandwiches, not caring what kind they were. He was hungry.

"This has been fun," Tilly said, as Ronin approached her and Trinity at their small round table.

"Great job with the edging. You have a steady hand," Ronin told her.

"Only because Trin did such a great job with the taping."

"We're the best. Go, team!" Trinity said, raising her hand for high fives. Her long blonde ponytail swished side to side with each hand-slap.

Ronin smiled. Trinity's enthusiasm was a bonus. He was glad she wasn't working her lifeguard job today.

Michael approached their table, soft drink in hand. "Almost done with the offices?"

"They're done," Ronin answered. "All hands on this open space now. Looks like it's close to being finished."

"Yes, once you guys join us, it won't take long. Glad to knock all the painting out in a day."

"Many hands," Tilly said.

Ronin nodded. "Right. Thank you."

He thought back on the date with Tilly's roommate Saturday night. Mackenzie had been engaging and funny, but she wasn't Tilly. There was no spark between them. They'd spent the time talking about Tilly and Michael. Ronin wanted more insights into who Tilly was as a person now, and Mack was interested in similar details about Michael, though it wasn't clear how serious she might be about Tilly's brother.

Everyone finished eating and was anxious to get back at it. Ronin's mom said sitting too long would make it even harder to get going again, and everyone agreed.

As Tilly tossed her napkin in the trash, Ronin stopped her. "Hey, were you able to schedule any venue appointments for Thursday or Friday?"

"Yes. I work Friday so I scheduled them for Thursday afternoon."

"Great. Hope we find the right one this week. I have to decide soon so we can send out invitations."

"And when you say we, you mean…"

"Tiny, Vaun, and me. Not you, Emmy. You're off the hook for the invitations."

"All right, just checking."

"Oh, and Em."

"Yes?"

"I told Emzee that I'll drive to Oz Fest."

"Emzee?"

"Sorry, I couldn't call her Mack and Mackenzie was too pedestrian."

"Emzee….it might grow on me. Anyway, thanks for offering to drive. It's going to be amazing. They have prizes for costumes, and as a group with most of the main characters, we'll have a good shot at a prize."

"Who else do you need?"

"It would be great to have the Wicked Witch and Oz. But maybe next year."

"Did you ask my sisters?"

"No, I didn't think they would be interested. But I'll ask."

Ronin wondered if that was a smart move. Having his sisters around might hinder his ability to spend as much time as possible with Emmy. And that was the plan—spend more time with her, get to know who she was today, not the child he grew up with, not the teenager he'd left behind when he went to college. The young woman she'd become. And he needed to get her to see him as the man he was becoming as well, not just as her brother's friend.

TILLY PULLED THE handkerchief off her head. She examined it, figuratively patting herself on the back for wearing the head covering because it was covered in paint splatters. She looked at Shevaun's short, bleached-white hair and smiled at the spots of pale blue paint scattered throughout.

"Shevaun, your hair!" Tilly said. She looked about the main office space. Three of the four walls were complete, and the last wall was almost done.

"I know." Shevaun shimmied her shoulders. "It's a look. I may ask my hair stylist if he can replicate the look permanently."

"You're such a trendsetter."

"I try. Middle-child stuff. I need to fight to stand out."

"I don't think that's the case. I think you naturally stand out. In a good way," she added. "Hey, I wanted to see if you would like to go with a group of us to *The Wizard of Oz* Fest a week from Saturday. We're dressing up and would love to have a couple more characters represented."

Everyone was stretching and starting to pick up their used lunch items. Almost time to get back to work.

Shevaun nodded. "That sounds fun. What characters do you need?"

"Well, we could use a Wicked Witch, Miss Gulch, or the Wizard. A female wizard would be a fun gender twist."

Shevaun's eyes lit up. "I would love to be the Wicked Witch. Let me guess, you're Dorothy."

"I am. And my roommate Mackenzie is Glenda the Good Witch. Would be great to have you as the Wicked Witch."

"Are Michael and Ronin going?"

"Yes. Ronin agreed to be Scarecrow and Michael will be the Tin Man. A friend of Mackenzie's will be the Cowardly Lion."

"Wow. Ronin really does have it bad for you, if he's agreed to dress in denim overalls and shove straw under his clothing in the sweltering August heat."

"There you go again with that silly idea." Tilly felt her face flush. "We're just friends."

Shevaun rolled her eyes, and Tilly noticed a fleck of blue paint on her eyebrow. *Shevaun's a messy painter.*

Shevaun glanced around before replying. "Maybe you've only ever been friends, but that doesn't mean he doesn't have a thing for you, Tilly."

"He's told you this?"

"No. And he denies it—" Shevaun leaned across the table and lowered her voice. "But I know what I know. And I'm sure I'm right. I think he doesn't act on it because of Michael, to be honest. Dude-bro honor or something stupid like that." She stood and picked up her paper plate and can of Sprite. "My only question is, do you feel the same way?"

She didn't wait for an answer; she walked away and tossed her plate in the trash can.

Tilly stared after Shevaun, her mind raced with the girl's words. *Could Ronin really have a thing for me?* Her mind started shuffling through images from the last few weeks; him holding her hand during fireworks, the wire with the bells strung from his apartment to her bedroom, when he didn't correct the lady at the Vrooman Mansion, and his apparent irritation when she suggested he take Mack out.

That would explain his deepening the kiss when I impulsively kissed him on my birthday. Tilly remembered the way he'd put his hand on the back of her neck to pull her closer or keep her in place; she wasn't sure which. She'd tried to forget the kiss and her humiliation at the action, but with Shevaun's declaration, she decided to study his actions more. Starting with the kiss. If she were being honest with herself, she hadn't done a good job forgetting it. It was on her mind every night when she went to bed and closed her eyes.

A movement next to her startled her back to reality. Ronin rested his hand on her shoulder. "Ready to get back at it, Em?"

"Um." Ronin's touch sent a shiver down her spine, and Shevaun's words echoed in her head. "Yes."

Ronin chuckled, it was as if he could sense her discomfort from her one-and-a-half words. "You don't sound so sure. Was Shevaun being a pain in the neck?"

Yikes! Does he know what Shevaun was talking about? "No, we were just talking. I think she's going to join us for Oz Fest."

Ronin didn't look pleased. "Oh, you asked her."

"I did." Tilly stood and gathered her trash. "She likes the idea of being the Wicked Witch. I'm surprised. Didn't think it would be cool enough for her."

"Nothing is, and she won't let you forget it."

Tilly laughed as she walked towards the trash can with Ronin following. Siblings. Like her and Michael, usually bickering. "She is way cooler than me."

"I think you're pretty cool," Ronin said softly.

Tilly blinked at him. What was that supposed to mean? Could Shevaun be right? He must be saying that to be polite. "You're the coolest." Ugh, could she be more ridiculous and befuddled around this man?

"Not everything is a competition."

"Isn't it?" Tilly wanted to challenge him to a competition on the spot, but now the office-space environment wasn't conducive. Earlier in the day, they could have raced to paint the offices.

"No. And I see that gleam in your eye, Em." Michael was trying to get everyone to huddle up by the large supply table in the center of the open space. Ronin didn't seem to notice his shouts and hand gestures. "Your wheels are turning. Care to explain?"

"It's nothing. I was just…" she paused, knowing Ronin wouldn't buy whatever she said, and went completely blank. "Never mind."

Ronin smiled slowly, and Tilly wanted to bask in his smile for hours. "You seem rattled. That's not like you. We should get to the huddle before Michael loses his mind. Thanks again for helping. Don't know what we'd do without you."

Tilly knew he meant what he said. She was contributing to the cause. But she couldn't help thinking maybe he meant something more. Shevaun's words circled in her brain. If she was right, it could be more. Tilly would need to guard her heart, though. She didn't really have time to start a relationship. School would be starting in a few weeks, and she wanted to come up with a career plan ASAP, so she could take the right classes this year.

Putting those worries aside, the idea of a relationship with Ronin appealed to her heart. He'd shown her who he was this summer. A considerate, smart, and handsome man who was becoming harder and harder to ignore.

CHAPTER NINETEEN

To SAVE TIME, Ronin picked up Tilly from In Bloom on Thursday to visit the cultural center. Tilly wished she'd had time to freshen up after working her long shift but understood Ronin's limited availability.

Under the building's canopy, which was part of the former gas station's original architecture, Ronin parked his sedan. Tilly gave him a quick wave from the counter at the back of the retail space and went to the office to grab her bag. In the bathroom, she changed her shirt, replaced the jeans she'd been wearing with a pair of shorts, and spritzed on a light body spray.

She told Anna Lee goodbye and walked out the front door.

"Ready?" Ronin asked as she climbed into his clean car.

"Yes. What did you accomplish today?" she asked, buckling her seatbelt.

"We ordered furniture and met with a couple of applicants for an IT position. We'll need someone on site for security and troubleshooting. We scheduled interviews for tomorrow for a cleaning company."

"Wow. Busy day! Can't believe you have the energy to do another site visit."

"The timing is not optimal, but it must get done. Thanks again for coming with me. I'm hoping after today we can lock in the location for the anniversary party."

"I hope so, too."

"Is this too much for you?"

"No."

"Is it boring for you?"

"No! I'm enjoying it."

"Good," Ronin said, pulling out of the parking lot. "How was work today?"

If she'd been able to be open with Ronin, she would have said she was enjoying the time spent with *him*. Sure, it was nice to see these historic mansions around town, too, but the time getting reacquainted with him was the big draw.

She remembered Shevaun's words during the painting party. She was going to pay extra attention to Ronin today, to see if she could see any evidence of Shevaun's assertion.

"Work was great. I helped Anna Lee with payroll again. I think I've got it down now and could do it on my own if asked. I also helped her place a supply order for the first time. It was neat to see that some of the suppliers that she uses are Illinois farmers. There is this one, Four Seasons Farm, where she gets pumpkins and gourds for fall, and we placed a large order today."

"Mid-July, and you're thinking about pumpkins. That's wild."

"I know, right? Anna Lee says you must be ahead of the season and get your orders in early to get supremo product."

"Supremo?"

"Her word. We talked about taking a drive to their farm this fall to check it out. Anna Lee says she hasn't been there in over ten years, and she likes to check in once in a while, to make sure their operations are still up to snuff. She likes to have a personal connection to her suppliers when she can."

Stopping at a red light, he looked over at her. "She shares a lot with you, doesn't she?"

Tilly considered. "Yes, she does. But I think she would share with anyone who asked. I don't think I'm special."

Ronin reached over and squeezed her hand. "Oh, you're special all right, Emmy."

"If you say special ed, I will whack you." The childhood taunt came back to her.

"No, I wasn't teasing. I'm being serious. You *are* special. You've got the biggest heart of anyone I've ever known, you care deeply about people, and you always try to find good in every situation. Those are rare traits nowadays. The world needs more Tillys. Though no one could ever duplicate you."

Tilly swallowed hard. "Green light."

Ronin looked away and started driving again. Tilly debated whether his words were being spoken as a friend or as someone who was interested in more.

"You'd be hard to duplicate, yourself," she finally said. And she meant it. He was unique; anyone would be lucky to date him, and if someone did, she'd be jealous. Whoa. The realization hit hard. *I would be jealous if someone dated Ronin.* She had been so relieved when Mack had come home from her date with Ronin and said that had been a big, gigantic bust—there was no chemistry, and they'd spent the evening talking about Tilly and Michael.

"Oh, yeah?" he asked as he turned into the designated church parking lot across from the cultural center. He pulled into a parking space and turned toward her.

Tilly was thankful he left the car running. It was almost ninety degrees, and she thought the current conversation drove the heat level up another ten.

"Yes," she managed. How much should she elaborate? This was the moment if she were ever going to hint at her feelings for Ronin. Put herself out there. Expose her tender heart. "You're special ed."

She jumped out of the car when he leaned towards her, his eyes widening.

Ronin slowly climbed out of the driver's door. "Matilda Marie Miller. You are going to get it."

"Oh, no! You full-named me." Tilly laughed and ran through the parking lot. She had to wait at the crosswalk for the light, and Ronin caught up easily.

He stood beside her, pulled her into a side embrace, and mussed with her hair.

"Stop! Stop!" she cried. She playfully pushed him away, but she really wanted to hug him back. Have a moment where they hugged each other as they laughed. She sighed as he let her go.

"You can still be a brat, you know that, right?" he asked, tucking his shirt back into his shorts. It had come loose in the struggle.

"Well, you set me up perfectly. I couldn't resist."

"There are times you need to resist. And there are times you need to tell the truth." He leveled a serious gaze at her, almost like he could hear what her heart wanted to say. She looked up at the pedestrian light, trying to distract herself.

She wanted to tell him the truth, she really did. But what if he rejected her? Her bruised heart finally felt free of the burden of Kyle's rejection, but was it, really? If Ronin turned her down now, it would be years before she could open herself up again to someone else.

Now's not the time. We're here on a mission. Ronin needs to find a place to host his parents' party. It wasn't time for declarations, not even tentative ones.

"I'm looking forward to seeing the Japanese garden on the grounds here," she said, changing the trajectory of the conversation before it got weird.

"Emmy…" Ronin's voice was low and slow, like a warning. She looked ahead, trying to ignore the soft plea in his voice.

The light changed, and she started walking; Ronin followed close behind, not speaking again until after they'd crossed the street and entered the edge of the center's gardens. He lightly grabbed her elbow to stop her. Turning to look up at him, she bit her lip.

He took a visible breath before speaking. "Em, before I push *you* to tell the truth, I need to tell my truth. Not only do I know you're special, but there's also more to it. I…" He paused and looked away, as if to think through what he was going to say next. "I like you. More than as a friend. I have for a while. Occasionally, I think maybe you might feel the same. I don't know, maybe I've imagined it. Or maybe I'm seeing what I want to see."

Tilly opened her mouth, but nothing came out. She shut it and glanced down at the pretty ground cover.

"Asking you to help me check out these locations was really a ploy to spend more time with you. To get reacquainted. To get to know you as you, as the woman you are, Tilly, not as Michael's sister. And I like you even more every time we're together. I see your joy in life, in people, and it makes me want to smile from ear to ear. I also see your uncertainties, and I want to encourage you to just keep going. You'll figure everything out. And you will be amazing in whatever you decide to do. I would like to see you every day because you're that amazing. This feels awkward. I don't know why. But I want to ask you out. On a real date."

"A real date?"

"Yes. Dinner. A movie. Dancing. Anything you'd like to do."

Tilly smiled. "Careful, Ronin. I could get pretty creative."

"I bet you could. But will you go out with me? On an actual date?"

Tilly knew she'd say yes, but she could drag this out a little longer. It was fun to see Ronin unsure of himself. To see all her doubts answered was overwhelming, but there was one thing she needed to know. "How long, exactly?"

"How long, what?"

"How long have you liked me as more than a friend? You said, 'a while'. I'm curious how long that while has been."

Ronin closed his eyes and shook his head slightly. Tilly prodded. "How long?"

"Years," he whispered.

It was Tilly's turn to shake her head. "No way. There's no way that it's been years. You've dated other people."

The left side of Ronin's mouth lifted. "Yes, I did. We were physically apart; it didn't seem possible to date you before now. I didn't know what Michael would think. I never had a hint that you might feel the same way until recently, and I didn't want to make things weird between us."

"Wow. That's a lot to take in. What does Michael think?"

"I don't know. I haven't brought it up with him. I'm surprised he hasn't figured it out."

"Shevaun has."

Ronin raised a questioning eyebrow.

"She said something to me yesterday while we were on a break from painting. I didn't believe her, but—"

"What, Emmy? But what?"

"I wanted to."

"Why?"

"I like you, too. It's new, though, and I'm trying to figure it out. I'm sort of overwhelmed right now. Between figuring out what I'm going to do with my life, helping my mom with adoption research, and you…it's a lot."

"I know what you mean."

"Right! With everything on your plate now, too. Is this really a good time to start a relationship?"

"Maybe not. But I think with the right relationship, having the right person by your side, can help with all the other craziness. And I don't mean that I'm looking for a partner to dump stuff on.

I want a partner that I can share my life with—the ups and the downs. But in partnership. I want to help you, Em. Figuring out life goals, figuring out your ancestry, whatever is on your mind or in your heart, I want you to share those burdens with me."

His words reminded her of Anna Lee referring to John as a sounding board. Tilly stepped forward and threw her arms around Ronin. He grunted at the impact but held her close. She rested her cheek on his chest and closed her eyes, taking him in through all her senses. Listening to his rapid heartbeat, smelling the clean cotton of his shirt and his cologne, feeling the ridges of his chest against her cheek. In her mind's eye, she saw the sweet look in his eyes as he said he wanted to share her burdens. She thought about all the times Kyle had dismissed her worries. It was comforting to believe that Ronin wouldn't do that to her.

Ronin hummed and rocked her back and forth. He hummed! A sound of contentment and joy. It filled her heart and made her dizzy.

"Ronin?" she asked, continuing to hold on.

"Yes?"

"We should probably tour the property and talk to someone about the party. It's too warm to stand out here hugging." She squeezed before she started to let go.

He held her tighter for a moment. "Never too hot to hold you." He released her. "But yes, it's hot. And we have a task at hand. But you still didn't say, with words, that you'll go on a date with me."

"Yes, just say when."

"When."

She laughed. "An actual day for a date."

"Okay. How about Saturday night? Dinner and something. I'll work on the something and let you know."

Tilly sighed. She'd always been the one to put the work into a date with Kyle. It was nice having someone else make the effort.

Everything seemed perfect.

Then she thought about Michael.

"Hey, Ronin. Who's going to talk to Michael?"

"Oh. Right. I'll do it. Tonight."

THE EVENTS COORDINATOR for the center was a man of about sixty who wore a checkered bow tie with a white shirt. Tilly commented on the tie, and the man's face lit up.

He showed them around the grounds and the pertinent areas of the building's interior. Ever since he'd told Tilly how he felt, Ronin couldn't stop smiling. He heard about a third of what the tour guide told them. Luckily, Tilly kept the conversation going.

Before they even saw the inside, Ronin knew this was the place to host the anniversary party. All the properties had been beautiful and accommodating, but this one just felt right. Maybe it was knowing that Tilly had agreed to go out with him here that gave it an extra-special feel.

"Everything is just beautiful," Tilly declared. Ronin knew she was talking about the historic manor and the grounds, but he was thinking about her. *She's beautiful, inside and out.*

He thought about the conversation he needed to have with her brother. He didn't expect it to be easy, but he hoped it wouldn't lead to anything dire. *Luckily, we're not Montagues and Capulets.*

Whatever happened with Michael, they'd have to work it out. They were roommates and business partners, and Ronin was going to date Tilly for as long as she'd let him. So, Michael would have to deal with it.

"READY TO GO?" Michael asked, grabbing his keys off the hook by the door.

Ronin glanced at his watch and stayed seated on the couch. "We have a little time. Can we talk?"

"Don't we do that all day?" Michael smiled and sat in the armchair. "What's up?"

Ronin glanced at the bell hanging under the window. "I asked Emmy out. On a date."

Michael's brows knit together. "Emmy who?"

"Your sister Emmy." Ronin hadn't anticipated that question. They didn't know any other Emmys.

"But, but—she's my sister." Michael leaned forward in his chair. "Does she know this?"

"I said I asked her out, not that I was going to ask her out." Ronin chuckled softly. "Yes, she knows."

"And she said yes? My sister said yes?"

"She did." Ronin watched Michael closely. He didn't look angry, but he didn't look pleased, either. "And I didn't coerce her. She agreed on her own."

Michael stood up. Not a good sign. "I can't wrap my head around this. Ew. I can't think about you kissing her. That's just wrong."

Your sister kissed me first, dude. Can't say that. But I can remember it. "It's not wrong. It's just new. You'll get used to the idea. Eventually."

"Are you sure about that? You're my friend, my best friend. My brother from another mother. I just can't. If you break her heart, so help me…."

"I have no intention of doing anything to hurt her. It's a first date." Of many, Ronin hoped.

"When?"

"Tomorrow night."

"Who else knows? Did you ask our parents?"

"It's a date. Didn't think I had to ask for her hand to date her."

Michael paced. "When did you ask her out?"

"Today."

"But how long have you…" He paused and shuddered, raising his hands. "…liked her? You must like her to ask her out."

"Yes, that's how that usually works." Ronin wanted to say, "for years", but he didn't think Michael was ready to hear that. "Spending time with her the last few weeks has been enlightening. I've gotten to know the grown-up Emmy, not just the kid."

There. Don't answer the question, just say words.

"I am floored, man. I didn't see this coming. You've never said a word about this. She's never said a word about this. I can't comprehend."

Michael sat down, looking as though he'd run a mile.

"I get that you're shocked. Maybe I should have said something to you, but I wanted to figure out where her head was first."

"And? Where *is* her head?"

"She's interested in giving it a go. See what happens."

"Wow. She was so into that Kyle dude. At least I thought she was. She seemed heartbroken when they ended. I'm glad she's willing to date again. I'm just not sure how I feel about it being you. I mean, if it works, fantastic. It would be great knowing you'll always be around. But if it doesn't work, then guess who's smack dab in the middle of the kerfuffle? Me!"

"Kerfuffle? Word of the day?"

"Maybe. I used it right, right?"

"I think so, but I didn't read your word-of-the-day calendar." Ronin looked at the time again. They should go or they'd be late. "Well, is your head clear enough to head over for movie night?"

"I think so. Does Mackenzie know?"

"I don't know. Maybe don't bring it up unless Emmy does. Just in case."

"All right."

"Speaking of Emzee, I thought you were flirting with her last time we were there."

There, get attention off him and Emmy.

"No, just being friendly."

"Mmm, hmm." *Right.* Ronin stood, walked over to the window, and pulled on the wire. "Let's go."

Michael walked to the door and opened it. He pointed back to the window. "Whole new meaning to the wire and bell contraption. Too bad we couldn't have put that in your bedroom."

Ronin just smiled and followed him out the door.

CHAPTER TWENTY

RONIN PULLED THE chair out for Tilly and helped her scoot in when she sat down.

"You good?" he asked.

"Yes, thank you." She watched him sit across from her. He wore dark slacks and a light blue knit shirt which made his eyes pop. His beard was neatly trimmed. His hair was loose and wavy, and she thought about the joy she'd take in running her hands through it.

After the waiter took drink orders and left, Ronin reached across the table, hand open, and she threaded her fingers through his.

"Yes?" Tilly waited.

"This is nice. Dinner, I mean. You look beautiful."

"You said that at the apartment when you picked me up."

"Just reminding you." He squeezed her hand and pulled back, opening his menu. "What's good here?"

"Everything I've eaten here has been scrumptious. I love the scampi and the fillet. I'm not sure which I'll pick tonight."

"Get both. Take leftovers if you can't eat it all."

Tilly laughed. "Are you the spoiling type, Ronin?"

"For you, yes. I am."

Tilly looked up from the menu. His tone was much more serious than she expected. He was watching her intently. The corner of her mouth tilted up. "That's sweet."

"I'm serious. It's not a line."

"I'm not surprised. You seem like the kind of man who would spoil someone."

"Not just someone. The one I really care about."

Tilly melted inside. She knew he was serious about this. He had already stated as much when he'd asked her out, but it was all still a little hard to believe.

"Any girl would be lucky to be spoiled by you. Forgive me if I act silly. I'm still having a hard time believing we're here. Together. I feel like I'm in a different dimension or something. Maybe I'm in a tesseract."

"You're here. With me."

With me. Those words made her heart soar; she pictured Snow White dancing with little birds circling her head.

"So, it's weird being on a first date with someone I've known for…" She paused and her eyes darted up, thinking. "…sixteen years?"

Ronin nodded. "Something like that. But, while we've known each other that long, we don't know each other deeply. We've known each other superficially. We've not shared our deepest secrets."

The waiter placed their salads on the table.

"Oh, you don't want to know mine."

"Come on. They can't be that bad."

"You're right. They're not. I'm pretty lucky. Great parents, and a decent older brother. Really good friends. Access to higher ed. Though I worry I've wasted time on a few classes."

"It's still learning. All of it's good."

"Even geometry?" She stabbed a grape tomato with her fork.

"You got a point there." Ronin grabbed a dinner roll from the basket between them. "There's time for us to get into the deep secrets. But as you said, it's a first date. Let's keep it somewhat light for tonight. Tell me, what do you most look forward to during your fall semester?"

"Hmm, school-wise, to meet some new people in my classes. Have great professors. To pass all my classes..."

"Good goals. What about on a personal level?"

"Well, I hope I can learn more about running a business from Anna Lee. I hope she opens a manager position and that I am qualified for it."

"That's more career. What about personal?" he pressed.

"Well, I hope my mom can find her birth parents. You know she was adopted, right?"

"Yeah, Eminem has mentioned it. I bet you have a lot of curiosity there."

"I do! I'm so curious. It will be fun to see what our ancestry is, our nationalities and things. Honestly, I'm always kind of afraid of getting married and finding out later that I'm related to my husband. Isn't that weird?"

"Wow. That's a lot to process. You're not worried we're related, are you?"

"No, but...how do I know? When there are gaps, you don't know. I'm on Ancestry and I get notifications sometimes about cousins, but we've recognized everybody who's come up. No one new."

"Really? Maybe we should take some kind of DNA test or something. Make sure we're not related."

"Don't even go there." *But how do I know?* "I hope we find answers soon. Mom thought she had a break, but we're not sure." She sighed. "Now, tell me your deep, dark secrets."

"My deepest secret is that I've had a crush on my best friend's sister for a number of years. But don't share that broadly."

"It's a secret, right?" She pretended to lock her lips with a key and throw it over her shoulder. "I don't believe you. You dated several women in college. That can't be true."

"Yes, it's true, I dated others. I was hundreds of miles away from you. Besides, I've debated the question of whether I should ask you out for years."

"Why?"

"Well, Eminem for one. Our families for another."

Tilly thought about Shevaun's words. She wondered how long Shevaun had known. "Did you ever tell Shevaun? She told me a few times this summer that you liked me. I didn't believe her at first…"

"No, I never told her. She's just perceptive."

"Wow. Remind me never to try to hide something from her." Ronin laughed.

Tilly laid her fork on her salad plate. "Seriously, though. How long?"

"How long?"

"Have you thought about me in that way?"

Ronin looked chagrined. "Maybe since your sweet sixteen."

"Really?"

"Yes. I was at your house, helping your parents set up, and you came down the stairs in that tight pink dress. You had your hair pulled up and your makeup done. I guess, at that moment, I noticed *you*. Not Michael's little sister."

Tilly sat back in her chair. "Whoa. That's a long time. Five years," she whispered.

"Oh, man. That didn't freak you out, did it?" He ran his fingers through his hair.

"Maybe. A little. I wish I'd known."

"No, you don't. I was getting ready to leave for college then. It wouldn't have worked. I needed time to grow, and so did you. I'm glad that it's worked the way it has."

"I hear what you're saying, and you're probably right. But if we had started dating then, I wouldn't have gone out with the jerks that I did. Especially Kyle."

"Now, that I can regret. And it would have spared me a couple of bad dates, too."

His brow furrowed, and Tilly longed to reach out and smooth his forehead. She didn't like seeing the pain on his face.

"Maybe…" She paused, searching his face. "Now is a good time to get into that conversation."

"What conversation is that?"

"Past girlfriends. Michael has never shared anything with me."

"I knew I liked him for a reason." Ronin took a breath. "Just a couple of serious girlfriends. Kristy was the last. We broke up just before I moved."

"Why did you break up?"

"I was moving away. We weren't serious enough to try a long-distance relationship."

"Is that all?"

"That's all I'll share for now." He gave her a look that told her part of the reason was her.

"Before her?" Tilly prodded.

"A couple of years ago, I dated a girl named Sherry for a few months. Then I realized she wasn't…"

"Wasn't what?"

"You."

Tilly sucked in a breath and leaned back in her seat just as the waiter put their plates in front of them.

"Can I get you anything else?"

"No, we're fine," Ronin said quickly, dismissing the waiter. To Tilly, he said, "Don't spazz on me, Emmy."

She shook her head. "What did you see in me, Ronin?"

"Your kind heart and how much you love those around you. You always stand up for the underdog, even when it causes you pain. You always want to help others. You listen. You're incredible."

"Wow. Thank you." She blinked rapidly to keep the tears from messing up her makeup. She should have worn waterproof!

"Don't cry, Em."

"You don't understand. Sometimes being the youngest, being a girl...I don't always feel seen, you know. And you...you see me."

"I have," Ronin said. "For a long time."

Her journal was coming out tonight. This was a lot to process. A shiver ran down her spine.

"Are you okay?" Ronin asked, seeing her movement.

"Just got chills."

"Wish I could offer you a jacket."

She remembered him offering his jacket at Paige's wedding. She knew if he'd had one, it would be on her in a flash.

"I think we should eat before it gets cold," she said, with a smile, trying to lighten the mood.

This was not what she was expecting. Of course, she'd never anticipated a first date with someone she'd known for over fifteen years before, either. She ate her food and listened to Ronin's benign chatter about the co-workspace and his family antics.

Tilly appreciated the way Ronin "read the room" —her— and kept her from falling off the deep end. She'd felt a flash of panic at one point. Not from his confession that he'd liked her for so long. No—with his kind words, she easily envisioned a future with him—marriage, kids, the whole thing. And she feared she would somehow manage to mess it up. All on her own.

RONIN COULDN'T BELIEVE he'd let her talk him into going to the new *Barbie* movie. He'd never be able to tell Michael, and hoped she wouldn't, either.

But Ronin had to admit, he'd enjoyed it.

He pulled up to the curb in front of her apartment. "I'll walk you up."

She turned in the seat to look at him. "You don't have to do that."

"I do."

He came around and opened her door, holding out his hand to help her out of the car and he didn't let go as they walked to the door.

"This was an amazing first date. Isn't it sad that we don't get to have more than one?" She pulled her keys from her purse and unlocked the door but didn't open it.

"Who says we can't? We just had our first dinner-and-a-movie date. We can still go on our first bowling date. Then our first mall-shopping date. Then our first museum date…."

Tilly laughed, leaning into him. He took advantage of her closeness and put his arms around her. She shifted and hugged him back. "That sounds perfect," she said into his chest.

He put his hand on her cheek to get her to look at him. "You're perfect, Em. Thank you for a perfect first date."

He shifted his hand to the back of her head and bent down to kiss her cheek.

She murmured softly. "What's next?"

Ronin paused. Did she mean next for tonight or the next step in their relationship? "Do you mean our next date? I haven't got that planned yet."

She leaned back to look up at him. "You are coming to work on costumes tomorrow, right? Mack's costume-designer friend will be here by noon."

"Yes, I will be here. And I'll have Michael in tow."

"Good. Are you still planning to go to your family dinner?"

"I'd like to if we're done in time. Would you like to go with me?"

"If we're done in time, yes, I'd like that. Is it time to tell everyone?"

"Nothing would make me happier. I can't wait until everyone knows."

"I hope they don't have a problem with it. I should probably call my mom in the morning and tell her. I need to check in on her adoption research anyway."

"It would be great if you told her...if Michael hasn't spilled the beans already."

"Right. Well, good night, Ronin. I had an amazing first date."

She squeezed him before letting go, and his arms felt bereft when she stepped back. "Emmy?"

"Yes?"

"I'm going to kiss you now."

Holding her face in his hands, he drew her close, moving slowly; this was new for them both. But when his lips touched hers, all his worries vanished. This was right. This was sweet. This was Tilly.

Knowing better than to let things go too far, too fast, he pulled back and grinned. Her eyes were wide, and her smile even wider.

"Our first kiss on a date," she said.

"Good night, Emmy. Expect a jingle when I get home."

"I'll be in my room in three minutes. Good night, Ronin."

He left his car parked in front of her house and ambled home. As he walked, he looked at the line strung between their apartments, pleased that it hadn't been detected and ripped down yet. He hoped it would be up as long as they lived in these apartments. He smiled, thinking about someday hanging a similar wire between two rooms in their shared home. *Not that I'm getting ahead of myself or anything.*

CHAPTER TWENTY-ONE

*O*N TUESDAY, TILLY put together the In Bloom schedule for the next two weeks and reviewed it with Anna Lee, who approved it.

"That was a little harder than I thought it'd be," Tilly said, looking over the columns and rows.

"A few more day-off requests than normal. You girls are taking advantage of summer break to do so many fun things. Like your Oz Festival on Saturday. Good thing Nica was available, so you and Mack can both be off."

"I know. And I'm glad you only have the one wedding that day, it'll be manageable."

"Well, thanks to you for agreeing to come in Friday, on your day off."

"I'm glad it worked out. Ronin picked a venue for his parents' party, so we're done visiting places."

"That's real good. How's their new office place coming along?"

"Great! They're set to open in a week and a half. Can't believe they've made so much progress in such a short time! But they are determined and focused."

Well, Tilly thought to herself, *mostly focused.* The date on Saturday night, Sunday working on costumes, and Sunday dinner at his parents' house had meant a full weekend, but Ronin had said things were well under control, and he could take the time for weekend fun. Michael had seemed relaxed as well during Sunday dinner at the McGuires', so it must have been true.

"Good qualities," Anna Lee said, flipping through her date book. "Hey, I called Four Seasons Farm and asked for a visit in early October to tour the place again. Would you still like to go with me?"

Tilly beamed. "Of course!"

Anna Lee shook her head. "Great. You'll get to see where we get our spring tulips and the fall pumpkins, and the sunflowers, and well, everything else we get from there." She waved her hand dismissively, like the details weren't important.

"I'm so looking forward to it."

The bell above the door chimed, and Tilly thought of the little bell that hung in her room. She looked up to see Ronin enter. *What's he doing here in the middle of his workday?*

"Welcome. You look familiar," Anna Lee said. "Do I know you?"

Tilly laughed. "Yes, this is Ronin. He was my date for Paige's wedding."

"Ah, yes. Hello, again."

Ronin walked up to Anna Lee, putting out his hand to shake. She batted the hand away and pulled him into a side hug.

"Hello, Ms. Anna Lee," Ronin said, laughing at her embrace.

"What brings you in today? Here to see Tilly?"

"Yes." He smiled. "And you. I would like to talk about ordering a weekly arrangement for delivery to our new co-workspace."

"Tilly's told me about that space. Interesting concept. I wish you years of success. Now, what did you have in mind?"

"I don't know. A pretty arrangement, like if I sent flowers to a friend for a birthday or celebration."

"Where are the flowers going? Who will see them?"

"They'll go on our reception desk in the front, so everyone who walks in or walks by the front door will see it. The front wall is mostly glass, so people walking by can look in."

"You may need a statement piece—something taller. Let me get my sample book, and we can talk through options and cost."

Anna Lee walked away, and Ronin turned to Tilly and gave her a hug. "Hi."

"Hi, yourself." Tilly loved the smell of his pressed shirt and his cologne and didn't want to let him go. "I wasn't expecting you."

"Surprise. This was necessary, though Eminem doesn't agree with me, and I missed you. Didn't get to see you at all yesterday."

"I know. Missed you, too."

Anna Lee walked in with a three-ring binder under her arm. Salty followed her with his tail in the air. He walked up to Ronin, sniffed him, and rubbed his orange and white fur against Ronin's black pant leg.

"Oh, no!" Tilly cried. "Your pants!"

Ronin looked down and saw the cat fur decorating his pant leg. "That's cute."

"Hold on," Anna Lee said, reaching below the counter. "Got a lint roller here. It'll do."

"Thanks," Ronin said, reaching for the tool, while Salty moved to the front window and jumped into his favorite sunny spot. "Is Nica working today?"

Anna Lee flipped open the binder as she answered, "No. She'll be in on Thursday."

"I have her phone number," Tilly said. "What do you need her for?"

"We were thinking about a statement piece for the lobby, and I know she's creative and thought maybe she could design something for us."

"She'd do great with that," Tilly said. "Maybe we could stop at her apartment tonight and talk to her."

"That would be great. I'll take you for dinner after. Will you text her to see what time would work?"

"Yes."

Anna Lee began showing them some ideas for the weekly flowers, narrowing in on size and budget. Ronin decided to alternate a statement piece with a centerpiece to keep in line with the budget he had in mind. Anna Lee agreed to bill monthly and deliver each Monday morning.

"Thank you, Anna Lee," Ronin said, signing the agreement she wrote up. "I appreciate your advice and your flexibility."

"You're most welcome." Anna Lee placed the order on top of the binder and picked them up. "I've got something to attend to in the office. Nice seeing you again, Ronin."

She turned away, winking at Tilly.

"I think the flowers are a great idea," Tilly said to Ronin when Anna Lee had closed the office door.

"Thanks." Ronin reached out and took her hand. "It's nice to have a flower lady around. I need to run a few more errands. Text me if you work something out with Nica. Either way, I'd love to take you to dinner."

"Sounds good. I'll let you know. I think Anna Lee stepped out so we could have some privacy."

"I wondered." Ronin pulled her into a hug, and she was thankful for the moment alone. He kissed the top of her head before pulling away. "Later, Em."

Tilly followed him to the front of the store and stood petting Salty as she watched him get in his car. He waved before pulling away.

"Salty," Tilly said to the sleepy cat, scratching behind his ears, "What do you think of Ronin? You rubbed up to him. Maybe that means you see the good in him, like I do. He's kind and supportive. And handsome." The cat thumped his tail. Hard. "Not as handsome as you!"

Salty purred softly and closed his eyes. Tilly smiled and shook her head. *This cat may be a good judge of character, but he is still purr-ty self-centered.*

TILLY ARRANGED FOR them to meet Nica, and Ronin picked her up for the drive over. Arriving at Nica's building, they walked up the steps to her third-story apartment.

"These stairs are really sturdy," Ronin noted.

"I think they're new." Tilly turned around and smiled at Ronin. "You should ask Nica about her landlord sometime."

"Isn't…"

"Yes, her boyfriend Grady is her landlord." She laughed.

"Right."

At the door, Tilly called hello through the screen.

"*Hola, chica!*" a voice called from inside. A moment later, a tall blonde in a purple T-shirt and cut-off denim jeans appeared. "Come in."

"Hi, Izzy!" Tilly said, opening the door. "Nica is expecting us."

"*Sí, sí.* She'll be out in a moment. She's on the fire escape, spray painting something. *Hola,*" she said, holding out a hand to Ronin. "I'm Isabel, but everyone calls me Izzy."

"Nice to meet you, Izzy," Ronin said, shaking her hand. "I'm Ronin McGuire."

"Ah, Tilly's man. I've heard." She smiled, and Tilly felt a tingle, hearing someone call Ronin her man. Even though they'd only had one official date, it seemed like they'd been together longer.

"Can I get you a drink?" Izzy asked. "I make an amazing sun tea."

"Sounds refreshing," Ronin said, and Tilly agreed.

As Izzy got glasses out, she chatted about the heat. Nica entered, wearing a paint-spattered jumpsuit. "Hey, there. Sorry, I was in the middle of something. Nice to see you both. What can I do for you, Ronin?"

Nica was not one to beat around the bush; Tilly appreciated that about her.

Ronin accepted the glass of tea before turning to Nica. "I've heard a few stories about your artistic talent, and I wanted to see if you would be interested in designing a cool decorative piece for the reception area of our new business. It's a co-workspace…"

Nica pushed her black bangs out of her eyes. "I've heard. What are you looking for?"

"Something unique that can be hung on a wall," he replied. "We've got a wall behind the reception desk that's ten feet wide by ten feet tall. The counter is about four feet high, so six feet of wall are visible."

"What's the name of the business?"

Ronin chuckled. "M and M Spaces. We're Miller and McGuire."

"Is it the word 'and' or the symbol?" she asked.

"The word and. If we used the symbol, we'd risk copying the candy logo. Don't want that."

"Right. Do you have a logo?"

Ronin reached for his wallet. "Yes, let me grab a business card. The logo is a tandem bicycle. Our motto is 'together we go farther'".

Nica nodded. "Nice. Would you be open to something using different types of wheels? Maybe with an actual tandem bike? I've seen one around town. I'll have to think where I saw it. I go to a lot of thrift and consignment stores. Off the top of my head, I think it would be neat to have different wheels—wagon wheels, skateboard wheels, and car wheels—to represent different types of workers. We don't all work the same way. We don't all take a bike to work, for example."

"Wow. That's ingenious. I love it. We open in less than two weeks. Do you think you could pull something together in that time?"

Nica scrunched up her perky nose. Izzy glanced at Tilly, raising her eyebrows. "Maybe? I have a piece to finish for Grady by Friday. But it's almost done. I need to scour the stores for that bike and more wheels. If the stars align, I think I might be able to do it. Can I stop by tomorrow and look at the place? I want to look at your paint colors and take some measurements."

Ronin was nodding before she'd finished. "Anytime. We'll be there whenever you need us to be."

"Fabulous. Let me get your number, and I'll text you when I have a time frame."

When Izzy offered to feed them, Ronin politely declined, saying he'd made dinner reservations.

In the car, Tilly asked where they were going for dinner.

"My place. I ordered takeout."

"So, no reservation?"

"Well, I considered the takeout delivery time a reservation. Can't be late."

"Is Michael home tonight?"

"Not until later. He joined a gym and was going for a workout."

Tilly laughed. "He needs it."

"The great thing is that the gym is in the building next to our business. It's convenient. I'm thinking about joining, myself."

"Oh, I don't think you need it."

"Thank you, but…health."

"Right. But you bike so much."

"I like to lift and use the machines. I visited the gym with Michael today. It's pretty nice."

Tilly thought about all the single people who used gyms as a dating-app alternative. "What's the clientèle like?"

"Well, it was mid-afternoon, so it was quiet. Only a couple of meatheads today."

"I see. So, it seemed like Nica had a cool idea for the lobby."

"I know. I'm excited. I talked to Grady at your party, and he was bragging about Nica—told me about several things she'd done in his properties and for some other clients. Sounds like she's really talented."

"She is. She's going to repaint the mural on In Bloom. I don't know if you noticed, but it's faded a lot. Anna Lee said it was done ten years ago and needs a refresh."

Ronin parked across from his apartment building, and they walked over. "Sounds like it's time, then."

In his apartment, Tilly went to the window and looked at the bell hanging there. "I still can't believe this works. Crazy."

"I hope it stays up for the next year."

"Next year?"

"Yes, until our lease is up."

"Right. Well, if it comes down, we could hang it back up. You know, if someone finds it, it's not hard to figure out who did it. It leads right to the guilty party."

"Don't you mean parties?"

"I didn't have anything to do with it! Except let you guys into the apartment and my room, where you hung a bell. I didn't string the string."

"I'll take the blame. I'd never let you get in trouble for it." Ronin wrapped her in a hug and placed a soft kiss on her forehead.

ON FRIDAY NIGHT, Tilly placed the order for pizza on her phone app and finished applying her makeup. Mack was in the kitchen, preparing a salad, and the familiar chopping sounds floated through the slightly open door.

Scrolling through social media, she glanced at the time. Ronin and Michael would be there in about thirty minutes, and Mack had things under control in the kitchen, so she had enough time to call and check in with her mom.

Her mom answered quickly, sounding rushed.

"Hi, Mom." Tilly leaned back on her bed and tapped the bell lightly, comforted by knowing she could alert Ronin that she was thinking about him. "Did I catch you at a bad time? You're not still at work, are you?"

"No, dear. Was just away from the phone. How are you? Having a good week?"

"Yes, very good. What about you? I wanted to see if you made any progress in the adoption search."

"Not much new. I don't think there will be, either. Well, not until I can go to the hospital and talk to someone in the records department in person. I'll do that when we're down there for the McGuires' anniversary party."

"What days will you be here?"

"Your dad couldn't take Friday off, so we'll come down Friday night and stay through Tuesday. Hopefully, I'll be able to find something out Monday or Tuesday. I plan to go to the hospital on Monday to check the records office and then I have an appointment with an adoption advocate who will help give me some direction."

"That's great news! I'm hoping you find something."

"Me, too. What are you doing tonight? Friday night...going out?"

"No, Ronin and Michael are coming over for movie night. And we're watching *The Wizard of Oz* because tomorrow is the best day ever, and we're going to an Oz Festival. Woot! Woot!"

Irena laughed. "Now, *that* I'm sorry to miss. Are you dressing up?"

"Of course! How could I miss that opportunity?" Tilly picked up the stuffed "Toto" dog that Ronin had given her. Maybe she should tell her mom about that development.

"Nice, Matilda. Who are you going as?"

Ignoring the question, Tilly took a steadying breath. "Mom, Ronin and I are dating."

She paused, waiting for her mom's reaction. There was none. "Mom?"

"Oh? When did this come about?"

"Our first date was last Saturday, but we've been hanging out. I told you I was helping him look for a venue for his parents' party and—"

"Does Michael know?"

"Yes..." *They're roommates, how could he not know?*

"I see."

"You don't sound pleased about it. Why not?"

"I'm absorbing. It's a lot to take in."

"But you like him, right?"

"Yes, of course! He's Michael's friend. We've known him forever. He's a great kid. But I was thinking about how crushed you were over your last breakup. If things go badly with Ronin, it would have a lasting impact—on everyone."

Not the vote of confidence Tilly was hoping for. Maybe this should have been an in-person discussion.

The doorbell rang.

"Mom, the boys are here. I should go. We can talk more later, right?"

"Yes, we will. Have a good evening and a great day tomorrow. Send pictures."

"Will do. Tell Dad hi for me."

Tilly hung up the phone and tossed it on the bed. That was not what she'd hoped for. Not by a long shot. She'd expected her mom to be thrilled with the news.

She wasn't going to worry about it now; there was pizza, and Ronin, and the Wizard. She left the phone on the bed and took Toto to the living room.

CHAPTER TWENTY-TWO

RONIN TOOK TILLY'S hand in his. "This way, Dorothy. I see the yellow brick road."

Tilly laughed and followed. "What do you think we'll find, Scarecrow?"

"Either a pot of gold or a trip home."

"I hope it's home."

"Kansas or Bloomington?" he asked.

Tilly beamed at him. "Why can't it be both? Let's take the magic of today, and this festival, and take it home with us to Bloomington."

"That means you want a souvenir, doesn't it?"

"Of course. Something great."

The Oz Festival was everything Tilly had hoped it would be. There were hundreds of people dressed in costumes, fun games, and delicious food.

And the fact that her friends had dressed up and attended with her made it even more special.

The only regret Tilly had was not breaking in the ruby slippers. They'd been at the festival for only two hours, and her feet were aching. She knew blisters were inevitable.

"Ronin, I have to sit for a few minutes. My feet are hurting like a house landed on them!"

"Oh no, Auntie Em! Let's sit."

"You can't call me Auntie Em when I'm dressed like Dorothy."

"Yes, but you're Emmy. So, Auntie Em is a better name. Maybe next year you should plan to dress as Auntie Em. It'll be easier on me."

"Maybe so, but Dorothy is my favorite."

"And you make the most adorable Dorothy. How are your feet feeling now?"

"Feels good to get off them. That's for sure."

Mackenzie, Michael, and Shevaun approached. Mack was eating a tractor tire, also known as a cruller donut.

"Ooo, that looks yummy!" Tilly cried.

"It tastes even better than it looks." Mack popped the last piece in her mouth.

"Where did you find those?" Tilly asked.

Mack pointed. "That way. It's a food truck that looks like Professor Marvel's wagon. So cute, you can't miss it. You have to check it out."

"We will," Ronin said, "as soon as Dorothy's feet allow her to skip down the yellow brick road."

"Forget skipping, I'd be happy to walk."

Shevaun pointed to Tilly's shoes, and screeched in a Wicked Witch voice, "I'll get those not-so-comfortable-but-pretty shoes!" She cackled with evil laughter.

Ronin scratched his wrist where the straw was taped around it. "How are you doing, Eminem?"

Michael rolled his shoulders and the tin of his costume clanked. "I'm contemplating buying ice to stick inside this costume, if that gives you an idea."

"I hear ya. Well, Dorothy, let's go get a donut and look for a souvenir, so we can head home soon, okay?"

"All right." She took his hand and stood up.

Michael shook his head. "I still can't wrap my mind around the two of you as a couple."

Ronin laughed, squeezing her hand. "Get used to it, buddy."

Tilly sighed. Setting the aching feet aside for a moment, she hadn't been this happy in a long, long time. To be enjoying an Oz Festival with her friends was an absolute blast, first of all. And being here with Ronin by her side was the icing on the donut. *Do crullers come with icing?*

Ronin made the day extra special. Earlier, as they walked into the park where the festival was held, a girl about four-years-old ran up to them, fascinated by the walking and talking Scarecrow. Ronin knelt to talk to her, and the girl's father snapped a photo. The little girl was curious about the straw coming out of his clothing.

After they finished talking, the little girl gave Ronin a kiss on the cheek and came away with face paint on her lips. "Yuck," she said, pulling up her T-shirt to wipe away the makeup.

"Oh, look at that, someone who isn't as fond of kissing you as I am," Tilly said, teasing Ronin.

The father and daughter walked away. Throwing an arm around Tilly's shoulders, Ronin wobble-walked, pulling her along. "There's only one lady I want to kiss or be kissed by."

"Yeah?"

He pulled her behind an evergreen tree. "Yes, you." Then he kissed her—a lazy Sunday kind of kiss—slow and meaningful. When he pulled away, Tilly no longer worried about her tight shoes.

She smiled up at him. Even in heels, she had to look up. "That's what I want to hear. Hey, you were awfully cute with that little girl. You have a way with kids."

He took her hand and pulled her along. "I like kids. They're cool."

Tilly knew it was too early to start fantasizing about having kids with Ronin, but she couldn't help it; her mind went there. She imagined Ronin riding a bike with several mini-Ronin's pedaling behind. Shaking away the adorable image, she changed the subject. "I talked to my mom last night."

"After the movie?"

"No. Before. I told her we started dating."

"Yeah? What did she say?"

"She was quiet. Then she asked if Michael knew. That was about it. We didn't have a lot of time. I'm sure we'll talk more when they come for your parents' party."

"Good. Glad you mentioned it at least. It's interesting to see how everyone reacts. We're charting new territory."

"Yes, and sometimes it feels like we're in the Land of Oz!"

Ronin shook his head, laughing. "We *are* in Oz, Dorothy!"

CHAPTER TWENTY-THREE

"CHICA, YOU LOOK gorgeous!" Nica hugged Tilly then stood back to admire her friend. Tilly's dark blue dress was covered in large white, pink, and yellow tulips and she wore sling-back heels in the same shade of blue. She had curled her hair so it hung in long loose waves.

"Thank you," Tilly said, hugging her back. "You look pretty scrumptious yourself. And my goodness, your art installation is amaze-balls."

She turned to point to the wall behind the reception desk, where a grouping of miscellaneous blue wheels was mounted. Nica had crafted wooden "M" letters out of thin plywood, painted them white, and mounted them to the front of the wheel display.

"Thanks." Nica beamed, pushing her dark hair behind her ear. "I think it came together well."

"Better than well," Tilly continued. "So many people have commented on it. It's striking. You need to give Ronin a stack of business cards to hand out when people ask. Because they're gonna ask."

They were joined by Michael and Ronin, who thanked Nica for her contribution to the space and for completing it before opening day.

Grady walked in, and Ronin led the couple on a tour of the facility. Michael and Ronin were taking turns leading visitors through the space while Tilly helped greet them and put them into the database if they signed up for a workspace membership.

Michael escorted a visitor to the front door, then joined Tilly behind the counter.

"It's finally here, big brother. How are you feeling?"

"Good. I wish Mom and Dad could have made it down today, but I know they'll see it this weekend."

"This is so exciting. We had such a busy weekend, and Ronin refused to talk about opening day, so it feels like this snuck up on me."

"How could he talk about work?" He threw his hands up in mock surprise. "He was busy picking straw out of—never mind."

Tilly playfully punched his arm. "Watch it, mister, or next year you'll be the scarecrow."

"Ah, naw."

"Anyway, I bet you're hoping for a lot of foot traffic today."

"Yes!" Michael replied. "Three people already signed up before today and we've had others interested who've said they would check out the launch today and decide."

"That's a good start."

"It's just an okay start, not good. But let's see what the rest of the day brings."

The door opened and two twenty-something men entered. Michael greeted them and led them on a tour. Tilly straightened the stacks of fliers on the reception counter as she waited for Ronin to return with Nica and Grady. She took a picture of the flower arrangement Anna Lee had created and posted it to their social media accounts, along with the caption, "Join us today for our Grand Opening! Sandwiches at noon and Cocktails at 5!"

Ronin, Nica, and Grady returned to the reception area where they chatted for a few more minutes. As they were leaving, Ronin shook Grady's hand and thanked him for his investment in the business.

Grady smiled. "I know a good thing when I see it. Like Spicy here." He pulled Nica into a side hug. Nica and Grady left, promising to return with friends for cocktails later.

It thrilled Tilly to see her friend with a great man. They were a perfect pair, both focused and driven.

Tilly smoothed the lapel on Ronin's suit and leaned against him for a moment. "Congrats again, Ronin. I'm so excited to see this dream come true."

"Thank you, Emmy." He smiled, and the warmth in his eyes heated her body. "Though it's not really the best dream to come true this month."

"Oh, yeah?"

"Yeah." He brushed her hair back over her shoulders.

"At the risk of sounding dense, what dream are you referring to?"

"You. This." He indicated their closeness.

She had hoped that's what he meant, but to hear him say it, felt like Fourth of July sparklers were popping and crackling under her skin.

The front door opened, and Tilly hopped backward. She didn't think it was professional to be seen hugging the business owner on opening day!

Two young ladies strolled in with brilliant smiles on their faces. Tilly felt a pang of jealousy and was glad she and Ronin had been hugging when those two walked in. *I hate to feel like I'm marking my territory, but...*

Ronin gave them a warm hello and reached out to shake their hands. "Hi, I'm Ronin McGuire. Welcome to M and M Spaces."

The ladies introduced themselves as Laura and Melanie, and Ronin led them on the tour of the workspace. Tilly tapped her foot on the ground, thinking about the way the women had blatantly looked Ronin up and down, ignoring her presence. She whipped out her phone and searched for the pictures of her and Ronin at the Oz Festival on Saturday. She smiled as she saw the Scarecrow and Dorothy walking arm-in-arm down the faux yellow brick road.

She took a deep breath, remembering the way Ronin had looked at her moments before, with something like love in his eyes. Tilly was trying not to rush things, and knew it was very early in their relationship, but it felt right. Ronin was everything she wanted in a partner—sincere, attentive, kind, and immensely amazing.

When Michael returned with the two men, he was smiling broadly. Both of them wanted to sign up, so Tilly handed each of them a clipboard with the sign-up form and a pen. They sat on leather chairs in the lobby area to complete the paperwork. Behind the counter, Tilly held out her hand for a "low five" and whispered, "Well done" to her brother.

Michael leaned towards her. "Did you see the two hotties Ronin was talking to?"

Tilly wanted to send the high-five across his cheek. "Yes," she hissed out. "Don't remind me."

"Oh, Sis, Ronin only has eyes for you."

He could say that all he wanted, but Tilly wasn't so sure. Those young women were professionally dressed, and in a position to consider a coworking space. They probably had important jobs, or even worse, were entrepreneurs in their own right. They were probably back there telling Ronin all about their intelligent investments and breakthrough ideas that were about to change the world. Her prior confidence in Ronin's affection was eroding. Doubt was creeping up her spine like a dangerous snake.

She sighed. "I wish I had your conviction."

"Well, remember, I'm your assigned protector. If he hurts you, I kick his—"

Just then, the first young man stepped to the counter. "Here's the form. Whose butt are we kicking?" he asked with a grin.

"Let's keep both of you out of jail, and not worry about that right now," Tilly said, taking the clipboard. "I can get you entered into the system and take your first month's payment." She looked at the clipboard. "Jonah."

He handed her his credit card. "Will I get to see you every time I come in?"

"Oh, no. I don't work here officially. I'm just helping for today."

Another man entered, and Michael greeted him.

"That's too bad," Jonah continued.

Ronin finally returned to the reception area with the two young women. He handed each of them a clipboard and introduced himself to Jonah and his friend, Raja.

As Tilly continued to sign up the new clients, another woman walked in. She was tall, blonde, and wore a beautiful blue suit with a skirt that fit all her curves perfectly.

Why does Ronin keep getting the women and Michael the men? Tilly fumed to herself while smiling and thanking Jonah and Raja. Ronin greeted the new woman and chit-chatted with her. When he led her to the back, Tilly wanted to kick the desk but decided that was a bad idea with open-toe shoes. She bit the inside of her lip instead.

"Hi," said the pretty brunette who'd been filling out the sign-up form. "Do I give this to you?"

"Yes. I'll get you set up and assign a badge to you. Just a moment." She sat down at the computer and began entering the woman's information. *Jill Shayne. What a name. Rhymes with shame.*

"So," Miss Shayne whispered, leaning over the counter. "Are both of the handsome owners single?"

Tilly bit her lip again. "Michael is."

"Is that the one that showed us around?"

"No. That was Ronin."

"Oh, and he's not single?"

"No, he's not. He's my boyfriend."

"Oh. That's...nice."

Tilly knew from Miss Shayne's tone that she didn't mean it.

"So," she continued, "you're the receptionist?"

Her tone sent a shiver down Tilly's spine. "No, they're hiring someone. I'm just here to help today. I may help when they're shorthanded. I hope to see you around."

To keep an eye on you, make sure you keep your talons out of Ronin.

"That would be great."

No, not great. Tilly nodded, though she wanted to shake her head. "And what do you do, Jill?"

"I started a software company."

A tech start-up. Gosh. Tilly looked down at the woman's driver's license. This lady was just two years older than her. "That's amazing. What type of software?"

Tilly wanted to keep the young woman talking so *she* wouldn't have to.

"I wrote a program that suggests hairstyles based on face shape. Would you like to try it? You look ready for a new 'do."

Actually, Tilly wasn't ready. After a horrible haircut in sixth grade, she'd vowed never to cut it short again. "No, thank you."

Jill looked disappointed. Tilly decided that was not her problem. The other woman walked up to them with her own clipboard. "Hi. I'll take that," Tilly said.

RONIN LOOKED AT his watch. Halfway through cocktail hour. He surveyed the crowded reception area. Two servers circled around with trays of finger foods, and a bartender stood behind the reception counter serving drinks.

Guests mingled throughout the lobby and the coworking space. He saw Tilly across the room and wanted to go see how she was doing, but just as he took a step towards her, someone touched his arm. He'd ditched his suit jacket at 5 p.m. and rolled up his sleeves. The touch landed just above his wrist. He was thankful the air conditioning was keeping up with the size of the crowd, and his arm wasn't sweaty.

He turned to see a woman smiling at him. She wore a red dress that didn't leave much to the imagination.

"Hello, are you the owner?" she asked.

"One of the owners. I'm Ronin. How can I help you?" He held out his hand. He wondered if she was a reporter. She looked overly made up, and he could imagine her with a microphone in her hand.

"I wanted to congratulate you on your opening." She'd taken his hand but held on after shaking it. "I've kept an eye on the place while you've been preparing."

"Do you work nearby?"

"I own the building across the street."

Ronin paused. The building across the street had several thriving businesses on the ground floor and multiple floors of apartments above. "Oh, do you live in one of the units?"

"Yes, the top one."

Only one unit on the top floor? The building took up half a city block. Must be a penthouse. "That's great. Thank you for coming out and supporting the grand opening. Have you met my partner, Michael, yet?"

Ronin needed to mingle. And find Tilly.

She shook her head and pouted her lower lip. "I haven't. But I was curious about the setup. Can I ask you a few questions?"

Ronin set his teeth. "Certainly."

"Could a certain single woman exclusively rent one of the office spaces? I would love to set up my own office and not have to carry things back and forth."

"Yes. We've designated two of the offices for permanent tenants, but we want to keep several open as flexible spaces."

"Very nice. And pricing?"

"It's on the info sheet, which you can find on the reception desk in the lobby."

"I'll be sure to pick one up on my way out. Now, will you be here full-time, or do you have other locations to manage?"

"For now, full-time, but we have plans to expand."

"Perfect," she practically purred, reminding Ronin of a cat with very sharp claws.

"I need to mingle." *I need to run.* "It was nice meeting, you Miss—"

"Sampson. Gena Sampson. Please call me Gena."

"Gena." Ronin nodded and walked away. He knew trouble when it approached that closely.

A server walked by with a tray full of fried deviled eggs. "Hold up," he said, reaching for a napkin.

"Great party," the server mumbled.

"Thanks. Keep up the great work."

Walking across the room to where Tilly stood, Ronin said hello to twenty more guests. He looked about the room for his parents but didn't see them. They should be arriving with his sisters soon.

Tilly's face lit up as he approached, but he caught a flash of sadness first. "Hey," he said, leaning towards her ear, brushing a kiss to her temple. "Is everything all right?"

She looked down quickly, and Ronin knew something was wrong, even when she smiled at him. Her smile didn't reach her eyes.

"Everything seems to be going well. Are you happy?" she asked.

"I'm a little overwhelmed, if I'm being honest." He shifted to stand next to her where he could survey the room. "There are so many people. I didn't expect this."

"It's really great…"

Ronin spotted his parents walking in. "My family's here! Let's go."

He grabbed her hand and led her through the crowd.

CHAPTER TWENTY-FOUR

TILLY WAS EXCITED to see Ronin's family again. She needed time with the family she'd known almost as long as her own. The room was full of beautiful, successful women who seemed to be auditioning for a dating reality show, not shopping for a drop-in workspace, and it was really shaking her confidence.

"Ronin!" Elizabeth shouted, throwing her arms around her son. "This is amazing! I can't believe it's the same space we saw just a few weeks ago."

"It takes a village," he said, hugging her back. "Thank goodness for all of our friends and sisters," he said, putting his arms around Trinity when Shevaun pushed him away.

Elizabeth hugged Tilly. "Tilly, it looks fantastic. Can you believe it?"

"Yes! I knew they would get everything done on time and do it well. Even Michael." Tilly hugged Bruce, Shevaun, and Trinity. "So glad you all came."

"We wouldn't miss it," Bruce said, "and we are looking forward to taking you all to dinner when you wrap up."

Tilly looked at Ronin. "I didn't know about dinner. I was stuffing my face with appetizers."

"Oh." Ronin threw his head back and groaned. "I forgot to tell you. I'm so sorry."

"It's okay, I'll be a cheap date."

Everyone laughed, and Tilly felt her emotional reserves being replenished. "Did you see Michael in the lobby?"

Trinity nodded. "He was helping the bartender."

"I'll go see if he needs any more help." Tilly wanted Ronin to have time with his family, and she needed her brother.

In the reception area the crowd had begun to thin. When she walked up to Michael and the bartender and saw the "Sorry, we're out of beer" sign, she understood why.

"Need a hand?" she asked.

"No." Michael stepped out from behind the counter. "It's under control. You're looking a little tired, Sis. Are you all right?"

"Yeah, I'm fine. Just a long day, you know?"

"Do I! I'm looking forward to dinner with the McGuires."

Tilly considered. She'd love time to visit with them and rehash the day's events, but she was exhausted and needed to open at In Bloom on Tuesday. "I think I'm going to beg off for tonight. I've got a headache. I'm going to call a ride-share and head home."

"Oh, does Ronin know?"

"No. Will you tell him and send my apology to his family?"

A stunning woman in a red dress, who Tilly had seen talking to Ronin, approached Michael. He looked at Tilly. "Sure." Then he turned to the woman in red and gave her a gigantic smile. "Hello. I'm Michael. And you are…"

"Gena."

Tilly grabbed her purse from under the receptionist's desk and walked out the front door.

Seeing all the successful women at Ronin's launch party was a blow to her psyche. Women who were put together, who knew what they wanted, had big dreams and goals, and were executing those goals. Tilly's head spun thinking about all the possibilities for her life. So many possible paths to take, and none of them felt perfect. She wanted desperately for the universe to point her to the right path. Her emotions were crushing her spirit, and she didn't want her mood to put a damper on Ronin's success and the celebration. She hoped he would forgive her for leaving suddenly. Even more, she prayed he would find her to be enough and wouldn't fall for one of the driven women he was sure to run across in his business.

DIPPING HER SPOON into her Neapolitan ice cream, Mack held it up to punctuate her words before taking a bite. "I don't care how beautiful and put-together those women seemed, you've got nothing to worry about. Ronin likes you. Like for real. A lot."

Tilly swirled the spoon around her bowl, the strawberry, chocolate, and vanilla flavors melting together. Ordinarily, she loved this ice cream and could devour two bowls in minutes, but tonight it tasted bland, and her stomach wanted to reject it. She placed the bowl on her nightstand, catching a glimpse of the bell hanging there.

She knew it was unreasonable to expect it to ring; she'd just left their office thirty minutes ago, and they were going out to eat after closing it. Ronin wouldn't be home for a couple of hours, at least. But it didn't stop the longing in her heart for it to ring—to know that Ronin was thinking of her.

"But does he? Really?" She pulled on her pajama top, picking at a loose thread. "We've been around each other a handful of days this summer, and before this past month, it was sporadic at best. We don't really know each other now. I knew Ronin best seven or eight years ago."

"Which is so romantic! I bet your parents have pictures of you as little kids. That will look so, so cute at your wedding. I can see the video montage before the toasts now." Mack held up her hands and mimed running an old fashioned, wind-up video camera. She smiled as she dropped her hands and picked up her bowl again. "It'd be the crime of the century not to have that video montage."

"Can we go on a second date before you start planning the wedding, please?"

"All right." She smiled warmly. "At least you've not given up hope if you're talking about a second date."

Tilly yawned and rubbed her eyes, hoping Mack would take the hint and leave.

"No, no, no." Mack was shaking her head. "Those dramatics won't work with me. You're a lousy actress."

"I'm lousy at everything." Her heart pinched, and she could feel the fire in her soul sputter.

"Stop!"

"You should have seen these women, Mack. They were so put together, with professional clothes and real jobs. Real aspirations. Ronin is going to be surrounded by that type of woman all the time—women more like him than I am. He'll quickly see what he could have and dump my sorry butt on the curb. He won't even have to drive far from home to do it."

She looked out her bedroom window toward their apartment. Their living-room window was still dark. Ronin and Michael weren't home yet.

"Hold up." Mack waved her spoon. "There's something else going on here. I've never seen you this unsure of yourself. What is it?"

Tilly rolled her shoulders. "There's just a lot to be unsure about. What am I going to do with this college degree? Should I switch majors? My mom is getting closer to finding her birth parents, and then what? If she finds her birth parents, what will that be like? Are they alive? Will we get to meet them? Could

I have more cousins? More aunts and uncles? Sometimes," she continued, "it feels like a dark wave is rolling over me and I can't get up for air. I've never had a panic attack before, but it feels like one is waiting just outside. Trying to catch me off guard. And then Ronin. I don't want to ruin this by imagining the worst. But I don't want to be caught off-guard like I was with Kyle, either."

Mackenzie put her empty ice-cream bowl on the floor next to the bed and leaned forward, taking Tilly's hands in hers. "Take a deep breath. We're going to do a relaxation exercise I learned in drama class. We'll focus on different body parts, feel how heavy they are, and then let the weight go. Starting with our feet. Ready? Close your eyes. In your mind, observe your feet. Feel the weight of them. Think about how they move you around all day long. They do so much work. They are tired. Feel how heavy. Thank them and relax…"

Soon, Mack's voice was just a pleasant whisper of words. Tilly listened to the instructions and let the words soothe and relax her. She wasn't even aware when Mack left the room because she was fast asleep.

CHAPTER TWENTY-FIVE

ONIN CLUTCHED THE glass of beer in his hand, slackening his hold when he realized it could break. He watched Michael flirting—flirting! with Shevaun across the table. *I'm going to beat him into a slimy little pile of pulp when we get home.*

To his left, Trinity was talking to their mom about back-to-school readiness. On his right, his dad was telling him about a new bike path that he wanted to explore on their next outing.

Ronin could barely keep up his end of the conversation; he was hyper-focused on whatever line of baloney Michael was feeding Shevaun. *And why in the devil was she eating it up?*

Was this how Michael felt when he found out about Ronin asking Tilly out? Like every drop of testosterone in his body had expanded a thousand times, cutting off all synapses from the logic portion of his brain? Ronin set his glass down and turned towards his dad. He had to remove Michael and Shevaun from his line of vision.

"Sounds great. Let's do it," Ronin said, hoping his timing was right.

"Maybe Tilly could come." His dad put the utensils across his plate.

"Yeah." But Ronin wasn't thinking about Tilly right now. He was thinking that Michael was too old for Shevaun. He was also remembering all of Michael's most unseemly escapades over the years. *He's not good enough for my sister!*

"Ugh," he groaned.

"What's that?"

"Nothing, Dad. Just remembered that I have to be up and in the office at six. I need to think about calling it a night."

"That's early."

"Well, our business hours are 6 a.m. to 10 p.m., so Michael and I are working shifts. I have the earlier shift…" *so I have evenings free for Tilly* "…and he's got two to ten." Good, Shevaun was rarely awake before two. And she'd be leaving for college on Sunday. Less than a week and she'd be safely away; then Ronin could relax.

What a day! He felt the launch of M and M Spaces had gone well, the turnout was great, and they'd had a good number of people sign up. But the fact that Tilly had left early without saying goodbye worried him, and now seeing Michael and Shevaun flirting, he had a weird taste in his mouth. He was crazy about Tilly, there was no debating that, but realizing how he felt about Shevaun and Michael laughing and chatting so closely gave him pause. *It's going to take extra effort to navigate our new relationship dynamics. As long as Michael keeps his hands off Vaun, everything will be fine.*

TUESDAY HAD BEEN a blur for Tilly. She'd had an emotional hangover from the Grand Opening, and she had a long day at In Bloom. By the time she got home, Ronin had crashed, and they didn't get a chance to see each other. So, on Wednesday she decided to pack lunch for the two of them and meet him after his shift to go on a picnic. *I'll feel better when our relationship is more established,* she tried to convince herself. *I just have to see him, to be assured that my fears are unfounded.*

She'd texted him and told him she'd bike to his office, knowing that he had a bike rack in the trunk of his car, and she could ride home with him. She liked the idea of exercise, not using the expensive gas in her car, and getting to ride home with Ronin.

He was on board, and she pulled up in front of his building just after two. He and Michael were in the reception area talking to the evening receptionist. Tilly had been pleased to hear that this receptionist was a former Army National Guard who they'd met at the gym. Ronin and Michael liked the fact that he could help handle things if something got out of hand. The morning receptionist was a former teacher who was ready for a second career.

"Good afternoon, all!" Tilly entered the lobby after parking her bike.

"Hi, Emmy," Ronin said, walking towards her. He kissed her cheek and introduced her to Travis, the receptionist/guard.

"Hi, Travis. It's nice to meet you."

"Thank you. Likewise." He shook her hand and Tilly decided he would be very effective in his role.

"Ready for lunch?' she asked Ronin.

"Yes, I'm hungry. I hope you packed plenty. If not, we'll drive through somewhere."

At the park, they spread a black and white checked blanket, and Tilly laid out the food she'd prepared—sandwiches, chips, pasta salad, sugar cookies, and strawberry cheesecakes she'd made in a muffin tin.

Ronin grabbed a sandwich. "I got worried when you left Monday night without saying goodbye."

"I'm sorry about that. I wasn't feeling well."

"That's what Michael said, but I still don't get it."

Tilly looked at the traffic passing by—anywhere but at Ronin. This was going to be hard to share. "To be honest, I felt intimidated. There were so many beautiful, professional women flocking around, that I freaked out a little bit. I started feeling poorly about myself."

"Emmy…" Ronin leaned towards her and rested his hand on her thigh, sending a flash of warmth through her body. "I have to interact with women at work. I don't want you to be worried or feel bad about it. I am not interested in anyone else. Just you."

The words were a salve to her bruised heart. And ego. "Thank you for that. It helps."

"Good. I don't want you to worry about that. And," he stressed the word, "you can't run off when you're upset like that. You have to talk to me. Tell me what's wrong so I can fix it, or at least make it better. If we don't communicate, we'll have all sorts of problems."

Tilly looked down at where his hand still rested on her leg. She put her hand over his. "You're right. I should have addressed it and not run from it. That probably brought on the headache."

Ronin hunched his shoulder and winced like he was in pain. "I don't like hearing that. Always talk to me, Em. Promise?"

"Promise. All right. Let's eat."

Ronin laughed and unwrapped the sandwich. "You won't have to tell me twice."

Tilly dished up a bowl of pasta salad. Ronin was right; she had to tell him when something was bothering her. He couldn't read her mind.

And I can't read his. "Same for you," she said.

"What?"

"You have to tell me when something's bothering you. We can't read each other's minds."

"You got it, babe."

Babe. He'd called her babe! The first time he'd used a romantic pet name. She was glad she'd planned the picnic for him. Her confidence was building up again—not to where it had been before Kyle broke up with her, but it was on the right trajectory. Ronin's attention and attraction to her were filling the fissures in her heart.

CHAPTER TWENTY-SIX

TILLY SURVEYED THE venue. The centerpieces that she'd helped design with Anna Lee were in place; they popped like crown jewels at every table, their tall stems of white irises and shorter stems of blue hydrangeas were set off with bunches of green foliage holding everything in place. She couldn't wait for Ronin to walk in and see the pretty tables. The venue supplied beautiful place settings with a dainty floral pattern featuring blue hydrangeas. The tablecloths were silver, and white napkins were tucked in the white glasses and resembled more irises.

The door opened and Ronin walked in, causing Tilly's breath to hitch. He wore a black suit with a white shirt and had added a silver tie in recognition of his parents' twenty-fifth anniversary.

He looked more handsome every time she saw him, now that she saw him as a man and not just Michael's best friend. As each day went by, she thought of him less as Michael's friend and more as her *boyfriend*. Maybe someday soon that would be her first instinct when she saw him.

She strode across the room, smiling as his eyes swept over her. She knew her lavender knee-length dress was stunning, and she was excited about the silver brooch sparkling with rhinestone balloons that she'd found at an antique shop.

"Hi!" she said, stepping into Ronin's outstretched arms.

He hugged her, and Tilly was pretty sure he sniffed her hair. "Hi, gorgeous! Everything looks fantastic! What can I do to help?" he asked, kissing her softly.

Tilly forgot they were in a large room, where several people bustled about, placing silverware at each place setting. The only thing that mattered was that she was in Ronin's arms. She returned his kiss and sighed when he cupped the back of her head with his hand. He pulled back and smiled at her. She grinned, feeling effervescent joy.

Whoa. That was scrumptious. "Nothing. We're ready to go. Just need guests. When is your family arriving?"

"Any minute now. Vaun sent a text fifteen minutes ago that they were leaving home."

"Good. And Michael? He didn't ride with you?"

"No. He wanted to have his own car tonight. I wish I could have picked you up. I hate that you drove yourself."

"I had to be here early to set up." She gestured around the room. "It's fine. I don't mind."

"You knocked it out of the park. Did I tell you how much I appreciate your help with this party?"

She couldn't stop smiling. "Here I thought it was all a ploy to get me to fall for you."

"Well." He leaned toward her. "Is it working?"

"Yes," she whispered, just before his lips found hers again. Tilly closed her eyes. It felt like she was floating.

Ronin's family entered, followed closely by Tilly's parents. She squealed when she saw them and ran towards them, flinging her arms around first her mom, then her dad.

"Hi! I'm so glad you're here! It's been too long."

"Agreed, dear," Irena said, embracing her. "Is Michael here?"

"Not yet," she said. "He should be, soon. Can I get you a cocktail? It looks like the bartender is ready."

Tilly got the requested drinks and returned to find her parents talking to Ronin's parents—about them dating! *Ugh!*

"I always hoped," Elizabeth said, "that there'd be a relationship between our kids. I'm glad it's Ronin and Tilly."

Irena smiled and nodded, but the smile seemed forced. Tilly glanced at Ronin, hoping he didn't pick up her mom's vibe. He shouldn't be worried about anything except his parents having a great time.

The cocktail hour was filled with introductions and the sight of many familiar faces. Several of their neighbors growing up had made the trip to Bloomington to celebrate Bruce and Elizabeth. It felt like a transplanted block party.

The lights dimmed briefly, indicating everyone should take their seats. Tilly had helped Ronin and his parents with the seating chart. She was a little disappointed that she and Ronin wouldn't be sitting together through dinner but understood that Ronin needed to be with his family.

Michael was seated to her left and her parents on her right. Rounding out their table of eight were Lloyd and Betty Carrington and Miles and Tina Bright; both couples still lived on the same block as Tilly's parents. They asked Tilly about school and Michael about the new business, then all the older adults began to discuss a new zoning law that was being proposed for their neighborhood, and Tilly tuned them out.

As their dinner plates were being cleared, Tilly noticed a striking woman enter the room. She wore her long blonde hair curled to perfection, a shimmery gray gown that ran all the way to the floor, and high heels that seemed ridiculously tall.

Michael muttered a curse word under his breath, and Tilly leaned closer. "An ex-girlfriend, here to do you harm?" she whispered to him, with a lilt to her voice.

"No, not mine. Ronin's," he muttered back. "This can't be good."

"What? Who?"

"Kristy."

"The one he broke up with a few months ago?"

"That's the one. What the heck does she want? Was she on the invite list?"

Tilly knew that list as well as Ronin. "No."

Michael just grunted, watching Kristy approach the McGuires' table. He shifted his chair back, ready to spring into action if needed.

Tilly swept her eyes to Ronin and saw the moment he noticed Kristy. His brow furrowed in confusion, but he managed to stand and smile at her like nothing was wrong. *But everything is wrong! This should not be happening!*

Tilly kept waiting for Ronin's eyes to seek her out, but they didn't. He smiled as Kristy said hello to his entire family like she knew them; she was not being introduced to them. Tears rushed to Tilly's eyes, but she blinked rapidly, refusing to let them fall. She was not going to fall apart in front of her family or Ronin's.

Michael reached over and squeezed her hand. The gesture was both comforting and annoying. Part of her worried that Michael was trying to tell her that whatever was going on in her head, this was worse. *Maybe he knows that Ronin's gonna break up with me now that Kristy's back in the picture.*

"Why would she come?" She whispered to Michael. "Does he want her back?"

There, lay it out plainly. No mincing her words. The conversation with Ronin about being open about her feelings came back to her. The only way he would know something was bothering her is if she told him. *I have to tell him. But not now.* She didn't want to spoil the party for his parents. She hoped this Kristy would be shown the door before Tilly had to confront anyone. She probably could confront someone. There's a first time for everything.

Her stomach flip-flopped and she felt her heart race. Deep breath. She tried to remember Mack's relaxation technique, but she drew a blank.

"He does not want her back," Michael said adamantly. "I don't know why she's here, though. You sure she wasn't on the invite list?"

"I told you, no, she wasn't. How did she find out?"

"Don't know. Want me to go over and see what's what?"

"No. Don't cause a scene. I—I think it'll be all right. Dinner is almost over. They're clearing plates. He'll give a toast soon. Let's just get through dinner."

Michael grunted and stood. "I'll be back."

Tilly watched him cross to Ronin's table. She reached for her glass of wine, and when her eyes darted towards Ronin, she knocked the glass over. Red wine whooshed out all over the tablecloth and right onto her dress.

Oh no! Oh no! Not now! I'm such a klutz.

"Are you all right, dear?" Irena asked.

"Um, it's okay, I spilled. Excuse me."

She rushed to the hallway and found a server. "Can I get a little club soda and a cloth?"

"One second."

Tilly looked down and saw the red wine continue to spread over her pretty dress. *This is terrible! I can't go back there looking like this. And there is no way I'm meeting his ex-girlfriend with a wine stain across my dress.*

The server returned with the necessary items, and Tilly dabbed at the stain. She heard the music stop, and Ronin's voice projecting over the sound system. *His speech! I can't believe I'm not in there.*

She listened to the speech and shed a tear as he ended it. *He'll understand. We're gonna be all right.*

Dropping the glass and towel on the server cart, she left.

RONIN DIDN'T SEE Michael approach until he was just a few feet away. His eyes swept towards Tilly's table. She wasn't there. *This is not good.*

"Ronin, there's an issue with catering. Can I see you for a minute?" Michael asked.

Kristy reached in front of Ronin, stretching her hand to Michael. "Hey, how are you?"

He took her hand briefly. "How are you, Kristy? Didn't expect to see you," he said coolly.

"I came on a whim," she said brightly.

"I'll follow you," Ronin said to Michael, turning away from the table.

Michael led the way to the hall. Once they were out of sight of the guests, Michael turned with fire in his eyes. "What in the double-cross is going on here?" he spat out.

Ronin ground his teeth before catching himself. "I don't know! She wasn't invited. From the looks of my family, my guess is she's been in contact with Trinity. Trin is the only one who didn't look surprised when they saw Kristy. Where's Emmy?"

"I don't know. She was at our table when I walked over to get you."

"Did you tell her who Kristy is?"

"Yes. I'm not going to lie to my sister."

"Is she upset?"

"She's not in the room, so take a guess. I can't believe this. This is a frickin' mess, Ro. You guys aren't on the strongest of foundations yet, so something like this will shake her up, obviously."

"Obviously. I have to find her. Can you try to keep Kristy occupied?"

"No way." Michael held up his hands and backed away. "Your family can do that. I'm not risking my sister getting ticked off at me."

"Understood. When you see her, tell her I had nothing to do with this."

"Yeah. Of course."

Ronin's heart raced entering the reception. Not only was he freaked out about Tilly, but he couldn't believe the anger that burned in Michael's eyes. Of course, he would feel the same way if Michael hurt one of his sisters. *Although, I'm ready to hurt one of my sisters for creating this disaster. Where is Emmy?* He walked back into the reception hall and made his way back to his family's table.

Kristy had taken his seat and was telling his family about law school.

Elizabeth interrupted Kristy. "Sorry, Kristy. Ronin, what time did you say dessert would be served?"

"Soon. I'll make a toast, and then you two will cut the cake. Sound good?"

Elizabeth agreed, and Ronin searched the room, hoping Tilly had returned.

A few minutes later, the catering manager pulled Ronin aside and said they were ready to bring out the cake. Reluctantly, Ronin walked to the podium and turned on the microphone for his toast.

Servers began distributing glasses of champagne, and Ronin cleared his throat.

"Ladies and gentlemen. Friends and family. Mom and Dad," he began. "I would like to make a toast to the guests of honor, Bruce and Elizabeth McGuire. Mom and Dad, I speak for all who know you when I say that your marriage is one to admire, emulate, and tell others about. Twenty-five years is an incredible achievement, and I know in twenty-five years, God willing, we'll be back to celebrate your fiftieth.

"You've taught me and my sisters the meaning of love and family. You encourage each other, you listen to each other, you make time for each other. You've taught us to try to do the same thing. Though we may not always act like it, we are learning the lessons you're teaching. I thank you for those lessons and hope that I can take them with me as I embark on the most important relationship in my life, with Emmy."

There was an audible sigh at those words, and Ronin scanned the room, hoping Tilly had heard them. There would be no way she could worry about Kristy if she'd heard this part of his speech. He didn't see her anywhere, though Shevaun had returned to the family's table.

"I'd especially like to thank Emmy for helping plan this special occasion. She helped find this venue, plan the menu, and design and make the beautiful centerpieces on the table. I couldn't have pulled this off without her." He cleared his throat, feeling a surge of emotion. "Well, I hope they served my younger sisters sparkling grape juice and not alcohol." There was a hearty laugh. "If everyone would raise their glasses. Congratulations to Mom and Dad on twenty-five years. We love you, and we wish you many more anniversaries to celebrate. Cheers!"

Glasses clinked throughout the room. Ronin glanced towards Tilly's table. Michael had returned and was clinking glasses with his parents and friends at the table, but Tilly was still nowhere to be seen.

THE GUESTS WERE beginning to leave, and Ronin stayed by his parents thanking guests for coming, when he really wanted to begin searching for Tilly. He'd already sent half a dozen text messages and tried calling her twice, but Tilly was not returning any messages.

He asked her parents if she'd said anything to them before leaving. Irena said that Tilly had spilled her glass of wine on her dress and excused herself.

Ronin wished he had a number for Mack and made a mental note to get that as soon as he could.

He knew this was bad. If Tilly had been a little shaken up by the glamorous strangers at opening day, what must she be thinking about his ex-girlfriend showing up unannounced?

He excused himself for a minute and stepped outside. He checked his phone again. Nothing. He called again, and it went to voice mail. He sent another text.

> **RONIN:** Hey, you okay? I hope this doesn't have to do with my ex. I don't know why she's here. Remember, she's my EX. She's not important to me. You are.

This was awful. Not a conversation for coldhearted text messages. He put his phone back in his pocket and counted to ten. He needed to chill out before going back in and confronting both Kristy and his sisters. He'd get to find out how Kristy ended up here at the party so he could assuage any of Tilly's concerns.

CHAPTER TWENTY-SEVEN

TILLY WOKE UP Sunday morning, still embarrassed about spilling her wine and having to leave the party early. She rubbed her eyes before picking up her phone and turning it on. She'd turned it off after leaving the party—she didn't want to field questions about leaving, from Ronin or anyone else.

Before reading his text messages, she reached up and pulled on the bell several times. If Ronin or Michael were up, they'd know she was, too.

She began to read through the messages from Ronin. He denied knowing his ex would show up, and that didn't surprise her. She didn't think he had known, but as soon as he'd seen his ex, he should have sought Tilly out to calm her fears and ease her mind. But he hadn't. He looked as though he didn't even remember Tilly existed as he'd stood talking to his ex and his family.

She made it through the messages, text and voice, and still no response on the bell. The boys must still be in bed.

Tilly had plans with her parents today. They had created an itinerary for their visit, and as usual, it was packed with activities and lots of eating. Michael planned to join them for most of the activities, though he'd begged off breakfast.

Making a pot of coffee, she texted her mom, saying she'd be ready to go in an hour. While the coffee brewed, she took a shower.

Mack rose once the coffee was finished and sat on the edge of the bathtub drinking a cup while Tilly put on her makeup.

"I can't believe his ex showed up," Mack said. "That blows."

"I know, right? You should have seen her. It looked like she was dressed for a beauty pageant. A dress with a slit the length of her whole leg up the side. If she wasn't a knock-out, it might have been trashy."

"What did Ronin say?"

Tilly scratched her arm. "I didn't talk to him after she arrived."

"What?"

"Well, it shook me up when Michael told me who she was, and I spilled red wine all over my dress. It was a mess. I tried to use club soda to get it out, but that only made it worse. There was no way I was going back in there to show my face when I looked so terrible. Especially with her looking like perfection from heaven. I was so upset. I was crying, and I didn't want to make a scene or ruin his parents' party. They deserved a drama-free event focused on them. Not on me."

"But did you call him last night?" Mack had been out when Tilly got home.

"No," Tilly answered, putting on blush. "I came home and went to bed."

"Did he call or text?"

"Yes. Multiple times."

"Wow," Mack said, blowing on her coffee. "He's going to think you're mad."

"He'll *know* I'm mad, and that's fine by me. Look, I don't think he invited her. He seemed surprised when she walked in. But he didn't even look for me to see if I was all right."

"Okay, then. Let him sweat."

"I'm going to. I'll be with my parents all day, so if he stops by, tell him I'm out."

"You betcha."

RONIN TOSSED SHEVAUN'S duffel bag in the trunk. "All right. Anything else?"

"No. That's it. Thanks for helping me load everything."

"Quite all right."

They started walking back to the house. Ronin checked his phone, hoping for a message from Tilly. Nothing.

"Have you heard from her?" Shevaun asked.

"Nope. Radio silence."

"Ouch, severe." She ran her hand over her spiky hair. "Are you going to kick Trin's butt for inviting Kristy?"

Ronin considered. He wanted to, he really did, but a conversation was sufficient, and Trinity'd said she was sorry already. "No. It's not necessary. She said she'd talked to Kristy before she knew Tilly and I are dating and she forgot to rescind the invite, so I guess it was an honest mistake."

"Did you let Kristy down easy, at least?"

After the party guests had left, Ronin had told Kristy that he was seeing someone new and there was no chance of the two of them getting back together, even if things didn't work out with Tilly. Kristy apologized for the surprise appearance, but said she'd thought that since Trinity had invited her, there was still a chance for them. Ronin assured her there wasn't, and she'd left.

"I think so. I think she understands."

"Well," Shevaun said, opening the door to the foyer. "I hope Tilly can find it in her to forgive and forget, but she's pretty stubborn."

"Don't I know it."

Ronin reminded himself not to get too worried; things would be fine when he talked to Tilly. He'd explain that he'd been as surprised as she was, and there was no chance he was getting back together with Kristy. That was not an option. *I'm sure Tilly will understand. I just wished she'd send a quick text saying she's all right.*

"Not only is she mad at you, but I am, too," Shevaun added. "Tilly was supposed to be here to see me off today."

"I'm sorry she's not, but don't get mad at her. Remember, her parents are here, so maybe she got busy with them and just forgot."

"That's cute." Shevaun grabbed her favorite fall jacket out of the hall closet. "It's almost like you think she's not pissed at you. I can guarantee you; she is. Whether she's with her parents or not."

Ronin threw his head back. "I know, Vaun. I know. Isn't it time for you to get on the road?"

"Yeah, yeah. I'm just going to say bye to everyone. Hug me. Cheer up. That scowl will cause wrinkles."

"That's the least of my worries right now." Ronin hugged her and followed her into the kitchen where the rest of the family was gathered. They'd planned a family bike ride after Shevaun left, before meeting his mom's sisters for lunch. *How am I going to make it through this day without knowing how Tilly is? Just my luck that we both have family in town and can't see each other when we desperately need to talk.*

CHAPTER TWENTY-EIGHT

C LASSES BEGAN ON Monday, and Tilly's morning was jam-packed. She begged her mom to wait for her to get out of school before going to the hospital records office so she could go with her. Michael was going to spend the morning with their parents while Tilly was in class.

Pulling into the parking lot of the hospital, she checked the time. She was five minutes early. She parked and texted her mom, saying she'd arrived.

At the information desk, she asked for the records office and found it easily. Her mom was there waiting for her.

They met with a records specialist, who was able to find what they needed quickly. He brought out a folder and handed it to Irena.

"This has a copy of the original birth certificate. I hope you find what you're looking for."

Irena looked at Tilly. "This is it. I can't believe I have this in my hand."

"Do you want to meet with Dad and Michael before looking at it?"

"No. That's not necessary, but I don't want to do it here. Let's find a place to sit outside and look."

They exited and found a sitting area in a shady circle. Irena sat on a bench and Tilly followed. There seemed to be as many butterflies buzzing in her stomach as there were flying about. Tilly noticed the various plants and flowers surrounding them, many of which attracted butterflies.

Irena took a deep breath, and Tilly mimicked the action.

"Okay, here goes everything," Irena said, opening the folder.

There were several papers attached to the birth certificate. They appeared to Tilly to be adoption papers. Irena flipped the birth certificate around and peered at the information.

Tilly gasped when she saw the names. "Oh my gosh! Oh my gosh!"

The mother was listed as Anna Lee Foster, Tilly's employer at In Bloom.

Irena looked up at Tilly with a crinkled brow. "What's wrong?"

"The name! That's my boss! Anna Lee."

"What? You must be mistaken."

"No. That's her."

"Too much of a coincidence—there must be someone else by the same name."

"But what if it is her, Mom? Wouldn't that be amazing? I know her. She's wonderful."

"Don't get your hopes up, honey. We don't know enough. We can't march in there and ask if she's my birth mom."

"Why not? She'd tell us. She's always honest."

"That's not my concern. We don't know why she gave up her baby. It might be very painful for her to be confronted with the knowledge. It could bring up unpleasant memories. She might not want to know me." She looked down at the birth certificate again. "Oh, she named me Anita Gene. That's pretty."

Irena's voice broke, and Tilly remembered that this was her mom's quest, not hers. Yes, she was impacted by it, but not as much as her mother. She needed to support her mom, not try to force her into doing something she wasn't ready for.

"Oh, Mom," Tilly said, leaning over to put an arm around Irena. "Try not to worry about that. What do you need me to do?"

"Nothing." Irena sighed. "Let's talk to your dad and decide what to do next. Maybe I can have the adoption counselor reach out to her. First, we need to make sure it's her and not someone else. When do you work next?"

"I'm supposed to work tomorrow. I don't know if I can go in and face her if this hasn't been cleared up. Maybe I could ask Mack to take my shift."

"That might be a good idea. Have patience, dear."

Patience? How am I going to do that? I have so many questions, and I want them answered NOW! Now I know how Mom felt when she said she was excited and terrified. Will Anna Lee reject us? Will she reject me?

Tilly's mind raced with all the possibilities for positive and negative outcomes. Her stomach churned with warring excitement and nervousness. *This. Is. Amazing! We need to call Gigi and Pops and let them know. Do we wait until after talking to Anna Lee, if she is Mom's mom? Probably better to fill her in now, so she knows.*

They left to meet her dad for dinner, and since they spent hours talking about the possibilities of a real breakthrough in Irena's adoption research, Tilly didn't have time to think about Ronin at all until it was time for bed. In bed, she reached up and tentatively rang the bell. Seconds later, the bell in her room jangled. Knowing Michael was working, it had to be Ronin letting her know he was thinking about her, too. She debated sending him a text, but she was emotionally drained. She would wait until she could see him in person and have a heart-to-heart conversation.

ON TUESDAY, IRENA called the counselor, who said she would verify that Anna Lee was her birth mother and, if so, ask if she would be willing to be contacted.

To pass the time, Tilly's family drove to Starved Rock to hike. Michael drove separately so he could get back to work in time for his shift.

When they'd separated from their parents enough to talk, Tilly asked Michael how Ronin was.

"Whoa. Nope." He shook his head. "I'm not going to play the middleman here, Sis. You two need to talk."

"I'm not asking you to play middleman. We just haven't had a chance to talk. I'm just curious if he's okay."

"He'd be better if you'd respond to one of his messages."

Tilly glanced down at her feet. The wooden steps were worn from the elements, and she didn't want to trip. "I'm afraid something will get misconstrued over text messaging. I'd rather say nothing than the wrong thing."

"Grow up. If you're not going to call him, at least send a quick text."

"We need to talk in person. I have things to say. And I need to see his face when I say them."

"You do what you need to do. I just knew something like this would happen, and I'd be stuck in the middle."

"You're not stuck. This isn't about you."

Michael threw his hands in the air. "Whatever."

He jogged up the rest of the stairs, putting distance between them.

Who's acting like they need to grow up, Michael? You're being a baby. At least I want to work this out like an adult, with a real conversation.

As much as Tilly justified her radio silence, she knew that the longer it took to talk to Ronin, the harder it was going to be. But she couldn't worry about that now. She was more concerned with her mom's adoption research and finding out if Anna Lee was indeed her grandmother. Her mind flooded with what-ifs and fantasies. *How amaze-balls will it be if she is my grandma? I have so many questions.*

CHAPTER TWENTY-NINE

WHEN MICHAEL CAME in for his shift on Tuesday, Ronin was ready to jump him for information. Ronin knew his friend had gone hiking with his family that morning, and he needed to know how Tilly was holding up.

"Bruh." Michael pulled his head back so far, so fast, he looked like an emu getting ready to strike. "I'll tell you the same thing I told her. I am not a middleman. You guys got to work it out. You guys got to talk. You guys got to not put your burdens on me."

"So," Ronin said slowly, processing Michael's statement. "She asked about me. That's why you told *her* you're not a middleman. That's promising. I can work with that. Maybe I just ask you questions, and you make facial expressions, and I interpret them."

"No. Nope. Not gonna work. You need to leave. You're off the clock. This is my shift."

"We *own* this business; there is no on-the-clock or off-the-clock."

Michael playfully pulled his fist back.

Ronin held up his hands. "All right. I'm going. But just a general question. Any idea when they'll be home today? If I were to swing by…"

"I don't know. My Mom can shop for hours, and I know there are a bunch of little towns with shops near Starved Rock. They really wanted to fill their time while they wait on answers."

Ronin had turned to leave and paused with his hand on the door.

"Answers?"

"Mom's adoption. They're making progress. They have a name; they're just trying to find the person."

"Really? That's promising."

"Yeah." Michael looked down, and Ronin recognized the look of hesitant hope in his expression.

"Hey, I hope it's a real breakthrough. I know you all would like to know."

"Yeah. Thanks, man. Appreciate that. Keep that in mind when you think about Tilly, all right? She's preoccupied with this search. She'd be nervous and emotional right now even if your ex hadn't shown up and freaked her out. Be—gentle."

"Got it."

Ronin drove home, contemplating Michael's words. Giving her space was the last thing he wanted to do. Letting her worries and fears fester without addressing them—together—was like throwing gasoline on a fire. Add the unknowns with the adoption research, and she was probably ready to blow.

When he got home, he changed and lifted weights for an hour. He spent the rest of the evening catching up on business administration. He'd moved his rolling standing desk into the living room so he could watch Tilly's apartment, specifically her bedroom window. He'd hoped to see the light come on before he went to bed but it didn't happen.

THE FAMILY HAD plans to meet Anna Lee on Wednesday night, but Tilly couldn't wait until then to see her. Besides, she figured it would be easier on everyone if she broke the news to Anna Lee.

Per the adoption counselor, Anna Lee was indeed Irena's birth mom. The counselor had contacted Anna Lee to tell her that her daughter had discovered her and wanted to meet, but she hadn't disclosed the relationship with Tilly.

Mack was working Wednesday afternoon and texted Tilly to say that Anna Lee had left abruptly after getting a phone call. She'd called Nica to come in and help Mack manage the store.

Tilly knew that the phone call was about the adoption, but she hadn't told Mack the connection, either. She didn't want to risk Anna Lee finding out through anyone else.

Parking at the curb, Tilly looked up at Anna Lee's house. She'd been here several times, but the emotions that washed over her now were raw and intense. *Should I really do this alone? Maybe I should wait for Mom. Well, I'm already here. No sense in putting this off. Besides, Anna Lee might have looked out the window and seen me, and that would have been weirder. Here goes.*

She walked down the brick-lined driveway, knowing Anna Lee always used the back door. Walking up the steps to the screened-in back porch, she smiled to see Salty curled up on top of a bookcase enjoying the late afternoon sun's rays streaming through the porch window.

Knocking on the back door, she felt a wave of nausea and a shot of adrenaline.

Anna Lee walked slowly to the door, dragging her feet. *Oh no, I've never seen her look that tired. The news must have been a drain.*

Seeing Tilly, Anna Lee brightened. "What a surprise! Come on in, Tilly." Her eyebrows furrowed. "Are you okay? Is everything all right?"

Tilly opened her mouth, and nothing came out, but she managed a nod. Anna Lee had opened the door and was waving Tilly inside.

"Come into the kitchen and have a seat. Looks like you need to talk. This calls for hot tea."

Anna Lee bustled about the kitchen as Tilly sat on one of the built-in benches around the table. "Tea would be good," she managed.

"You look like you've seen a ghost, girl. Let me get the kettle on. Such a surprise to see you here! I left the shop early. I got some news today; I'll tell you another time." She waved her hand, and the movement made Tilly think about a butterfly, a flutter-by.

Anna Lee never babbled. She was always direct and to the point.

"Anna Lee," Tilly began, watching the woman on the bench across from her.

"Yes?" Her glasses made her eyes look bigger than they were. Tilly had never noticed that before.

Tilly clasped her hands and put them on the tabletop, leaning forward. "I know what your news is," she said softly.

"What? How could you possibly know? Did Mackenzie over-hear my conversation?"

"No, no. Mack doesn't know. I, um. Wow. My mom, Irena, has been searching for her birth mom."

Tilly watched as Anna Lee's hand fluttered to her mouth. Tears began to stream down her face immediately. Anna Lee shook her head softly. "No," she whispered. "It can't be."

Tilly felt her own tears streaming down her face. "Yes. We saw the birth certificate on Monday. The counselor did some more research to make sure it was you. She called my mom after talking to you today. My mom's been in town this week, hoping to find you."

"Then, you're—you're—," She couldn't get the word out.

Tilly smiled through her tears. "I'm your granddaughter. Yes."

"Oh, Heavenly Father!" Anna Lee looked up. "Thank you, thank you."

The tea kettle began to whistle, and they both jumped. "I'll get that," Tilly said, jumping up.

"She's coming over. Tonight. Right?" Anna Lee asked.

"Yes. She doesn't know I came here early. I, I…" Tilly paused, turning off the burner. "I thought maybe it would be easier if I broke the ice, so to speak. I couldn't believe it when I saw your name. I knew it was you. I knew it in my soul. Mom said to not get my hopes up, that they needed to confirm, but I knew."

She sat back down at the table, the hot water forgotten.

Anna Lee shook her head, still processing. "I just can't believe this. First, that my daughter looked for me, and second, that I know you. What are the chances? This is unbelievable! The greatest blessing. I just got off the phone with John a few minutes ago. He's coming over. I wasn't sure what to expect. I mean, I got the call—your daughter wants to meet you. And…and how many times over the years have I dreamt of this? Countless times. I'd given up hope. Oh." She shuddered. "This is a lot to take in."

"Are you okay, Anna Lee?" Tilly reached across the table and took the older woman's hand. "This isn't too much of a shock, is it?"

"Never. What time will your mother be here?"

Tilly smiled. "Soon. Very soon."

CHAPTER THIRTY

BY THE TIME the rest of the family arrived, Anna Lee had pulled out the couple baby pictures she had of Tilly's mother and spread them on the table.

When the front doorbell rang, Anna Lee looked at Tilly with excitement in her eyes. "You reckon' that's them?"

Tilly smiled. "Yes, I bet it is." She followed Anna Lee through the house and began crying before they reached the door.

Opening the door, Anna Lee threw her arms out wide. "Welcome! Welcome!"

Irena stepped forward tentatively. "Hello. It's very nice to finally meet you. I'm Irena."

"Irena? Why, that's a beautiful name," Anna Lee replied, and Tilly could hear the emotion in her voice, though she couldn't see the woman's face.

Irena stepped forward and hugged Anna Lee. Smiling at Tilly over Anna Lee's shoulder, she mouthed a silent "thank you".

"Come in, everyone. I'm excited to meet you all!" Tilly made the introductions, and Anna Lee invited everyone to make themselves comfortable in the living room.

"Tilly," Anna Lee asked, "would you run to the kitchen and grab those photos? Would anyone like a drink? I have fresh iced tea."

"We don't want to impose on you," Irena began. "We were thinking about ordering food to be delivered, if you don't mind."

"That sounds wonderful." Anna Lee nodded. "We have a lot to catch up on, and I'd be thrilled if you stayed all evening."

Irena smiled at her. "Our thoughts exactly."

Tilly motioned to Michael to follow her. She pointed out the pictures to him as she grabbed the pitcher of iced tea from the fridge and a stack of glasses from the counter.

"This is so wild, Sis," he said as he flipped through the pictures. "Hard to believe Mom found her and that you already knew her."

"I know, right? Serendipity!"

Back in the living room, Irena was sitting next to Anna Lee on the loveseat, and they were holding hands. Fresh tears sprang to Tilly's eyes at the sight. Irena was explaining the steps she'd taken to find her birth mother.

"Such a blessing. I'm so glad you looked for me."

"Well," Irena began as Tilly and Michael poured and handed out glasses of tea. "I've thought about it over the years, but life feels so busy. Building a career, raising kids. But earlier this year, they found a spot during my annual mammogram and asked about family history. Of course, I've been asked about that all my life at medical appointments and was always comfortable saying I was adopted and didn't know. I was healthy! But with the breast cancer scare, finding out took on new immediacy."

"Ah, I see. Well, as far as I know, cancers are not common in my family. My father died of a heart attack; he was a heavy smoker. And my mother was killed in a car accident at fifty-five."

Tilly's dad reached over and patted Anna Lee's knee. "I'm so sorry."

"Thank you. I didn't have the greatest relationship with my parents. When I got pregnant with you..." she paused and looked at Irena. "They disowned me for a long time. It was years before they reached out and tried to mend the relationship, but the damage was deep. We sort of patched things up, but we never really forgave each other."

"You were young, then?"

"Yes, I was seventeen. My boyfriend was drafted into the war, the Vietnam War," she clarified. "He never came home."

Anna Lee took a small sip of tea before continuing. "He was African American, and my parents could not accept him. I was in love and was looking forward to us becoming a family. But when he was killed, I couldn't imagine raising a baby on my own. I was so young, and without my family's support, I couldn't see a way to manage."

She teared up, looking down at her lap.

"Oh, please. Don't be sad. I understand," Irena said, putting her arm around Anna Lee. "I had a good life, great parents. Please have no regrets over your decision. Not on my account."

Tilly smiled, watching the exchange. She was proud of both these women.

Michael leaned forward. "Do you have any photos of our grandpa? I'd love to see him."

Anna Lee's face lit up. "Of course, I do."

Anna Lee left the room, and everyone in Tilly's family began talking at once, reminding each other of little facts they'd learned in the last hour. When Anna Lee returned, Michael asked for everyone's ideas about dinner and placed an order on his phone.

Anna Lee showed them a framed photo of Irena's father, and they all admired the handsome man. Irena pointed out Michael's resemblance to his grandfather, remarking that their eyes looked the same.

"Oh, yes. I see it, too!" Anna Lee declared, looking tenderly at Michael. "Anita—I mean, Irena—would you like to see my yard?"

"Go, Mom. Anna Lee has the prettiest flower beds," Tilly said, sensing that Anna Lee wanted a few moments alone with her newfound daughter.

As the two women left the room, Tilly sat back on the couch next to Michael. "Wow. Can you believe this is real? Now, we have more family here in Bloomington. We have to plan to spend lots and lots of time here visiting. Don't you agree?"

"Yes!" he answered. "Why don't we see if Anna Lee would be open to having Sunday family dinners, like Ronin's family has."

Tilly nodded. "That's a great idea." *Though I'd hate to miss the opportunity to go to the McGuires' house for dinner.* "Or maybe we could do Sunday brunch with Anna Lee."

Then she'd be able to spend time with Ronin and his family, too.

"Hey," she said. "I'm going to go and take a peek out the back window. Just to make sure they're okay. Can I get either of you more tea?"

"They're fine," her dad, Chris, said. "But I understand your curiosity."

"No to tea, but I'm coming with you," Michael replied.

Her dad nodded. "Me, too."

When they reached the kitchen, Tilly saw her mom and Anna Lee standing beside the small garage. Anna Lee was pointing at some flowers.

"Who's that man?" Michael asked.

"That's John, Anna Lee's sounding board. I mean boyfriend."

"Sounding board?" Michael asked. "You're so weird."

Tilly grinned as she wiped away happy tears. John was standing just behind Anna Lee, there if she needed him.

Salty jumped up on the seat in front of Tilly and nudged her hand with his head. "Oh, Salty. Do you need some attention?" Tilly began scratching the cat's head. "Dad, Michael, I'd like to introduce you to Anna Lee's cat. This is Salty. He's the shop cat. Anna Lee takes him to work in a backpack. Did I tell you she drives a scooter to work?"

"That's really cool," Michael said. "I'm going to enjoy getting to know Anna Lee."

"Hmm. 'Anna Lee' doesn't seem right anymore, now that I know she's my grandma. I'll have to come up with another name for her."

Her dad put his arm around her. "I'm sure you'll come up with the perfect name, honey. Why don't we head back to the living room and give them some privacy?"

Tilly's heart swelled. She couldn't believe this day was here—and that the journey led her to someone she knew, admired, and loved.

CHAPTER THIRTY-ONE

W HEN RONIN'S ALARM clock woke him on Thursday morning, he wanted to throw it out the window.

He'd waited until after midnight for either Tilly or Michael to get home, to no avail, so he'd gone to bed worried and frustrated, which resulted in a night of fitful sleep.

He rolled out of bed and headed straight for Michael's room. After knocking lightly, he opened the door and spoke into the darkness. "You awake?"

A moan came from the general vicinity of Michael's bed. "Is the apartment on fire?"

"No. Just curious how things went last night. You were out late."

The bed shifted and the bedside lamp clicked on. Michael rubbed his eyes and ran his hand through his curly hair. "Yes. It was late, but it was a great night. Mom found her birth mom, and we got to visit her. She lives here in Bloomington. So crazy that I moved to the same town as my grandmother. Whoa."

"No kidding! That's fantastic! Happy for you. Was Emmy there?"

"Yes." Michael shook his head and laughed. "You won't believe this. Tilly's boss at the flower shop is our grandmother."

"What? Anna Lee? I met her! At Em's friend's wedding a few weeks ago. That's unreal. How's Emmy taking it?"

"Great. I haven't seen her happier in a long time."

Ronin sighed. *I wish he was saying that about something I'd done to make Emmy happy.* "I'm glad. Hey, is there any chance you could cover me this morning for a couple hours? I have to see Emmy, and I can't wait any longer. I haven't seen her since Saturday."

Michael scowled. "Wait, weren't you meeting the chamber of commerce person this morning? That's an important meeting. We want them in our corner."

"I know. And you can handle it without me; you'll do great. I can't go another half day without talking to her and making sure we're good."

"What time's that meeting?"

"Eight."

"All right." Michael threw off his quilt. "But you *owe* me."

"Thanks."

After showering and dressing in less than ten minutes, Ronin grabbed his car keys and left. He drove to his favorite bagel shop where he bought a variety of bagels and two kinds of cream cheese spread. He wasn't sure what Tilly would like, and showing up just after the sunrise would require baked goods.

Knocking on her apartment door—with the bag of bagels and a carrier containing three coffees, just in case he woke Mackenzie—he hoped Tilly wouldn't run him off.

Light appeared under the door, and Ronin tensed as he heard the door chain slide through its track.

Tilly opened the door, rubbing one eye. She was wearing simple black shorts and a Queen T-Shirt that looked very similar to a favorite shirt he'd had in high school.

"Good morning, sleepy," he said. "Sorry to wake you. I brought bagels. Is that my shirt?"

She glanced down, and her eyes widened as they returned to his. "Um, maybe?"

He raised an eyebrow. "I always wondered what happened to that shirt. May I come in?"

"Of course." She opened the door wider and gestured for him to enter. "Wait a sec. What are you doing here at whatever unnatural hour this is?"

"I couldn't wait any longer to see you. It's been days." He walked to the kitchen counter and set down the things he was carrying before turning back to her. "I've been worried about you. First, with Kristy showing up at the party. Your mom said you spilled a little wine. And after talking to Michael, I know there's been a lot happening regarding your mom's birth mother. He told me this morning that Anna Lee is your grandmother. That's just incredible. Amazing. I want to support you. Help you anyway I can. Seems like we keep missing each other, and I thought, why not see you early—before the day gets crazy?"

Tilly leaned one hip against the counter. "Hold on a minute. Are you rambling, or am I still asleep?"

Ronin laughed. "Probably a little bit of both."

Stepping towards her slowly, he held out his arms. She smiled as she slipped into them.

"Hi." He squeezed her body against his and let out a sigh. *Finally.*

Leaning her cheek against his chest, she held onto him tightly. "Hi," she said. "I have so much to tell you. I'm glad you're here, even if it is before dawn."

Chuckling, Ronin released her. "It's after dawn. Now, come sit with me. Let's talk."

TILLY ADDED HER own creamer to the coffee Ronin had brought. *Ah, that's better,* she thought, lifting the cup to her lips.

She couldn't believe he was there. After a few tumultuous days, her heart felt like it'd been through its own tornado. She had missed Ronin. More than once she'd started to call him and then decided to wait. She needed to see him in person to say what she needed to say. Seven in the morning wasn't her ideal time. *But when opportunity knocks...*

"Can we sit on the couch?" she asked.

"Certainly."

Ronin grabbed his own coffee cup and followed her. She sat down, putting the coffee on the end table and covering her bare legs with a throw blanket.

"There's so much to talk about." She sighed. "I'm not sure where to start."

"Why don't we start with the party? It was the second time you've run out on me. I hope this isn't going to become a habit." His words sounded harsh, but the look in his eyes was of pain, not anger.

"I'm sorry." And she meant it. "I spilled wine all over my dress, it wasn't 'a little wine'. I was embarrassed and couldn't bring myself to walk around like that."

"If you didn't want to come back into the room, I wish you'd sent someone in to get me, so I could have seen you before you left. Then we could have talked about Kristy being there, and I could have told you that I had nothing to do with that."

"Well, yes. I was upset about that, too. How did she find out about the party?" Tilly reached for her coffee; she needed the caffeine for this conversation.

"Trinity said she'd talked with Kristy about the party before she knew about us and once she knew we were dating, she forgot to tell Kristy not to come after all."

"Oh."

"Look, I think it was an honest mistake. Trinity really liked Kristy. Not as much as she loves you, though. She's like me in that." Ronin smiled, and Tilly ached to lean into him and feel his arms around her.

"I see. I understand that. But Ronin, you didn't even remember I was there. I watched you. I would have expected you to realize right away how hurt I was and seek me out. But you didn't. Maybe my expectations are unrealistic."

Ronin shifted. "No. That's a perfectly fine expectation. I failed you there, I agree. But I was shocked. I couldn't understand why she was there, and the next thing I knew, Eminem was in my face, ready to kick my butt. Then you were gone. It couldn't have been more than ten minutes."

"It happened so fast; probably more like five minutes. For the record…" Her words were flowing now. "I want to be the one you think about first. Always. If that's not something you can sign up for, better to know now. I want to be respected. I deserve to be respected."

She felt a newfound confidence. She *had* learned from the wrecked relationship with Kyle.

"Yes, you do," he agreed, reaching for her hand. "I will strive to do that. Always. I am human and may make a mistake or two—"

"You're allowed two." She smiled.

Ronin laughed. "Fine. Two."

"You are the first thing I think about." She thought about Anna Lee saying John was her sounding board, and how romantic and amazing that would be to have. "All throughout the day. I want to tell you about things Mack says, or Anna Lee. I want to ask what you're eating for lunch and if you had trouble commuting to work. No matter what I'm doing, I'm thinking about you."

Ronin slid across the couch to be next to her. "Same. It's the same for me, Emmy. You are on my mind all day. It's been torture not seeing you the last few days, but Michael told me to give you space, and as much as I wanted to ignore his advice, I listened to him."

She shifted so she could lean against his chest, and he put his arms around her. "I know listening to Michael is torture."

Ronin laughed. "For real. Are we good?"

"Yes, we're good." She hesitated. "But if we're putting it all out there, I have one request."

"Name it."

"I prefer it when you don't wear the hair gel." She raised an eyebrow. "I like to run my fingers through your hair."

"Noted." Ronin grinned. "You won't see any product in my hair if there is the slightest chance you could run your fingers through it."

Tilly reached out and ran her hands over his washed and product-free head.

"Great. Now, tell me about discovering Anna Lee's your grandmother. How are you feeling about that? How did the meeting go with your family?"

Tilly pulled back and shifted on the couch so she could look at him as she shared the most amazing thing in her life. "And then when everyone was leaving, Anna Lee pulled me aside and suggested that after graduation, I could consider taking over In Bloom! She says she'll give me a family discount on the sale price!"

"What? What did you say?" he asked.

She smiled. "Anna Lee and I had a conversation recently about gut reactions to things—how sometimes it's better just to listen to your gut and not overanalyze things. I told her my gut was saying that it sounded amazing. And I meant it. It feels right. Like everything in my life has led me to this."

Ronin brushed her hair back behind her ear and rested his hand on her shoulder, the warmth of his touch filling her. "Funny how life does that. I think that sounds perfect, Em. Now, about that T-shirt..."

She threw her head back and laughed. "I found it in Michael's room after you'd stayed over one time. I'd always liked it, and

I snatched it. I like to wear it when I'm feeling all the feels and need the comfort it gives me."

"Well, it looks great on you. But I may have to borrow it sometime."

"Or maybe," she said, tilting her head, "you could just buy your own now. This one's been mine for years."

"It's a good thing I like you, Emmy."

Tilly nodded. "It's a very good thing." She leaned forward and kissed him.

CHAPTER THIRTY-TWO

Three months later

TILLY WAS IN the middle of making a pumpkin pie for Thanksgiving. Her parents were staying at Anna Lee's house, so she and Ronin were going there for dinner number one. Later in the evening they would head over to his parents' house for dinner number two.

Ronin had just texted to tell her he was walking over and had a surprise for her. She was excited to see what it was. *I mentioned needing a new cell phone. Could that be what he got me?*

A knock on the apartment door caused her to startle and drop the jar of pumpkin pie spice into the mixing bowl. "Ope!" she muttered. Luckily, it landed upright without spilling into the other ingredients. *Close call!*

She fished the little jar out and set it on the counter with the measuring spoon before crossing to open the front door, talking before she even opened it. "This better be good—"

She squealed at the sight before her. An adorable, fuzzy black puppy was in Ronin's arms, with a big bow wrapped around its collar. "Ronin! Did you get me a puppy?"

"How did you guess, my brilliant Em?" He handed the dog over, and it began licking her face. "I know this is a big deal. It's not the best gift to spring on someone, and I'm fully committed to keeping him myself if you can't. With us living so close, I thought we could manage it. The fact that Eminem and I work different shifts will help, too."

"Does he know?"

"Yes, he went to the shelter with me yesterday to help me pick out this little girl."

"That's why you couldn't do movie night last night."

Since Mack was going home for the holiday weekend, they'd planned to change movie night from Friday to Wednesday, but the boys had said they couldn't make it this week.

"Right. There you go again, Veronica Mars. Solving all the mysteries."

The puppy started wiggling in her arms, and she set her down. "Is she potty-trained?"

"Mostly. But she's a puppy, and they have accidents."

"Did you name her?"

"She's your dog. You get to name her."

"Right. A name. Hmm. Well, I'll have to talk to Mack. I don't know if she's allergic. And then the landlord, but I would *love* to have her if I can keep her."

"Remember, if you can't, you can always visit her at our place. And who knows, maybe someday my place will be your place and vice versa."

"Whoa. Let's not get too far ahead of ourselves...but my gut is liking the sound of that."

The puppy barked.

"I think she agrees," Ronin said.

Tilly scooped up the puppy again. "How am I going to finish baking the pie in time for dinner with this cute little distraction?"

"I'll help." Ronin walked into the kitchen, and Tilly followed with the puppy in her arms. "Now, any thoughts on a name? I think Toto has a nice ring to it."

Tilly laughed. "That may be too on the nose. I'll think of something. Now, let's get this pie completed. I want to get over to Anna Lee's as soon as possible. I better give her a call first and ask if Salty will mind a canine guest."

She stood on her toes to give Ronin a kiss. "Thank you for the gift. I'm completely shocked. And thrilled. You are the best!"

Ronin took the dog from her, set her on the floor, and wrapped Tilly in his arms.

Tears began to spill from her eyes, and she was thankful she hadn't put on makeup yet.

Ronin rocked her slightly. "Hey, now. No tears today. You know I can't stand to see you cry."

Tilly leaned back to look up at him. "Just think. You trying to stop my tears led me to kiss you. Right here, as a matter of fact."

Ronin grabbed her by the waist and swung her up onto the counter. "I'll never forget that moment as long as I live."

He brushed her tears away and stroked her cheeks. "I love you, Matilda, Emmy, Maria Miller."

"I love you, Ronin Lee McGuire."

EPILOGUE

One Year Later

"WOW! WHAT A year!" Ronin said, looking around the reception area of M and M Spaces' original location. "I can't believe it's the first anniversary of our business, and we're still going strong."

"I'd say better than strong. You're expanding!" Tilly straightened the flower arrangement that she'd brought for their original office space. The arrangement for the new location was still in her car.

Ronin stood behind her, wrapping his arms around her. "It's fitting that Anna Lee scheduled the sale and transfer of In Bloom to you for today, the anniversary of M and M Spaces' opening."

"She loves symmetry," Tilly said. "I hope you don't feel like it's overshadowing your celebration."

"Not at all," he said, resting his cheek on the back of her head. "I love that our business birthdays will share an August fourteenth date."

Tilly put her hands on his arms, enjoying the moment of closeness and peace. It was going to be a very busy day. She would meet Anna Lee at the bank to sign papers and make the business transfer official. Ronin would go along to support her.

Since Tilly's graduation in May, the mentoring and transitioning had been in full swing. With Anna Lee, she'd made several visits to suppliers for introductions. They'd completed a full store inventory and decided what would go to Anna Lee's and what would remain in the shop. Tilly had essentially been running the business on her own for the last month while Anna Lee took a much-deserved vacation with John. They'd made a three-week road trip to the Northeast coast.

When they'd returned last weekend, Anna Lee had invited Tilly and her family over to share their adventures and the hundreds of photos that they'd taken. There was a moment as everyone—Anna Lee, John, Ronin, Michael, Tilly, and their parents—sat around in the living room laughing and joking, that Tilly had remembered sitting in that room with the girls from In Bloom during an earlier time and being thankful that they'd found Anna Lee. She had been sort of an adopted grandmother as well as boss to all the girls, who were away from home attending college and working.

Now that Tilly knew Anna Lee was her biological grandmother, her heart swelled with love and gratitude.

Next week would be the one-year anniversary of finding out that Anna Lee was her grandmother. They had a large celebration planned to celebrate that, too. Tilly had been brainstorming ideas for a meaningful flower arrangement for their dinner table. She'd settled on an unusual bouquet including tulips, marigolds, and peonies. All the flowers symbolized family. The tulip represented both rebirth, which her family had undergone when they found Anna Lee, and unconditional love. Nica had told her how marigolds were used in Day of the Dead celebrations to honor loved ones who'd passed on, showing that familial love transcends even death. Since peonies symbolize happy marriages and prosperity, they were an easy choice to include.

In addition to the centerpiece, she was going to make corsages and boutonnières with red poppies to honor her grandfather who she'd learned had died in the Vietnam War. She hoped they wouldn't bring too many tears and that Anna Lee would share more stories about him.

"Right?" Ronin asked, leaning close to her ear.

"I'm sorry." Tilly shook her head, bringing herself back to the moment. "I was daydreaming. What did you say?"

"I said…" He chuckled, and she felt the gentle shake of his body, one of her favorite sensations. "We'd better be on our way to the bank. Don't want to leave your grandmother waiting."

Gosh, Tilly loved the sound of that. Anna Lee, her grandmother.

"Let's go."

AFTER TWO AMAZING anniversary parties at M and M Spaces locations, Ronin took Tilly out to dinner.

"What a day. My heart is full," she said, raising her glass of wine. "To continuations and to new adventures."

Ronin lifted his glass and clinked hers. "I agree. It was a fantastic day."

"I can't believe I own my own business!" Tilly leaned forward, eyes wide, body buzzing. "And I've never been more sure of a decision in my life. I'm so lucky. Grannie Annie built up a thriving business, and I will be able to build on that and leave my own mark. And I get to work with customers, and I get to create. I'm so thrilled!"

"I'm so proud of you, Emmy. So many things are clicking into place."

"I'm thankful you've been by my side during this journey." She brushed a strand of hair off her face. "I was a bit of a mess at your grand opening last year."

"Hey, don't beat yourself up about that. It was early in our relationship, and I hadn't shown you just how much you mean to me. I hope I've done that now."

She put her glass down. "Yes, you have. I still want to pinch myself. Hard to believe how far we've come in such a short time."

"And by a short time, you mean the seventeen years we've known each other, right?"

Tilly laughed. "Well, when you put it that way. What took us so long to fall in love?"

"We just had to wait for the right stars to align."

Tilly smiled, she'd thought those same words herself. "I'm glad they finally did."

The waiter dropped off dessert, a bowl of strawberry ice cream for Tilly and chocolate for Ronin.

Tilly scooped up a bite of ice cream and put it in her mouth. "Mmm. So good."

Ronin stood up, and Tilly stared at him, confused. "You can't leave now. Your ice cream will melt."

He stepped towards her and bent down on one knee.

"Ronin." Her voice broke. "What are you doing?"

"At the risk of August fourteenth not being memorable enough, Madeline Marie Miller, will you marry me?"

Tilly's eyes sparkled as her eyebrows lifted and a grin spread across her face. "But what about Emmy?"

"I want to marry her, too. What say you, Madeline Emmy Marie Miller?"

"Yes, absolutely yes."

She leaned over to kiss him, and several patrons around them began cheering and clapping. She blushed at the attention.

He pulled a ring from his pocket. "Then I'd like to place this ring on your hand, Emmy."

She looked at it and blinked quickly, trying to hold back the tears that threatened to escape. "Ronin McGuire, it's beautiful. So unique."

It was an antique-looking gold band with a large red center stone surrounded by green stones, making the piece look like a flower. *It's similar in shape to a daisy. Ha! Just like our puppy, Daisy.*

"Unique just like you. Anna Lee gave it to me to give to you. It belonged to her grandmother, who gave it to Anna Lee when she was sixteen. A beautiful ring for a beautiful lady."

"What?" she shrieked. "This was my great-great-grandmother's ring? When? When did Anna Lee give this to you?"

Ronin put his hands on her face and kissed her, a kiss filled with tenderness and love. Tilly wanted to throw her arms around him and not let go.

"Last weekend. I told her I was going to buy a ring, and she stopped me. Brought this out to show me; said she would be thrilled if I proposed with this. But if you want a diamond, I'll be happy to get you one. Maybe a designer could even add diamonds to this band."

"No! Absolutely not!" She shook her head so hard that her ponytail smacked her cheek. "It's perfect just the way it is. You know, it looks like a flower, which is perfect. And the red and green remind me of *The Wizard of Oz*, red for ruby slippers and green for the Emerald City. It's beautiful and *perfect*. I can't believe this belonged to Grannie Annie's grandmother. I want to cry."

Ronin leaned towards her and swiped a tear away. "Don't cry, Emmy. I'll cry."

"Not you, too. We can't cry, Ronin. It's the best day ever."

"Second best."

"Why the second?"

"The best day ever will be when we marry and become partners for, and in, life."

"Oh. Wow. We'll have to plan a wedding." She freaked out for a moment but took a deep breath. *No sense in getting ahead of ourselves.*

"There's no rush. I'd marry you tomorrow if I could. I know you have a lot on your plate with buying In Bloom right now. I'm not going to let you start stressing about a wedding. It'll happen when we're ready. Though we did see a lot of cool, unique venues, searching for a place for my parents' anniversary party. So, we have a little head start."

"Thank you. I love you, Ronin. Now, can we finish our ice cream before it melts completely?"

"We'll order new bowls. And some champagne to toast."

"Scrumptious!"

WHAT'S NEXT

I hope you enjoyed *Tulips for Tilly!* I have a bonus scene with a cute event for Tilly and Ronin shortly after the epilogue of *Tulips for Tilly*. Tilly has more big decisions to make about In Bloom—four-legged decisions. If you'd like to receive it, please join my newsletter by going to this web address:

https://dl.bookfunnel.com/ksm4h98f1p

If you enjoyed this story, I hope will consider leaving a review. A review helps a story get discovered and helps other readers know if a book is right for them. Leave a review wherever you normally do—Amazon, Goodreads, Barnes & Noble, The StoryGraph, etc.

There is an introductory novella called *Wildflowers for Anna Lee*. It's an exclusive gift for joining my newsletter. You'll learn about Anna Lee's history, meet the In Bloom ladies, and see the beginning of a sweet romance for Anna Lee. Get your copy at:

https://dl.bookfunnel.com/mmsejnrbbp

An expanded version of this story will be available in early 2024.

In case you've missed the other books in this series...